Readers love Alex Pine's Christmas Crime

'Alex Pine has done it again! Another excellent crime thriller . . . I was hooked from the first page. Read it – you won't be disappointed'

'HELP! I am addicted to this series! Unputdownable'

'Absolutely gripping. . . I was on the edge of my seat'

'A real page turner. . . I am now a firm follower of DI James Walker'

'A fast-paced gripping read with plenty of twists and turns. This series just gets better and better!'

'I loved every paragraph, every sentence and every word of this masterpiece! I was totally hooked'

'Impossible to put down'

'I loved this book! It is dark, gritty and thrilling . . . It is fast-paced and has you hooked from the first few pages. I devoured this book in two sittings'

'Dang! Now this was one heck of a story! If you want suspense, thrills and chills, then this is your book!'

'A chilling page turner'

'WOW! This book had me hooked from the first page, I didn't want to put it down and this was one of the twistiest and most complicated murder cases I've ever read about'

'Another fantastic book from Alex Pine!'

'I loved this book and enjoyed every minute of it. There were so many twists, turns and surprises on just about every page'

'DI James Walker is fast becoming a favourite of mine along with Alex Pine being one of my top authors'

Alex Pine was born and raised on a council estate in South London and left school at sixteen. Before long, he embarked on a career in journalism, which took him all over the world – many of the stories he covered were crime-related. Among his favourite hobbies are hiking and water-based activities, so he and his family have spent lots of holidays in the Lake District. He now lives with his wife on a marina close to the New Forest on the South Coast – providing him with the best of both worlds! This is his fourth novel.

THE
NIGHT
BEFORE
CHRISTMAS

ALEX PINE

Published by AVON
A division of HarperCollins*Publishers*
1 London Bridge Street
London SE1 9GF

www.harpercollins.co.uk

HarperCollins*Publishers*
Macken House,
39/40 Mayor Street Upper,
Dublin 1
D01 C9W8
Ireland

A Paperback Original 2023
1
First published in Great Britain by HarperCollins*Publishers* 2023

A catalogue copy of this book is available from the British Library.

ISBN: 978-0-00-862102-5

Typeset in Minion Pro
by Palimpsest Book Production Limited, Falkirk, Stirlingshire
Printed and Bound in the UK
using 100% Renewable Electricity at CPI Group (UK) Ltd

MIX
Paper | Supporting
responsible forestry
FSC™ C007454

This book is produced from independently certified FSC™ paper to ensure responsible forest management.

For more information visit: www.harpercollins.co.uk/green

To my brother Harry, with whom I share lots of fond memories of our years living in London and more recently the times spent at his home in Dubai.

Introducing DI Walker and his team

This is the fourth book in the DI James Walker series. For those who haven't read *The Christmas Killer*, *The Killer in the Snow* and *The Winter Killer*, here is a brief introduction to the man himself and the key members of his team.

DETECTIVE CHIEF INSPECTOR JAMES WALKER, AGED 42

An officer with the Cumbria Constabulary based in Kendal, recently promoted to DCI. He spent 20 years with the Met in London before moving to the quiet village of Kirkby Abbey. He's married to Annie, aged 38, who was born in the village and worked as a teacher. The couple have a young daughter, Bella, and Annie is now pregnant with their second child.

SUPERINTENDENT JEFF TANNER, AGED 48

Now based at Cumbria police HQ in Penrith. James took over from him as DCI. He's married with a son.

DETECTIVE INSPECTOR PHIL STEVENS, AGED 40

A no-nonsense detective who moved up the ladder to replace James as DI. He's married with two children.

DETECTIVE SERGEANT JESSICA ABBOTT, AGED 35

A highly respected member of the team and of Irish and East African descent. She's sassy, as sharp as a razor, and not afraid to speak her mind. She too was promoted to her current position as part of the department shake up. She got married to her boyfriend Sean, a paramedic, back in the summer.

DETECTIVE CONSTABLE CAROLINE FOLEY, AGED 29

The youngest team member and a new addition, having been transferred from Carlisle. Her three-year relationship to another woman had recently broken up and she's now living with her widowed mother in Kendal.

PROLOGUE

As the clock in her living room struck 5 p.m. on Christmas Eve, Maria Payne decided that it was time to call the police. She felt she had no choice, even if it did get her husband into trouble.

Dylan and his three pals had set out almost ten hours ago. They were supposed to have finished up early afternoon but no one had heard from them.

They all knew from experience that it wasn't safe to trek across the Cumbrian fells in the dark and had always made a point of returning before sunset. But this time they hadn't, and that wasn't right.

The other family members hadn't been overly concerned until Maria contacted them and it became clear that all the mens' mobile phones were either switched off or unable to receive a signal. That was when the fear started to set in.

Did it mean that something bad had happened to them? Perhaps there'd been an accident or they'd become stranded in one of the many mobile phone black spots that dotted the Lake District.

She had tried to persuade Dylan to stay at home this morning because the snow that was forecast would make the landscape particularly treacherous.

'You're being reckless,' she'd told him. 'And selfish. You said we could go for a pub lunch and you'd go with them on Boxing Day.'

'But the weather looks even worse then so that might have to be cancelled. Besides, it doesn't look like it will turn bad until this afternoon. This morning they're only forecasting a few rain showers. And we can go to the pub tomorrow. The Bugle is always open on Christmas Day.'

It was typical of her husband, of course. He was stubborn, uncompromising, and too often put his own feelings before hers. But she had to admit that he more than made up for it in other ways, which was why he remained the love of her life five years on from the day they'd tied the knot.

She went to the window for the umpteenth time, hoping to see their Range Rover pulling onto the driveway. But there was no movement outside except for the snow falling from the sky. The sight of it made her even more anxious and fearful.

Swallowing hard, she stepped away from the window and grabbed her phone from the coffee table. She'd held off long enough in the hope that she wouldn't have to do it. She knew that Dylan would be furious with her if it turned out that she'd overreacted, especially if the police got wind of what the guys had been up to. But, at the same time, she would never forgive herself if they suffered because of her inaction.

Seconds later she was through to an emergency service operator.

'I'm worried about my husband and his friends,' she said, while struggling to keep her voice steady. 'There are four of them and they're all missing. I think they might be in trouble.'

CHAPTER ONE

Day One
Christmas Eve

It had been a long day and Detective Chief Inspector James Walker was looking forward to going home. He wasn't looking forward to the drive, though.

It was twenty-five miles from police HQ in the market town of Kendal to Kirkby Abbey, the Cumbrian village he'd lived in for the past three years, and the brutal weather had turned the roads into potential death traps.

Looking out of his office window, he could see that the snow was thankfully easing off now and the gritters and snow ploughs were out in force. But they were having to contend with strong winds and sub-zero temperatures.

He was reminded of what Annie had said to him as they snuggled up in bed in the early hours.

'The weather forecast is pretty dire, James. Is there any chance you can get someone to cover for you so that you can start your Christmas a day early?'

It had been tempting, but he'd decided that it wouldn't have been fair on his colleagues, especially DI Phil Stevens and DS Jessica Abbott. They were taking charge through Christmas Day and Boxing Day, and he knew for a fact that they'd both made plans for today.

At least it hadn't been a stressful shift and there'd been no call for him to leave the office. DC Colin Patterson had attended the mugging of a pensioner in Ambleside and DC Caroline Foley had driven to Sedbergh to interview a woman who claimed she'd been threatened by her ex-husband.

They were both back now, and like him they'd be heading home in the next hour or so, after the night shift officers reported for duty. Hopefully they weren't going to be delayed by the inclement weather.

James returned to his desk and started tidying the paperwork that covered it. It still felt strange not to be out there in the open-plan office with the rest of the team, even after nine months.

It was back in April when he was promoted from Detective Inspector to Detective Chief Inspector, filling the shoes of Jeff Tanner, who himself got promoted to Superintendent and was now based at Constabulary headquarters in Penrith.

James's promotion was unexpected, but not unwelcome. Having served as a police officer for over twenty years, most of it with the Met in London, he'd felt more than ready to take the next step up the career ladder.

He often wondered where he'd be now if he'd stayed in the capital. The move to Cumbria came about after Annie's mother died, leaving her the four-bedroom family cottage in Kirkby Abbey.

By then Annie had lived in London for thirteen years, but it had got to the point where she'd no longer felt comfortable there.

Street crime, unbearable levels of traffic, and the urge to start a family – but in a safer environment – had persuaded her that they should relocate to the place she grew up.

James came around to her way of thinking after he started to receive death threats from a violent criminal and so they upped sticks and headed north.

At first, he feared he wouldn't adjust to being a copper in Cumbria, a county with one of the lowest crime rates in the country, but much to his relief he'd found the job far from boring. In fact, since moving here he'd had to grapple with three of the biggest and most disturbing cases of his career. And the fact that they had all taken place each year around Christmastime was the reason he'd come to secretly dread the festive season.

'Sorry to bother you, guv, but something has come in that you need to be made aware of.'

The voice snapped him out of his reverie and he looked up to see DC Foley standing in the open doorway. She was the newest recruit to the team, a tall twenty-nine-year-old who had transferred from Carlisle six months ago.

'What is it, Caroline?' he asked her.

'I don't know the details, but it doesn't sound good,' she said. 'Colin answered a call from Control and then signalled for me to come and get you. He's still talking to them but he held up his notepad on which he'd scribbled "four people missing".'

Those words sent a cold rush of blood through James's veins and he shot straight to his feet.

'Lead the way,' he said to DC Foley and then followed her out of the room and across the office to Colin Patterson's work station.

Patterson was still on the phone, scrawling notes on his pad as he listened intently. He now had the full attention of everyone in the office – one other detective, two uniformed officers, and three civilian support staff. James could see the tension etched into their features as they waited anxiously for Patterson to finish the call.

Another thirty seconds passed before he put down the phone and looked up, his face pinched with concern.

'Four men and their dogs who went for a hike early this morning have been reported missing,' he said. 'They set out between seven and eight and were supposed to have returned to their homes early this afternoon. The call came in from a woman named Maria Payne, who's the wife of one of the men. She says they're all experienced hikers so the fact that they've not been in touch to warn that they'll be late, and none of them can be reached on their mobiles, has given her cause for concern. Search and rescue have been alerted, but they'll have a lot of ground to cover because Mrs Payne doesn't know the route the men took.'

'It could be that they've just been cut off by the bad weather and can't get a phone signal,' James said.

Patterson nodded. 'Let's hope so. But we've been asked to get involved right away because of the worsening conditions. The group set out from a farm that belongs to one of them, a Mr Ted Rycroft. The other three men are his pals and all live within a fifteen-mile radius of the farm, which is just north of Kentmere village.

'Mr Rycroft, a widower, lives alone apparently, and though he has two employees, Mrs Payne doesn't have their names or contact details.'

James drew a tremulous breath as dread swelled inside him.

He was only too aware of the risks people took when they went walking across Cumbria's sprawling fells and bleak, boggy moors, especially during the winter. The number of deaths due to accidents had more than doubled in the last three years. And so far this year over twenty hikers and climbers had perished. The most recent tragedy was only two weeks ago when a man's body was found on Scafell Pike three days after he went missing during a lone hike.

'In view of how bad the weather has been all afternoon and how many people are involved, we need to treat this as a serious incident,' James said.

'How do we play it then, boss?' Patterson asked.

'We liaise with search and rescue and get in touch with the families,' James replied. 'We also need the mobile numbers of all four men. See if we can make contact even though the families haven't yet been able to. Meanwhile, the obvious place to start the ball rolling is the farm they set out from. I'll go straight there in a patrol car and you can come with me, Caroline. It shouldn't take us long assuming the roads are passable.'

James glanced at his watch and his heart skipped a beat when he saw that it was almost six o'clock already.

'We need to move fast,' he said. 'In a situation like this every second counts.'

CHAPTER TWO

James returned to his office to grab his coat and call Annie. He'd told her to expect him home around seven-thirty and they had planned to have a Christmas Eve dinner together. He'd also been hoping to see Bella before she was put to bed.

But, as so often happened, he was going to have to disappoint them.

'Is it likely to be another all-nighter then?' Annie responded when he broke the news to her.

'I sincerely hope not seeing as tomorrow is Christmas Day,' he said. 'But we have a serious situation to deal with. Four hikers have been missing for most of the day and can't be contacted.'

'Oh God, their families must be worried sick. Will you be joining in the search for them?'

'We'll be coordinating efforts to start with. Rescue teams have been informed and they'll soon be on their way to the area.'

'Well, don't waste your time talking to me,' she said. 'Go and do your best to find those men, but please don't place yourself in danger. It's a rough night out there.'

'I won't. How's Bella?'

'She's still full of energy and showing no signs of tiredness. Plus, she's learned how to say "snow" and keeps toddling over to the back window to look out.'

James couldn't help but smile. Bella was eighteen months old now and it seemed that with every day came another milestone. She was certainly a handful, but Annie was coping remarkably well considering she was five months pregnant with their second child. An ultrasound scan was booked for early in January, and they were hoping that would tell them if Bella was soon going to have a baby sister or brother.

'I made us a beef casserole,' Annie said. 'I'll leave yours in a bowl so if you're hungry when you eventually come home you can just put it in the microwave.'

'That's great, thanks. And don't wait up for me.'

'I'll probably go to bed about ten. Can you phone or text me just before then to let me know what's happening?'

'I will if I remember. But don't worry if you don't hear from me.'

'I'll try not to. Love you lots.'

'Love you too.'

After the call, James wrapped a scarf around his neck and pulled on his fleece-lined parka. DC Foley, who was now tucked inside a long, quilted jacket, was waiting for him as he stepped out of his office.

'The patrol car's warming up downstairs, guv,' she said. 'But first Colin wants to show us where the farm is.'

DC Patterson was still at his desk, looking at a map on his computer screen.

'There's Kentmere village,' he said, pointing. 'The farm is

a few miles north of it in a fairly remote location. You get there by following this narrow lane.'

'I'm familiar with the area,' James said. 'I know that it's popular with walkers but it doesn't get as busy as many other parts of the Lakes.'

Patterson nodded. 'That's right. And the latest info we have is that the roads from here to there are passable.'

'We'll get going then,' James said. 'Phone through any updates as and when you get them. And make sure the Constabulary press office is alerting the media. We need to spread the word about those missing men as quickly as possible.'

Minutes later James and Foley climbed onto the back seat of a sturdy Land Rover. The driver, PC Seth Malek, was the only officer of Egyptian heritage on the team. As efficient as always, he had the engine running and told them he'd already looked up directions to the farm.

As they set off, James took a deep breath and tried to push back on the foreboding that was growing in his chest. But it proved difficult because he knew that on a night like this the Cumbrian landscape was a dangerous place to be, even for experienced hikers. Trails got lost in the snow and tiredness-induced errors were more likely to occur.

The task facing the volunteer search teams was not going to be an easy one. It would take them time to respond and when they did it seemed they weren't going to know where to start. Plus, if the weather got worse as the night progressed, they would have to be mindful of their own safety. Only light snow was falling now, but one thing James had learned since moving to Cumbria was that the weather had a habit of changing dramatically from one hour to the next.

They drove through the brightly lit streets of Kendal, which were busy with people enjoying the Christmas break. The pubs and restaurants appeared to be doing a roaring trade and a festive atmosphere prevailed.

'Did you have any plans for this evening?' James asked Foley, knowing that she now lived in the town.

Shaking her head, she said, 'I was going to have a quiet night in. I really haven't been able to enter the Yuletide spirit this year, what with the break-up and my dad's passing.'

Her three-year relationship with a woman named Tessa had only just ended when her father died from sepsis back in early spring. It was what had prompted her transfer request from Carlisle to Kendal, where she now shared a house with her widowed mother.

She'd proved herself to be a real asset to the team and James was pretty sure that she'd go far on the Force if she stuck with it. James also admired the way she had made a conscious effort to build a rapport with DC Patterson, who had recently turned his own life on its head by coming out of the closet and admitting to his wife of four years that he was gay.

They'd split up in the summer and the divorce was pending. Foley saw how Patterson was struggling to deal with it and struck up a close friendship with him in a bid to help him rebuild his confidence. And it had worked.

'What about you, guv?' she said. 'Were you intending to do anything with the family?'

'Just dinner and early to bed,' he replied. 'Tomorrow is going to be all about our daughter. I can't wait to see her opening her presents. Having said that, my gut is telling me that neither of us will be going home any time soon.'

'What do you expect to find when we get to the farm?'

11

James shrugged. 'I'd like to believe that Ted Rycroft and his mates are already back there but for some reason they don't want anyone to know so they've switched off their phones.'

Foley raised her brows. 'That sounds highly unlikely to me.'

'Exactly. But any other scenario is as bleak as this bloody weather.'

It continued to snow as they drove out of Kendal and headed west along the usually busy A591. There was very little traffic this evening even though the gritters and snow ploughs had done a good job of keeping the road clear.

Soon they were passing through more countryside, but the lush meadows and rugged slopes were barely visible.

They were almost six miles into the journey and approaching the village of Staveley when James's phone rang. It was DC Patterson with an update and he put him on speaker for Foley's benefit.

'I've now got the names of all four hikers and I also managed to get through to one of the two people who work at the farm, a Miss Rebecca Carter,' Patterson said. 'She's employed as a part-time clerical assistant and lives in Windermere. She told me that she and the guy who works there as a farmhand were both off today and that they knew their boss was planning a Christmas Eve trek. She has no idea where they were going, though, and she wasn't aware they were missing until I told her.'

'Did she say anything else?'

'Only that she's worked at the farm for just a few months, but her colleague has been there for years. Her boss rents out quad bikes and organises hikes for tourists, and she handles the bookings and paperwork. He used to focus on dairy farming but scaled back on that after his wife died five years ago. He now has only twenty sheep and they provide a small income from milk, wool and meat.'

'Does she know if he's gone missing before?'

'She doesn't believe so. He goes on lots of walks even though he's almost seventy, and he knows the area well.'

'What about the farmhand? Have you spoken to him?'

'Not yet. Miss Carter gave me his name and number, but when I called it was busy. I'll try again in a sec . . . Guv, I've got the Constabulary press office trying to get through to me on another line and I should probably take the call.'

'You do that. We're about halfway to the farm and I'll phone you from there.'

The next stage of the journey took them off the A591 and through Staveley. From there they followed the Kentmere Road as it meandered northwards between hills, meadows and miles of dry-stone walls. Along the way they passed a few isolated farms and houses, but not a single vehicle.

They soon reached Kentmere village, a small, scattered community of fewer than a hundred homes. It was slow going beyond that on a narrow, twisting lane that lay under several inches of pristine snow.

Another lane took them off to the left and within minutes they came to Ted Rycroft's farm.

The gate was open and PC Malek drove onto a yard that was already occupied by four other vehicles – a Jeep and three cars. These were parked between the stone-built farmhouse and two outbuildings, one of which looked like a barn.

The farm was small and James sensed an ominous stillness about the place. It was in darkness and the only sound was the wind that swirled and howled around them.

'Oh my God, look at that,' Foley blurted suddenly, just as the Land Rover pulled up in front of the line of parked vehicles.

It took James a moment to realise what she was referring to and when he saw it every muscle in his body stiffened.

The windscreens and side windows of all four vehicles had been smashed and fragments of glass dented the snow that covered the bonnets.

'That's not something the wind could have done,' PC Malek said.

James knew he was right and a heavy weight settled in his chest.

Throwing open his door, he jumped out of the Land Rover. As he did so the cold air rushed into his lungs.

'Let's go straight up to the house,' he said. 'And Seth, bring a couple of torches.'

The three of them hurried towards the two-storey building and when they reached it, they got another shock. The front door was wide open and the windows either side of it had also been smashed.

'Brace yourselves because Christ only knows what we're going to find inside,' James said.

CHAPTER THREE

James had to stiffen his spine and take a deep breath before stepping through the front door, Foley and Malek right behind him.

'Is anyone here?' he shouted at the top of his voice. 'We're the police. Make yourselves known to us.'

After getting no response, he used a torch to cast a pale, yellow light into the short hallway ahead of him. What it revealed sent a rush of blood through his veins.

The carpet was a mess, littered with various objects, including a broken vase, a framed picture with shattered glass, and the remains of a plant that looked as though it had been crushed underfoot.

'The light switch is on the wall to your left, guv,' Foley said, but when James flicked it on nothing happened.

'Could be the power's been turned off,' he said. 'Keep an eye out for the fuse box.'

He dragged in a deep breath before taking careful steps along the hall. There were open doors on either side and at the end of it a staircase.

'We'll stick together and search the ground floor first,' he said. 'Keep close and stay alert.'

The first door on the left gave access to the kitchen and it was obvious that a degree of effort had gone into wrecking it. Chairs had been overturned and bottles, tins, plates and utensils were strewn across the tiled floor. The fridge door stood open and liquids had been poured over the worktops and table.

As the wind roared through the broken window, James made a mental note of the scene while questions raced through his mind.

'Who the hell was responsible for this carnage?' he said to himself. 'And do we assume it happened after Mr Rycroft and his pals left the farm this morning?'

'It's the same in here, sir,' Malek said and James turned to see that the PC and Foley were staring into the room opposite, a small office. A metal filing cabinet lay on its side and the floor was cluttered with plastic folders, loose documents, newspapers and a laptop. There were also a number of framed photos that had been ripped from the walls, which showed people riding quad bikes and hiking through the fells.

Malek tried the light switch, but again nothing happened.

The next door along led into the living room and the scene inside was much the same. No sign of life, but their torches highlighted more extensive damage.

The television screen was smashed; a large artificial Christmas tree with all the trimmings had been pushed over. Baubles were smashed into the carpet along with still-flickering Christmas lights and even a small, beheaded glass angel. Other objects were piled on the floor including several framed pictures that had been pulled off the walls, and bottles from a drinks cabinet. The only window was broken and cold air was rushing in.

'Whoever did this must have a serious grudge against the farmer,' James said.

Foley then drew his attention to a low table to one side of a long, deep leather sofa.

'There's the house phone,' she said, shining her torch at it.

There was one more door off the hallway, which turned out to be a toilet, but the room was intact.

'Now let's check upstairs,' James said.

He led the way and when he reached the landing, he saw that there were four doors leading off it and they were all open.

'We'll go from left to right,' he said. 'Stay behind me while I look inside.'

He was sure it was the safest approach given that they might well be in for another nasty surprise.

His heart shunted up a gear as he cautiously entered the first room. There was a double bed and a tall, freestanding wardrobe. But no occupants. Drawers had been pulled out and emptied of their contents. The duvet was on the floor and what looked like soil was sprinkled over the sheet covering the mattress. And yet again the glass was missing from the only window.

The second room contained a single bed and not much else, and there didn't appear to be any damage.

After that came a bathroom with a toilet in which the mirror behind the sink had been smashed.

Room four was the most vandalised, but that didn't stop James from realising straight away what he was looking at.

'This is Rycroft's trophy room,' he said.

He pointed to the far wall on which there was a tin sign that read:

MAN CAVE
HUNTERS ONLY

Another wall must previously have been covered with mounted fox heads and deer antlers, but most had been removed and dropped on the floor. They lay alongside a collection of trophies that had been tipped out of a glass-fronted display cabinet. The front to what looked like a tall gun cupboard had been wrenched open and it was empty inside.

This was all disturbing enough, but when James's torch beam landed on a framed print on the wall behind the door, he felt a sharp stab of alarm.

The picture depicted a group of red-coated fox hunters on horseback and surrounded by a pack of hounds. Scrawled roughly across it in what looked like black paint was one word: *Murderers*.

CHAPTER FOUR

DC Foley reacted to the sight of the defaced picture by letting her breath escape in a low whistle.

'This whole thing is becoming more bloody unsettling by the minute,' she said.

James nodded in agreement and shivered despite the heavy coat he was wearing.

What they were looking at was causing his mind to spiral with fresh fears and questions. He was well aware that fox hunting was a controversial subject. Despite the fact that it had been banned across England, Scotland and Wales since 2005, he knew that illegal hunts still took place in many areas, including the Lake District. As a result, opponents of blood sports were as active as ever, making clear that they saw hunters as cruel animal killers.

'Given that Farmer Rycroft is obviously a keen hunter himself,' Foley said, gesturing at the scene around them, 'perhaps some local animal rights activists decided to seize the opportunity to wreak havoc here while he was out hiking.'

'Or perhaps he and his pals didn't go on a hike,' James said. 'Maybe they went hunting instead.'

'But that's not what Mrs Payne told the emergency operator when she rang in.'

James shrugged. 'Well, she could have been lying so she wouldn't get them into trouble. Or maybe her husband thought it best not to tell her the truth.'

Foley nodded. 'I suppose that's possible seeing as more and more hunts are taking place these days across the whole of the Christmas period.'

Fox hunting had played an important part in rural life for years but had always provoked serious opposition. In fact, earlier today, James's colleagues in another part of the county had been called out to a gathering after violent clashes broke out between hunt supporters and protesters. And the Constabulary was now bracing itself for Boxing Day, which was by far the busiest day on the hunting calendar.

The problem was that although conventional fox hunting was no longer permitted, it had been replaced by so-called trail hunting. This involved people on foot or horseback with hounds or beagles following a laid-down trail of animal-based scent along a pre-determined path, effectively replicating traditional hunts but without the animals being chased and killed.

However, this was frequently being used as a smokescreen for illegal hunting. The hunters in question only pretended to lay down the scent and instead went after the real thing, just as they did before the ban was introduced.

'It's too soon to draw any conclusions,' James said. 'First, we need to get the lights on in here and check the rest of the farm. Then I'll call for backup and forensics. You go and look for the fuse box, Seth, while Caroline and I check the other buildings.

And keep an eye out for any shotguns and rifles. I think it's safe to assume that cupboard wasn't empty before today.'

Outside it remained a cold, unpleasant evening. There were still no breaks in the cloud cover and the wind continued to tear across the yard.

James wondered with mounting dread how Ted Rycroft and his pals were coping. Right now, he didn't care if they'd been hiking or hunting. He just wanted to hear that they were safe. If they hadn't managed to find shelter in a bothy or cave then he reckoned they'd be in real trouble. The search would soon be under way, of course, but it was going to be seriously hampered by the arctic conditions.

They went to the barn first, which had stone walls and a thatched roof. It wasn't locked and inside there were about twenty sheep looking cosy and comfortable in rows of small, individual pens. James couldn't see any signs of vandalism and none of the sheep appeared to have been harmed.

There were double doors at the back that opened onto a small, fenced-in field. Beyond it they could just make out the dark fells in the distance.

The other outbuilding had clearly once been a stable housing up to a dozen horses. But there were no horses now and between the stalls were four mud-spattered quad bikes.

'These must be the ones he rents out,' Foley said. 'They're all the rage nowadays, especially around the Lakes. I've been out on them a couple of times and I know of several farmers who invested in them as a way of supplementing their dwindling incomes.'

As soon as they stepped back into the yard, they saw that the lights were on in the farmhouse so PC Malek must have found the fuse box.

'You go and start taking some photos while I phone Colin,' James said to Foley. 'But tread carefully because we don't want to compromise anything. Like it or not, this is now a crime scene.'

He took out his mobile and climbed into the Land Rover to make the call.

Patterson answered straight away and the first thing James told him was that Ted Rycroft and his friends had not returned to the farm.

'But you need to send a forensics team here pronto along with some uniforms,' he said. 'The place has been deliberately trashed and there's evidence to suggest that it was carried out by one or more people with a grudge against Mr Rycroft. And it appears that several guns or rifles have been taken.'

He described what they had found in the house and made specific mention of the trophy room and picture daubed with the word *murderers*.

'It makes me wonder whether those men went out on a hunt and not a hike. If so, then—'

'Can I stop you there, guv?' Patterson interrupted. 'You should know that a couple of things have come to our notice that suggest you could be right and they did go on a trail hunt, or even an illegal hunt.'

'Really? What have you got?'

'Well, after the details started to circulate about the men, Ted Rycroft's name rang a bell with one of the team. He ran a check and found that about a month ago a guy contacted us claiming that Rycroft had vandalised his car outside a pub. The bonnet was scratched with a sharp object, probably a knife, and all four tyres were punctured. The two men had apparently got into an argument inside the pub. Rycroft left first and when the other guy left an hour or so later, he discovered the damage and naturally assumed it was Rycroft who did it. Uniforms attended and spoke to Rycroft. He denied it and since there were no witnesses or security footage, they had to take his word for it.'

'I vaguely recall it being brought to my attention at the time, but I was working on something else and didn't get across it. So, who was the bloke who made the allegation?'

'He's also a farmer. His name is Neil Hutchinson and he's Rycroft's nearest neighbour. The report that was filed says the pair have been involved in a long-running feud and it's occasionally boiled over into acts of aggression and even vandalism.'

'Do we know what the problem is between them?'

'It's all about fox hunting apparently,' Patterson said. 'Rycroft loves it and Hutchinson hates it. And since they live so close to each other, I suppose clashes are inevitable.'

'We'll need to talk to this Neil Hutchinson then,' James said. 'Find out his address and text it to me. If he is responsible for trashing the farm – and it's a big *if* – then he might well know where the group was headed this morning.'

'Will do,' Patterson replied. 'Meanwhile, we've now contacted all the next of kin and they're worried sick.'

'That doesn't surprise me, but try to make sure that no relatives come here. They'll only be in the way. If the men haven't turned up by morning, we should make arrangements to bring the families together at headquarters. We can then update them on the search and tell them about the state of the farmhouse before the news gets out.'

'I'll put the wheels in motion, guv.'

'DC Foley and I will have to stay here for now so if

there are any developments at your end then let me know immediately.'

Before getting out of the Land Rover, James checked the time. It was after seven so he decided to let Annie know that he'd probably be working through the night after all, which would not have been such a big deal if tomorrow wasn't Christmas Day.

After sending her a message, he used his phone to take photos of the registration plates on the four vehicles in the yard. There was the Jeep, a Range Rover, a Ford Explorer and a battered Skoda. He forwarded the pictures to Patterson, asking him to confirm who the owners were.

He then returned to the farmhouse and when he stepped inside, he experienced another blast of shock and outrage. With all the lights on the extent of the mess was more evident. It surely would have taken quite a while to inflict so much damage, and it had presumably happened this morning either before or after Ted Rycroft and the others had set off.

And that raised a disturbing question – did the person or persons responsible for the mess also have something to do with why the men were missing?

CHAPTER FIVE

'Take a look at this,' Foley said when James entered the living room. She held up a framed photograph, adding, 'I'm guessing this is Mr Rycroft and his late wife. It was one of several lying on the floor.'

James snapped on latex gloves before taking it from her. The couple looked to be in their late sixties and were bundled up in thick coats. He had grey hair and a square, craggy face, and she was much shorter with thin, pale features and narrow eyes.

'Seth is looking around upstairs, but I'm not sure we'll find anything that will help lead us to the missing hikers,' Foley went on. 'And we haven't come across any shotguns or rifles. It might be best to leave it to forensics and wait outside for the search teams to arrive. They should be here soon.'

James nodded. 'You're probably right.'

He told her about the feud between Rycroft and his neighbour and how the other man had claimed Rycroft had vandalised his car.

Foley nodded knowingly. 'It comes as no surprise to me that two farmers are at war over it. Having lived in Cumbria all my life, I know well that fox hunting is a very divisive issue around here.'

'We'll interview Neil Hutchinson as soon as we can,' James said. 'Given their history, it's easy to believe that he could be responsible for all this, but harder to accept that he knows where the men are. We need to be careful not to go down the wrong track and waste valuable time.'

He placed the photo he'd been holding on the coffee table and snapped a picture of it.

'I'm going upstairs to check in with Seth. When I come back, we'll carry out a quick recce of the fields around the farm just to be on the safe side.'

He took some photos of the trophy room, including one of the framed picture with the word *murderers* painted on it.

PC Malek pointed to a small tin of black paint on the floor and a brush that was lying next to it.

'If we're lucky, forensics might find some prints on them,' he said.

James shook his head. 'I very much doubt it. Whoever did this put a lot of thought into it. I don't suppose for a second that they didn't think to wear gloves.'

They went back downstairs and before stepping outside, James took some more photos in the living room, kitchen and office. He then attached all those he had taken to an email and sent it to Patterson.

Foley was standing in the yard with her phone pressed against her ear. James walked over to her while Malek took it upon himself to venture out into the fields surrounding the farm.

The snow was still falling lightly, but the wind was increasing in strength. James didn't like to imagine what it must be like out on the moors and fells that stretched for miles in all directions.

When Foley came off the phone, she said, 'I just checked in to see what's happening with the Mountain Rescue Teams. They should be here at any minute but because of the bad weather it's unlikely a helicopter will be able to take part in the initial search. Oh, and the press are now across the story and appeals for people to be on the lookout for the men are being broadcast across social media and the radio.'

James swallowed hard as a tremor of unease rippled through him.

'Things are not looking good for those poor sods,' he said. 'I just wish we knew which direction they went off in.'

Just then both their phones pinged and they opened them up to see an email from Patterson, which provided information on the missing men.

Ted Rycroft, 67, a widowed farmer. No next of kin.

Nigel Marr, 57, a farmer near Selside. Has a wife named Francesca.

Rhys Hughes, 60, a gamekeeper near Ambleside. A widower who lives with his son Owain.

Dylan Payne, 49, runs an outdoor clothing and equipment store in Kendal. Wife Maria.

Registration check as follows:

Jeep belongs to Mr Rycroft
Range Rover belongs to Mr Payne
Ford Explorer belongs to Mr Hughes
Skoda belongs to Mr Marr

They've all known each other for some years appar-ently and often meet up and go on hikes and trail hunts. Mr Hughes owns three hounds and he took them with him, according to his son. Mr Marr owns the other dog that's with them.

They both finished reading the email but before they could discuss it their attention was suddenly drawn to a pair of approaching headlights.

James immediately assumed it was a rescue vehicle, but when it pulled into the yard, he saw that it was a silver Ford Escort, and a man and a woman were in the front seat.

It came to a stop, the lights were turned off, and the couple got out. As James approached them the woman, who was wearing a fur-trimmed puffer jacket, fixed her eyes on the broken windows of the farmhouse.

'Oh my God,' she yelled. 'What's happened? Who did that? Is Ted inside?'

She started to walk towards the building with the man in tow, but James rushed forward to intercept them.

'Please don't go any closer,' he said. 'I'm Detective Chief Inspector Walker and I'm afraid I can't let you enter the farmhouse.'

They stopped and looked at him, the shock evident on their faces.

'We both received calls from the police to tell us that Ted and the others were missing, so we came to see if they're back,' the man said, and then pointed to the front of the building. 'But we didn't expect to see this. What the hell is going on?'

'I'll tell you in a moment,' James said. 'But first I need to know who you are.'

'I'm Greg. Greg Pike. This is Rebecca Carter. We both work here with Ted. He gave us today and tomorrow off.'

'Well, Mr Rycroft and his friends are still missing, but a search is about to get under way. The damage you can see is another matter and unfortunately extends inside. I'll explain the situation in a moment, but first I have to ask you both some questions.'

CHAPTER SIX

The yard wasn't the ideal place to have a conversation, but they didn't have much of a choice and James intended to keep it short.

Greg Pike and Rebecca Carter were clearly concerned and keen to help. They both appeared to be in their late twenties or early thirties, and James learned that after the police phoned Greg, he'd called Rebecca from his home in Ambleside. They decided to come straight to the farm and he picked her up from her place in Windermere.

Greg was short and slim, with sandpaper stubble coating his chin, and he told James he had worked as a farmhand for Ted Rycroft for six years.

'I used to have a lot more to do,' he said. 'Since Ted and his wife never had children there was just them and me running the place. But after Lisa died, he lost interest in farming and decided to scale back and opt for an easier life. He sold most of his land along with his chickens and reduced the number of sheep he bred.'

'We were surprised not to see any horses in the stable,' James probed.

'He used to have several but he decided they were too expensive so he cut back to just the one, but she had to be put down three months ago after breaking a leg during a hunt. Ted hasn't got around to replacing her. The same has happened with his dogs. He used to have eight, but now he doesn't have any.'

'And he now makes extra money from day trippers to the area?'

'That's right. Hiking used to be his hobby but he turned it into a nice little earner by arranging walks. Then he invested in some quad bikes, which he rents out.'

'That's how I came onto the scene,' Rebecca said. 'He advertised for a clerical assistant to handle bookings and accounts, and I applied and got the job. That was just over four months ago and I've really enjoyed it here. I work three days a week and Ted has been like an uncle to me. I just hope that he and the others are all right. I can't help thinking that if nobody has heard from them then they're in trouble.'

Rebecca was tall, with a thin face and short dark hair, and James could tell that she was trying to control the emotion in her voice.

'We know the group set out early this morning,' James said. 'And I appreciate that neither of you were here at the time, but do you have any idea of the route they were going to take?'

'When I asked Ted yesterday, he told me he hadn't decided,' Greg said. 'But that's not unusual since they always leave it until the last minute. That way they know what the weather is going to be like. Some trails are more difficult than others if it's raining or snowing. But it wouldn't surprise me if they followed the river towards the Kentmere Reservoir. It's a popular route that he often takes hikers on.'

'Was Mr Rycroft more specific with you, Miss Carter?'

She shook her head. 'No, he didn't tell me and it didn't occur to me to ask him.'

'So, when was the last time you both heard from him?'

'Yesterday!' she replied. 'He gave us each a gift and a card and told us to enjoy our break. We'd made sure there wasn't much work for him to do. I finished all the paperwork and Greg sorted the sheep.'

'And would I be right in assuming that you're both familiar with Mr Rycroft's friends who are with him?'

Greg nodded. 'Yes, he mentioned that he was going with Dylan Payne, Nigel Marr and Rhys Hughes. Another mate, Johnny Elvin, was due to go, but pulled out at the last minute.'

'Do you know why?'

'I wasn't told.'

'Have you got contact details for him?'

'I haven't. All I know is that he lives in Shap.'

'And is it possible that someone else was invited to go along after he said he wasn't going?'

'It's possible, but I can't think who it would have been.'

James made a mental note to check up on Johnny Elvin, before adding, 'Have you met all the guys?'

'Sure. They regularly get together here and at the local pubs. Ever since I've known Ted, he's organised the trail hunts, which they never miss, and they always go out on both Christmas Eve and Boxing Day if the weather permits. They gave up wearing the red coats years ago, though, so they don't draw attention to themselves.'

James was quick to seize on the answer. 'Then it's a trail hunt they've been on and not a hike?'

Greg frowned. 'I thought you knew that.'

James shook his head. 'Dylan Payne's wife told us they were hiking.'

'Oh, I see. Well, she probably didn't want it to get out. It's often easier for trail hunters to say they're hiking if they go out on foot. But please don't take that the wrong way, Inspector. Ted and the guys stick to the rules and follow a scent, usually a fox's urine. Others, as you know, continue to chase foxes and get away with it.'

'I should have been clearer when I spoke to one of your officers over the phone,' Rebecca said. 'But I got confused and I think I described it as a trek.'

'But why is it a problem if trail hunting is legal?' As soon as James said it, he realised that he knew the answer already, but decided to let Greg continue.

'Because it isn't permitted on land owned by the Lake District National Park Authority. And private land owners must give permission, which many don't. It's why Ted and others like him have such a hard time of it these days. Since he sold most of his land, he has to take the crew way beyond the farm. And it doesn't help that the guy he sold the land to refuses to give permission for him to use it now.'

'And who might that be?'

'His nearest neighbour to the east. Neil Hutchinson. His farm is much bigger than this one and he runs it with his wife and two daughters.'

'Actually, he's someone we intend to speak to,' James said. 'We understand that he and Mr Rycroft don't get on.'

'More like they hate each other's guts,' Greg said. 'It's been going on for ages because Hutchinson – or Hutch, as we call him – vehemently opposes hunting of all kinds. But it got much worse about a year ago over the sale of the land.'

'What do you mean?'

Greg shrugged. 'Well, Ted didn't know that it was Hutchinson who bought the land off him until after the deal was done. You see, Hutch knew that Ted wouldn't want to sell it to him so he got a relative to buy it on his behalf through an estate agent and his name was kept out of it. Ted was furious when he found out, but there was nothing he could do and Hutch went on to tease him about it.'

'Are you aware that Mr Hutchinson recently accused Mr Rycroft of vandalising his car?'

'Yes, but Ted said he didn't do it and we believe him. It was probably some other local who the bastard had upset.'

James gestured towards the vehicles on the other side of the yard.

'You've seen that the farmhouse windows have been smashed, but I don't think you've noticed that the same has happened to the vehicles over there.'

Greg and Rebecca turned and were both clearly taken aback.

'Jesus Christ.' Rebecca gasped as her hand flew to her mouth. 'I don't believe it. Who would have done such a thing?'

'That's what we need to find out,' James said. 'Whoever it was has also caused extensive damage inside the house, which is why we can't let you go in there. But there's a picture I'd like to show you.'

He took out his phone and pulled up the shot he took of the framed photo that Foley had picked up off the living room floor. They both confirmed that it was indeed Ted Rycroft and his late wife, Lisa.

'There's one more I want you to look at, which was taken in the trophy room,' he said and held up the defaced hunting picture.

They both reacted with shock and incredulity.

'That's bloody sick,' Rebecca blurted. 'I can't believe someone is actually accusing Ted of being a murderer.'

'Have you any idea who might have written that?' James asked.

'I think I get it,' Greg offered. 'This is looking like the work of a bunch of anti-hunt extremists. They're doing this sort of thing all too often these days. I've heard about them physically attacking hunt supporters, damaging their cars and daubing slogans on the outside of their homes. It's got out of hand.'

'But it works both ways,' Rebecca pointed out. 'Protesters are also being attacked when they try to disrupt hunts. It's so sad because it's driving communities apart all over the country.'

James shoved his phone back into his pocket and said, 'There's something else I need to ask you about the trophy room. It contains what we believe to be a gun cupboard. Are we right?'

'Yes, you are,' Greg replied. 'Ted has a small collection of shotguns, which he uses from time to time for game shooting and pest control.'

'Exactly how many are kept in the cupboard?'

'Five. And they were all there the last time I went into the room.'

'Well, the cupboard is empty now,' James said. 'The door was forced open and it appears they've been taken.'

Rebecca's eyes grew wide in their sockets. 'What about the ammunition?' she asked. 'He also kept several boxes of twelve-gauge shells in there.'

James shook his head. 'They're gone too.' He then took out his notebook and added, 'Would you both mind hanging around until the search teams get here? I'm sure that whatever you can tell them will be helpful.'

After jotting down their phone numbers and addresses, and establishing that they were both single and lived alone, he suggested they go and sit in their car while they waited.

'Sure thing,' Greg said. 'But first can you just clarify something for me, Detective Walker?'

'If I can.'

'Am I wrong to assume that you think Hutchinson might have come here today and vandalised the place?'

'At this stage we don't know what to think,' James replied. 'But in view of what we've learned about the pair of them he will have to be questioned.'

'Then you need to be aware that the guy is a close friend of the Spicer brothers. I'm sure you must have heard of them since they're a couple of nasty hunt saboteurs, or sabs, who spend their free time and their own money monitoring hunting groups and disrupting meets. They've been making mischief for years. They've had a few run-ins with Ted and I know for a fact that they've threatened him at least once. What's more, they live not far from here, just outside Kendal.'

CHAPTER SEVEN

'How much do you know about the Spicer brothers, guv?' Foley asked as they watched Greg Pike and Rebecca Carter climb back into his car.

'Our paths have never crossed, but I'm aware they've come to our notice,' James said. 'If my memory serves me right then one of them was convicted of abusive behaviour a few months ago.'

'That's correct. It was the younger brother, Warren. He was arrested after scuffles broke out at a hunt near Keswick and he got fined by the court. It stuck in my mind because about a year ago he was beaten up by two hunt supporters when he tried to disrupt a meet. The attackers were wearing balaclavas and we were never able to identify them.'

'Was he badly hurt?'

'He suffered a broken arm and a bruised face. Could have been much worse, though.'

'What was your impression of him?'

She shrugged. 'He struck me as a passionate animal rights

activist who assumes that everything he does is justified. At the time he was in his mid-twenties, working as a plumber, and single.'

'What about his brother?'

'As I recall Liam is about five years older. I met him briefly when he arrived at the hospital to pick his brother up. He came across as loud-mouthed and arrogant. At the time they were living together, but I've no idea if they still are.'

James stroked the stubble on his chin and nodded. 'We'll add them to our list of potential suspects then and get the team to check them out.'

Just as he finished speaking the yard was lit up again as two vehicles arrived at once and James was relieved to see the distinctive colours of the Mountain Rescue Land Rovers. Within seconds doors were being flung open and figures were jumping out.

James waved his arms and called out to draw attention to himself. Soon he was surrounded by a group of about a dozen rescuers. After explaining who he was, he said, 'The four men who are missing set out from here over twelve hours ago with four hounds and they were due back six or seven hours ago. They haven't been in contact with their families and it seems their mobile phones are either turned off or unable to get a signal.

'My colleague and I arrived a short time ago and we've learned that the men did not go on a hike as we were first led to believe. They went trail hunting, but it's not known in which direction they headed. This farm, which for some reason has been seriously vandalised, is owned by a Mr Ted Rycroft, who is one of the hunters. Two of his employees, who were not here this morning, have just turned up. They're waiting to speak to you and might possibly be able to help you decide where to begin the search.'

He pointed to the vandalised vehicles and then to the front of the farmhouse.

'The damage inside is extensive and one possibility is that animal rights activists were responsible.'

'Does that mean they might also have something to do with why the men haven't returned?' asked the team leader, a big man with a dark, bristly moustache who gave his name as Craig.

'We don't know yet and probably won't find out until we've spoken to Mr Rycroft and the others,' James said. 'But I need to point out that several shotguns may have been taken from the house. We have no idea what's happened to them. I'm not suggesting you should feel in any way threatened by that, but it's something I have to make you aware of.'

He was still answering questions from the team when PC Malek returned to inform them that he'd found nothing in the fields surrounding the farm. As he was speaking more vehicles turned up, this time two patrol cars and a forensics van.

James told Foley to brief the officers while he took the rescuers over to meet Greg and Rebecca. He then listened in as Greg explained that his boss usually headed through the Kentmere Valley on his guided walks and trail hunts. The rescue team said they were familiar with the area. To the south it consisted of rolling hills and meadows, but to the north the slopes were steep and rugged, leading to the high summits of the fells.

'We'd better get going,' the team leader said to James. 'Another team is on its way, but this is going to be a real challenge. We'll head north along what we know to be one of the easiest trails, but visibility is poor, the wind is vicious, and the forecast is for conditions to get progressively worse during the night, with more heavy snow.'

'Any thoughts on what might have happened to them?'

'That's anybody's guess, but it is rare for contact to be lost with such a large group of people. Mobile phone coverage is poor to non-existent in places, but those guys are experienced and would have taken that into account. We have to hope that they're curled up in a safe place somewhere, keeping warm while waiting for the weather to improve before making their way back here.'

'And what are the odds on that being the case?' James asked.

'Not as bad as you might imagine, Inspector. We'll just have to keep our fingers crossed.'

James thanked Greg Pike and Rebecca Carter for their help and promised that they'd be among the first to be contacted when there was news about their boss.

'You should go home now because there's nothing more you can do here and it's going to get much busier,' he said. 'But if Mr Rycroft and the others have not turned up by morning, we'll probably ask you to come back so you can tell us if anything apart from the shotguns is missing from inside the house. Would that be all right?'

'It won't be a problem for either of us,' Greg said. 'But can I check on the sheep first? I want to make sure they're okay for the night ahead if Ted isn't back.'

'Of course you can.'

James switched his attention back to the rescuers as they got their gear together, which included torch helmets and radios. When they set off minutes later, he felt the urge to go with them, but he knew he couldn't. He wasn't prepared and he didn't have the qualifications and experience.

Searching for people on and around the fells was a dangerous, gruelling task on nights like this. The Cumbrian Mountain Rescue Teams were self-sufficient and committed, and they knew how to navigate the difficult terrain away from the marked paths.

The volunteers he now watched walking onto a dark, hostile landscape were about to risk their own lives in a bid to save others, and he had nothing but respect and admiration for them.

CHAPTER EIGHT

James was glad to see that scene of crime officers had responded in force to the call-out. This was a case they needed to get stuck into from the outset even though there was no sign of bloodshed at the farm.

The extent of the damage inflicted on the property, the missing shotguns, the defaced picture of the red-coated hunters and the fact that Ted Rycroft clearly had enemies, was enough to trigger plenty of alarm bells.

DC Foley was standing in front of the farmhouse speaking to Tony Coppell, the Chief Forensic Officer, who had already donned his protective over-suit. As James approached them, Coppell turned towards him and raised a brow.

'I should have known that we wouldn't get through the festive season without having to deal with yet another shocking event,' he said, his tone mocking. 'This is the fourth year running! You know, we were able to enjoy Christmas and New Year before you arrived on the scene.'

James stifled a grin and replied, 'That's always been my

problem, Tony. Bad luck follows me around. It's really unsettling.'

The good-natured banter the pair often engaged in was something that James welcomed. It was a defence mechanism that helped them both deal with the disturbing and painful situations that all too often confronted them.

He reached out and patted Coppell on the shoulder. 'I'm glad you were on call, mate. I've got a bad feeling about this one. Has DC Foley filled you in?'

Coppell nodded. 'She has, and three of my team are already inside. I can see the mess through the windows, and I gather the owner of this place is one of the men who are missing.'

'That's right, and I'm hoping you might find a clue as to their whereabouts among the wreckage.'

'Caroline told me about the missing shotguns. Do you know if anything else has been stolen? Could it be that the damage was done to cover up a burglary?'

'I very much doubt it,' James said. 'My money is on a revenge or grudge attack.'

Coppell pursed his lips. 'I can see why, given that the word *murderers* was painted on that picture.'

'That is pretty troubling and suggests that it could be the work of anti-blood sport extremists. Mr Rycroft and the others are huntsmen and they've been on a trail hunt. So today would have offered their opponents the perfect opportunity to make their feelings known.'

Coppell, who was in his mid-fifties, had been doing the job for over twenty years and viewed every case as a challenge. James could tell from his expression and demeanour that this one had already piqued his interest.

'Well, let us get on with it and I'll give you a shout if anything turns up,' he said. 'This looks set to be a long, horrible night, so will you be hanging around?'

'Probably not,' James answered. 'The uniforms will stay here but DC Foley and I need to follow up a couple of potential leads.'

As Coppell nodded and then pulled on his face mask and headed into the farmhouse, James turned to Foley and was about to ask her if she'd received any more communications from headquarters. But before the words came out of his mouth, he noticed she'd wrapped her arms around herself and was visibly shivering.

'Are you okay?' he asked her.

'I would be if it wasn't so flipping cold,' she replied, her breath clouding in front of her face. 'But it's my own fault. I should have put a jumper on over the shirt I'm wearing under the coat before we left the office.'

James sympathised with her. His own body was also numb from the cold.

'Go and sit in the Land Rover,' he told her. 'I'll get Seth and join you. We can put the heating on while I call the office.'

'Are you sure, guv?'

'Absolutely. I think we're about done here. The search is under way, the SOCOs are cracking on, and I need to decide what our next step should be.'

Once the three of them were seated in the Land Rover, it didn't take long for their bodies to warm up thanks to the heater and a flask of hot coffee that Malek had brought with him. He also shared a packet of chocolate biscuits and a bunch of bananas.

James chewed on one as he exchanged updates with DC Patterson over the phone.

'We've informed all the families that the men still haven't returned to the farm, and we've told them what you found there,' Patterson said. 'As we speak uniforms are dropping in on the wives of Nigel Marr and Dylan Payne, and on Rhys Hughes's son. And they'll stay to offer support for as long as is necessary.'

'Good. We've had it confirmed that the men had been on a trail hunt and not a hike. His farmhand has assured me that the dogs were chasing scent and not foxes, but it's possible he's covering up for them.'

'All the more reason to speak to the neighbour, Neil Hutchinson. I've now got the address of his farm and I'll text it to you. Someone is sifting through the database to see what else we have on him.'

'It makes sense to go and see him, especially given what we now know about him,' James said. 'We've been told he's a friend of a pair of anti-hunt saboteurs who are known to us. Warren and Liam Spicer.'

'Yeah, I've heard of them,' Patterson said.

'Run a check then. They live in Kendal apparently. Get their address and we'll pay them a visit too.'

'Anything else, guv?'

'One other thing. A fifth man was intending to join the hunt but pulled out at the last minute. We should find out why. His name is Johnny Elvin and he lives in Shap, but that's all I know.'

'Leave it with me. Are you staying at the farm for much longer?'

'There's no need. Tony Coppell and the uniforms have got the place covered and the Mountain Rescue Team have just headed out. But we do need to prepare for them to return if the weather gets much worse.'

As soon as he ended the call, James's phone pinged with a text from Patterson. It contained Neil Hutchinson's address, which Malek tapped into the satnav.

'It's about two miles from here by the looks of it, sir,' the PC said.

'Then let's get going. We need to find out if he took a wrecking ball to his neighbour's farm and, more importantly, if he knows where Mr Rycroft and the others are.'

CHAPTER NINE

The first half mile of the journey to Neil Hutchinson's farm was back towards Kentmere village. They then took a sharp turn onto yet another long, narrow lane.

The punishing wind buffeted the trees on either side of the car and swept the snow into a frenzy. It served to conjure up a vision in James's mind of the four missing men cowering against rocks up on the fells while fearing – or knowing – that they weren't going to survive the night.

A knot tightened in his throat as yet another spike of dread worked its way under his ribs. It was becoming increasingly difficult for him to believe that they hadn't met with misfortune.

'That must be the farm up ahead,' PC Malek said.

It was off the beaten track, it's interior lights piercing the darkness. As they drew closer, they saw a curl of smoke rising from the chimney. Beyond it, snow-covered hills loomed large against the horizon.

'At least we know that someone's at home,' Foley commented.

James checked his watch. Eight fifteen. In under four hours it'd be Christmas Day and this Christmas Eve would linger in his mind alongside those other morbid memories from the last few years.

His first Christmas in Cumbria was spent hunting a serial killer. A year later he had to investigate the slaughter of an entire family on Christmas Eve. Then, twelve months ago, it was the murder of a maid-of-honour at a New Year's Eve wedding.

And now this, a case involving four missing men, a smashed-up farmhouse, and a likely link to the highly controversial blood sport of fox hunting.

He puffed out a breath and wondered why he ever thought that being a copper in the Lake District would be any less challenging than it had been in London.

'How should we approach this, guv?' Foley asked him. 'Do we start with the mispers or the trashing of the farmhouse?'

'We'll do it in order of priority,' he said. 'Mispers first.'

Foley nodded. 'That makes sense. Plus, the narrative of events must surely begin with those guys setting out this morning. I take it we're ruling out the highly improbable scenario that they did the damage themselves for whatever reason before leaving the farm?'

'That has occurred to me and no, I don't reckon we can rule it out this early on. One thing I know from experience is that we should never shy away from thinking the unthinkable. Some of the most bizarre acts of criminality I've come across made perfect sense after the motives were established.

'In this case it's not inconceivable that Mr Rycroft and his pals got drunk and thought it'd be fun to wreck his farmhouse and the cars. Then, once they sobered up, they realised they needed a cover story so that they could claim on the insurance. So, they wrote the word *murderers* across that picture to make us believe a bunch of animal rights activists did it while they were out hunting.'

'I'll be astonished if that is what happened.'

'Me too, but we need to keep an open mind until things start to come together.'

The farm consisted of a collection of grey buildings surrounded by sprawling fields and patches of woodland. There was no gate and they drove straight onto a large tarmacked yard.

As they parked close to the house, James was surprised that no one emerged to see who was paying them a visit so late in the day.

He told PC Malek to wait in the Land Rover while he and Foley got out and walked up to the front door. He rang the bell and within seconds heard a voice from inside call out, 'Did you forget to take your bloody key again?'

The door was then opened by a woman who was clearly shocked to see them.

'Oh, shit, I'm sorry. I thought you were my sister and her fella coming back from the pub.'

She was slim with sharp features and short blonde hair, and James guessed she was in her early thirties.

'Apologies for disturbing you at this time,' he said, showing her his ID. 'I'm Detective Chief Inspector Walker with Cumbria police and this is Detective Constable Foley. We've come to speak to Mr Hutchinson. Is he at home?'

Her eyes darted between them and she had to clear her throat before responding.

'He's watching television in the living room with my mum.'

'And you are?'

'Naomi. Their daughter.'

'Then would you mind asking them if we can come in and have a word, Naomi?'

'What's it about? Has something happened to Faye, my sister?'

He shook his head. 'No, not as far as we know. We're here to discuss a matter relating to your neighbour, Mr Rycroft.'

She drew in a breath, then turned and shouted out, 'Dad, you need to come to the door. It's the police and they want to talk to you.'

Naomi stood to one side, allowing James to see a couple wearing dressing gowns come rushing out of a room and along the hall.

It was Hutchinson who spoke first when the pair reached the door. He was a thick-set man with a fleshy face and a head of silver-grey hair.

'What's going on?' he demanded, his voice rough and clipped. 'Is this about Faye? Is she okay?'

'Please don't be alarmed, Mr Hutchinson,' James said. 'As I've just explained to your daughter, this is not about Faye.'

His body stiffened and suspicion shaped his features. 'Then what is it about? Why are you here?'

James introduced himself and Foley. 'We want to ask you some questions about your neighbour, Mr Rycroft. Are you aware of what's happened to him? I believe it's been on the news.'

He furrowed his brow and exchanged a look with his wife. She then responded with, 'We don't watch or listen to the news.'

'In that case I should tell you that Mr Rycroft and three of his friends have been reported missing,' James said. 'They set out from his farm early this morning on a trail hunt and no one has heard from them since. So, there's growing concern that something might have happened to them.'

'But why have you come here to tell us?' Hutchinson said. 'We don't have anything to do with that lot. And you shouldn't believe they went trail hunting. I guarantee they're out killing foxes. It's what they do.'

'There's more to it than that, Mr Hutchinson. We really need to have this conversation inside rather than on the doorstep. May we come in?'

'But me and the wife were about to go to bed. Can't it wait until tomorrow? I'm sure that Rycroft and those other pricks will have turned up by then with animal blood on their hands.'

'Oh, grow up, Neil,' his wife snapped. 'There's no need to make things difficult for them. They wouldn't have come here if it wasn't important. Let's listen to what they have to say.'

And with that she ushered James and Foley inside and along the hall with her husband and daughter following behind.

They entered a large, soulless living room where the air stank of cigarette smoke. A few Christmas decorations hung around the doors and there was a small, brightly lit tree in one corner.

Mrs Hutchinson invited them to sit on a large, leather sofa while she perched herself on one of two armchairs facing them. Her husband then sat on the other chair and their daughter remained standing.

'My name is Sheila, by the way,' Mrs Hutchinson said. 'Allow me to apologise on behalf of my husband. You see, he can't abide Ted Rycroft and whenever the man's name is mentioned the red mist descends and he behaves like a child.'

Hutchinson heaved out a sigh and gave a resigned shake of his head, but he chose not to contradict what his wife had said.

James took a moment to size the couple up. He sensed that it was a marriage of equals and that Sheila gave as good as she got. They both appeared to be of pensionable age, but she didn't look as healthy as he did. Her face was pale against her shapeless brown hair, and deep wrinkles fanned out from bloodshot eyes.

'Well, get on with it then,' Hutchinson said, without trying to conceal his irritation. 'What more do you want to tell us?'

He sat back, took a half-smoked cigarette from the table next to him, and re-lit it.

'When was the last time any of you saw Mr Rycroft?' James asked.

'I haven't seen him in weeks,' Hutchinson said. 'Not since our paths crossed in a pub and we got into the usual slanging match. You'll know about that because afterwards he went outside and vandalised my car. I reported it, but he managed to convince your stupid colleagues that he didn't do it. But I know he did. It was so fucking obvious.'

James nodded. 'I'm aware of what happened. I also know about your long-running feud with him, which got worse after you bought his land without him knowing.'

He dragged heavily on his cigarette and let the smoke out of his nose.

'We were looking to expand our business here and when the land was put up for sale, I wasn't going to pass up the opportunity to buy it even though I knew he wouldn't want me to. So, I pulled a little trick and it worked.'

'I don't understand what all this has got to do with Ted

and the others going missing,' Sheila said. 'We've told you we haven't seen him in ages.'

James leaned forward, resting his elbows on his knees. 'Well, the mystery surrounding the whereabouts of Mr Rycroft and his friends is only one aspect of our investigation,' he said. 'We also want to find out who vandalised his home after he left it this morning. Most of the windows were smashed and severe damage was done inside almost every room. Vehicles belonging to the men were also damaged.'

Sheila's eyes spread wide and her nostrils flared alarmingly.

'Are you serious?' she shrieked. 'Do you actually suspect that my husband was responsible?'

James started to speak, but Hutchinson got there first.

'As much as it pleases me to know that Rycroft's home has been wrecked, I can assure you that it wasn't me who did it,' he said.

'Then I take it you can account for your movements since this morning?' James said.

'He's been here all day.' This from his daughter who stepped forward and placed a hand on his shoulder as she looked at James. 'I swear it. We've all been hard at work and he hasn't left our sight.'

'And that's the truth,' Sheila said. 'I can't believe that you've come here to accuse him of something like that.'

James sat up straight and huffed out a breath. Before he could respond, Foley spoke up.

'Look, Mrs Hutchinson, we're not accusing your husband of anything. But in view of the toxic relationship that exists between him and Mr Rycroft, we're obliged to ask these questions.'

'And we've answered them,' Sheila replied. 'So now you can . . .'

She stopped mid-sentence, distracted by the sound of the front door opening and a voice from the hall calling out, 'We're back and you'll never guess what's happened.'

'That'll be my sister,' Naomi said.

Seconds later a young couple entered the room and it was Foley's reaction that took James by surprise.

'Well, I didn't expect to see you here this evening, Mr Spicer,' she said to the guy who stood there looking confused. 'You remember me, don't you?'

He squinted at her and gave a slow nod. 'You're the copper who interviewed me after those guys roughed me up.'

'That's right. Detective Constable Foley.'

In response he snorted dismissively and said, 'You never did catch the bastards, did you? But then I don't suppose you really tried to.'

James felt his pulse escalate and he wondered if Spicer's presence in the area today was more than a mere coincidence.

CHAPTER TEN

A heavy silence descended on the room and all eyes focused on Warren Spicer, including those of his girlfriend. But he didn't respond immediately to what DC Foley had said, which gave James time to satisfy himself that he'd never seen the man before.

He was wearing a padded waterproof jacket and tight drainpipe jeans that made his legs look like sticks. His face was thin and sharp, and he had dark hair that was spiked up with gel.

Some ten seconds passed before James broke the silence with, 'I'm Detective Chief Inspector Walker, Mr Spicer. My colleague told me earlier what happened to you. She also explained that you're an anti-hunt saboteur, that you and your brother have had run-ins with farmer Ted Rycroft and that you allegedly threatened him on at least one occasion.'

Spicer's jaw went rigid and he fixed Foley with a steely gaze.

'We've never threatened Ted Rycroft,' he said loudly, his voice dripping with contempt. 'And we've only ever got involved in verbal scraps with him when he's been out chasing and killing foxes. So, whoever has told you otherwise is a liar.'

Eager not to see something nasty develop, James stood up and said, 'Calm down, Mr Spicer. It's not our intention to antagonise you or anyone else.'

'Then would you mind explaining why the police have been talking about me and my brother? We've made a point of staying out of trouble. So, it's time you left us alone.'

James resisted the urge to put him in his place and said, 'Are you aware that Mr Rycroft and three of his friends are missing?'

Spicer shrugged. 'We heard about it in the pub. Faye was about to tell her parents. But so what? Have you got it into your heads that me and my brother had something to do with it?'

'It's not like that, Mr Spicer. After we learned that those men were missing, we went to Mr Rycroft's farm because that was where they set out from. While there, we were told about his long-running feud with Mr Hutchinson over their opposing views on fox hunting. We were also informed that you and your brother and Mr Hutchinson are close friends. That was the extent of it.'

'We're more than just *friends*,' Spicer said, coldly. 'Faye and me are moving in together soon. We're family.'

'Then allow me to wish you both well,' James said, hoping it would take some of the heat out of the conversation.

Spicer shrugged again. 'Thanks, but I still don't understand why you're here. So Rycroft and his pathetic mates have gone and got themselves lost while out hunting. That's their fault.'

'It's not just about that, Warren,' Hutchinson broke in. 'Someone dropped in on Rycroft's farm after they left and did a lot of damage to it. And it seems like I'm the prime suspect.'

Spicer pulled a face. 'But that's ridiculous. Why would you have done that?'

'I have to assume the police think I wanted revenge for what the slimy bugger did to my car outside the pub.'

That last remark prompted interventions from Hutchinson's wife and both his daughters. They all spoke at the same time, claiming that he'd been with them throughout the day.

James had to raise his voice to make himself heard and insisted that because of Mr Rycroft's views on fox hunting everyone who had clashed with him over it had to be considered a potential suspect for the vandalism.

'It's our job to investigate, to ask questions, and to eliminate individuals from our inquiries,' he said. 'And to that end, would you mind accounting for your movements today, Mr Spicer? I know that you and your girlfriend went to the pub. But what time was that and where were you earlier in the day?'

A shocked expression froze on Spicer's face. 'So, I'm suddenly in the frame because I just happened to turn up here?' he responded, indignation rising in his voice.

'Not at all,' James answered. 'We were intending to visit you and your brother as soon as possible, along with various other people. So please help us to move the investigation along by cooperating.'

James saw a defiant glint in the man's eyes, but it couldn't disguise the fact that he was clearly nervous. He looked first at his girlfriend and then at her father, his teeth tugging at his bottom lip as he did so.

'Oh for heaven's sake, Warren, just answer the question and tell them where you were,' Sheila pleaded with him. 'We all know you had nothing to do with what's happened.'

Spicer acknowledged her with a sharp nod and drew a breath before speaking.

'Okay, fair enough,' he said. 'Everyone knows I got here just before six to pick Faye up. I came straight from home where I spent all day with Liam. Neither of us had to go to work so we got up late and then chilled out doing nothing.'

'I find that surprising, Mr Spicer,' James said. 'You're a well-known hunt saboteur and I understand a number of meets were taking place today across the county. Why weren't you taking part in one of the protests?'

He shrugged. 'I've decided to give up on all that stuff now that I'm in a relationship. I can't risk being in the middle of it when situations become explosive, as they do all too often these days.'

'I can vouch for that,' Faye said. 'We've talked about it a lot and I made it clear that I wouldn't be with him if there was a chance he'd get arrested again and end up in prison.'

'The same goes for my brother,' Warren said. 'He's also in a serious relationship and he doesn't want to fuck it up.'

'And where is Liam now?' James asked.

'How would I know? I'm his brother, not his mum. He did say he'd probably go out for a drink in Kendal. We live on the edge of town.'

'We will have to talk to him,' James said, as he tugged his notebook from his pocket. 'Can you give me your phone numbers, address and vehicle registrations?'

'I don't know Liam's reg off hand.'

'Then give me yours.'

James wrote them down then asked, 'What do each of you do for a living?'

'We're both plumbers and we run our own company,' he said. 'Our dad passed the business on to us after he retired.'

James had already come to the conclusion that there wasn't much more to be achieved by dragging out the conversation. Hutchinson's family had given him an alibi and they would have to follow up what Spicer had told them.

He asked a few more questions, made some more notes and left his card with them.

'Please contact me in the unlikely event that you receive information on the whereabouts of Mr Rycroft and his crew,' he said.

'We will,' Sheila replied while her husband remained silent, his face set like granite.

She showed them to the front door and as soon as they stepped outside, they both received the same text message from DC Patterson. As James read it a cold shiver washed over him.

Bad news, guys. The rescuers have found them-selves in the midst of a blizzard and have been forced to call off the search and turn back.

CHAPTER ELEVEN

It was no surprise to James that the search had been called off so soon after it had got under way. The wind was even stronger now and the snow that was falling was thicker, heavier, with flakes the size of 50p coins.

As he sat beside Foley in the back of the Land Rover, he continued to be weighed down by concern for those four men. It was made worse by the fact that he wasn't sure that investigating the vandalism at the Rycroft farm would bring him any closer to finding them.

The most credible scenario was that a bunch of anti-hunt activists struck this morning because they knew that the property would be empty. But they didn't know that Rycroft and his fellow hunters would go missing and therefore wouldn't return hours later to be confronted by their handiwork.

'So, what's your take on what we were told, guv?' Foley said, breaking into James's thoughts as they drove away from the farm. 'They didn't convince me that they were being totally honest with us.'

'That was my impression as well,' James replied. 'Spicer was put on the spot and clearly wasn't keen to tell us how and where he'd spent the day. I find it hard to believe that he didn't go out protesting, despite what he told us. It wouldn't surprise me if he's on the phone to his brother now, making sure their stories tally. But if one or both of them are our vandals, I suspect it'll be hard for us to prove it without any conclusive forensic evidence.'

'I agree. It also struck me as slightly suspicious that the wife and daughters sprang so quickly to Hutchinson's defence. It was almost as though they'd been primed and knew what they had to say.'

James nodded. 'What came across too was the sheer level of animosity they feel towards their neighbour. They made it sound like they wouldn't give a toss if he didn't survive the night.'

'So where do we go from here?' Foley asked.

'We'll talk to Liam Spicer and see if the brothers' alibi stacks up. If they did leave their home earlier then there's an outside chance that we'll find them on a road camera. I also intend to ask Greg Pike to shed some light on the threat that the brothers allegedly made against Rycroft. The trouble is any avenue of inquiry relating to the trashing of the farm might not help us solve the mystery of those missing men.'

'That's my worry too. And now that the search has been halted, even if only for a few hours, it looks less likely that they'll turn up safe and well.'

Rycroft's farm was still a hive of activity despite the harsh weather. Crime scene floodlights had been set up around the yard and officers in hi-vis jackets were working at a pace to seal the shattered windows with insulating film and anything else they could find to do the job.

Another detective, DC Ahmed Sharma, had arrived from headquarters. He was a fairly new recruit to the team and like James had spent time in the Met before moving to Cumbria. He was busy making notes and taking photos of the damaged cars. Inside the house, SOCOs were working methodically through the rooms and taking stock of what exhibits to collect.

'You call the office and brief Colin on our conversation with Hutchinson,' James said to Foley. 'And get him to send officers to the Spicer home to find out what the elder brother has to say for himself.'

He then donned gloves and overshoes, and as he entered the house, tiredness tugged at his bones. It had been a long day and he knew it would be many more hours before he got to go home. This was a curious case that was unlike any he'd been involved in before. It was already playing with his head while throwing up questions at a blistering rate. Did Neil Hutchinson lie to them and trash the farm as an act of revenge against his neighbour who he believed had vandalised his car? Or did Warren Spencer, his potential future son-in-law, do it for him? And was it conceivable that one or both of them knew what had happened to the four huntsmen?

James threw out a loud sigh as he walked up the stairs to where he'd been told Tony Coppell had been inspecting the trophy room.

The chief forensic officer was inside taking photographs and when he saw James, he lowered the camera and said, 'I don't suppose I need to tell you that this room will probably be key to the investigation. I've already bagged the picture that had the word *murderers* scrawled on it, along with the tin of black paint and brush that was obviously used to do it. We'll check them for prints and DNA deposits. So far we haven't found any of the weapons that were in the cupboard.'

'What are your thoughts, Tony?' James asked him.

'Well, it's hard not to conclude that this is the work of extreme anti-hunt activists. I've attended a number of properties owned by high-profile hunters over the years where severe damage was inflicted. In almost every case, slogans of some sort were daubed on walls and mirrors. I recall one where the word *killer* was plastered across the front door. But you'll know yourself that hunt supporters can be just as destructive. They usually target cars and individuals, though.'

'Have you come across anything that might help us determine the whereabouts of the four men?'

Coppell shook his head. 'Not so far, but I did find these.' He reached down and picked up two small, framed photos from a cardboard box on the floor. As he handed them to James, he added, 'Would they be the men in question?'

In one, four men were standing together in a field, surrounded by a pack of hounds. They were wearing shirts and jeans and James recognised Ted Rycroft instantly from the photo he'd seen earlier.

The second photo had obviously been taken some years earlier because the same four men were clearly much younger. They were wearing red coats and sitting astride horses while waving at the camera. Once again, there were hounds in the foreground.

'That guy is Ted Rycroft,' James said, pointing at the second photo. 'I don't know who the other three are, but there's a good chance they're the men who went out with him today.'

James handed the pictures back after taking photos of them on his phone, which he promptly sent to DC Patterson.

'I gather the rescue team has had to turn back,' Coppell said.

'I'm afraid so. Hopefully they'll be able to set out again soon.'

'It's never a good sign when people go missing during such bad weather. And it doesn't help in this case that we don't know if and when they got into trouble. Was it early this morning or later in the day?'

'I know, and what's so strange about it is that they're all experienced hikers and hunters.'

'That only counts for so much in this part of the country,' Coppell said. 'Even those who are accustomed to the terrain can get into difficulties when the weather turns.'

'My team will be working through the night and well into tomorrow morning, and I've called for reinforcements so we can extend the search beyond the house.'

James left him to it and went back downstairs. Foley was waiting for him inside the front door, having just come off the phone to DC Patterson.

'He had no more updates for us, guv,' she said. 'But he did tell me that he'd arranged for the team to be prepared for an early morning call-out if there's no news on our mispers.'

Just then James's phone rang and when he took it from his pocket, he saw that the call was from Superintendent Tanner.

'It's the boss,' he said to Foley. 'While I take it, could you go and get our people together so that I can have a quick word before we go back to the office?'

'I'm on it, guv.'

Jeff Tanner usually made a point of going away at Christmas

with his wife and son. But this year, having been promoted from DCI, he'd decided not to, no doubt in order to make a good impression with the powers that be in Penrith.

'I've been briefed, James, but I thought I should have a quick word with you before I turn in for the night,' he said. 'Last I heard those men were still missing. Does that remain the situation?'

'Sadly, it does, sir. And the search has also been called off because of the weather.'

'Christ, it's going from bad to worse. Any developments in respect of the damage to the farmhouse?'

James brought him up to speed and gave him a detailed description of what it was like inside. He also mentioned the missing shotguns and the defaced hunting picture.

'It's my understanding that the press have only been told that the men set out from there,' Coppell said. 'It's not yet been disclosed that the place has been vandalised. When the newspapers do get wind of it, and they will soon enough, there'll be a media frenzy. Fox hunting is a divisive issue and all kinds of claims and counter claims are likely to surface. We need to prepare ourselves for that.'

'Agreed. It's going to be hard to control the flow of infor mation though. This thing, whatever it is, involves so many people,' he said. 'You've got all the individuals and groups who detest those men because they're convinced that they break the law by hunting foxes. And you've got the families who are living in limbo not knowing if their loved ones are alive or dead.'

'I want you to liaise closely with the press office and to call me at home if there are any major developments during the night,' Tanner ordered.

After the call, James went outside into the windswept yard where Foley had brought the officers together. There were twelve uniforms along with DC Sharma. He told them to remain at the scene until they received further instructions.

'Stay safe, keep warm and do what you can to assist the SOCOs and Mountain Rescue Team,' he said. 'And I'm sorry that your Christmas won't be as merry as you were hoping it would be.'

He then took some questions and made a point of asking Sharma to arrange for hot drinks and snacks to be brought to the farm.

'I'm going to the office now so I can start to pull things together, but I'll return in the morning at some point,' he said.

When he was seated in the Land Rover, he looked at his watch and was surprised to see that it was almost eleven o'clock.

'I have to say this is not how I thought we'd all be spending the night before Christmas,' James said to Foley.

'Well, it doesn't surprise me, guv,' she replied. 'This stopped being the season of goodwill years ago.'

Malek started the engine, but just as they were about to pull away DC Sharma banged his fist on the window to stop them. He then pulled open the rear door and said to James, 'There's been a development, guv. The Mountain Rescue Team have just been in touch. They were heading back here when they found a dog sheltering in a bothy. They think it could be one of the hounds belonging to the huntsmen. But that's not all. They also say there are stains on its coat that look like blood.'

CHAPTER TWELVE

They didn't have long to wait before the Mountain Rescue Team arrived back at the farm, and it was clear from their tight expressions that they'd had a rough time of it.

The team leader was the one cradling the small dog in his arms and James didn't need to be told that it was a beagle, one of the most popular breeds of hunting dogs in the UK. It had long, droopy ears and a smooth, dense coat that was a combination of black, tan and white.

'We found her purely by chance about a mile from here,' the team leader said as James and Foley approached. 'She was lying inside a small stone bothy and at first, we thought she was dead. But thankfully, she's very much alive. Exhausted and cold, but alive.'

They followed him to the team's Land Rover where he placed her gently inside the open boot. Her eyes were closed and James could see that she was still shivering.

'There was nothing else in the bothy and we did a quick search of the immediate area, but found no other sign of life,' the team leader continued. 'We couldn't stay there because conditions were getting worse by the second. It's my guess she got lost and managed to shelter there. But there's no telling where she came from or how far she walked before she got there.'

'And what about the stains you mentioned?' James asked.

The man pointed to several large red patches on the white fur below the dog's head.

'I hope I'm wrong, but that looks like blood to me,' he said.

James agreed. 'Have you checked for any injuries?'

The team leader nodded. 'There are no open wounds that I can see, so I reckon the blood isn't hers. But look, she is wearing a personalised collar with a name and a phone number.'

James noted that the name on it was Pixie and he immediately asked Foley to call Patterson.

'Can you get him to check the number and find out if it belongs to one of the missing men?' he said.

James took photos of the dog and her tag on his phone and emailed them to Patterson. Next, he asked Sharma if he would go and fetch Tony Coppell from inside the farmhouse.

While he waited for the chief forensic officer, he noticed that the wind was getting much stronger and he could well understand why the search had been temporarily abandoned even though the team had struck lucky by finding Pixie.

Thankfully, she was alive, and if she did go out with the four huntsmen then it encouraged him to believe that they too were alive and sheltering somewhere.

But what about the blood on her coat? If the dog hadn't suffered any wounds, then how did it get there and who did it belong to?

'I need the answers to two questions,' he said to Coppell when he came over to the Land Rover. 'Is that blood on the dog's coat? And if so, is it animal or human?'

Coppell leaned into the boot and inspected the stain. 'It certainly appears to be blood, but I won't be able to give you a definitive answer to either question until we've analysed a sample in the lab,' he said. 'I'll make it a priority, but it could still take forty-eight hours or more to get the result back.'

Minutes later Foley broke the news that James had been dreading.

'Colin just got back to me, guv,' she said. 'The number on the collar does belong to one of the huntsmen – Rhys Hughes. He took all three of his dogs with him this morning. And his son has confirmed that one of them is named Pixie.'

CHAPTER THIRTEEN

Day Two
Christmas Day

It was ten minutes past midnight when James and Foley hurried back into police headquarters in Kendal.

Speed was of the essence, not only because they wanted to move forward with the investigation, but also because they were both desperate to empty their bladders.

James made it to the loo just in time and breathed a loud sigh of relief when he was done. As he washed his hands he almost didn't recognise himself in the mirror. He looked more like fifty-eight than forty-eight. His face was pallid and drawn, the jawline rough with stubble, and creases had dug their way into the corners of his eyes.

On the way up to the office he helped himself to a large coffee from the vending machine in the hope that it would help him to revive his senses and keep him awake.

He wasn't surprised to find that none of the officers and support staff who had been on duty throughout Christmas

Eve had gone home. They were still working tirelessly alongside those on the night shift. Their strong commitment to the job and the way they rose to every challenge was one of the reasons James had been happy to take on the role of detective chief inspector.

Though he didn't doubt that they were as gutted as he was that they wouldn't be spending Christmas morning with their families.

After shedding his coat in the office, he went straight over to where DC Patterson was attaching photos to the evidence board.

The first thing he noticed was that the two photos he'd sent over of the four huntsmen together, though years apart, had been given pride of place in the centre of the board. And beneath them were individual photos of the men with name tags to identify them.

'We got those from relatives and social media accounts,' Patterson explained. 'They've been sent out to the papers and broadcast news operations as part of the appeal for information.'

Ted Rycroft, at sixty-seven, was the oldest. Rhys Hughes was seven years younger, but his face had more lines etched into it and his hair was completely grey. Nigel Marr, aged fifty-seven, was a short, sinewy man with a bald head and a crooked nose that looked very much as though it had been broken at some point. Dylan Payne, the youngest at forty-nine, carried more weight than the others and was the only one wearing spectacles.

'It's hard to believe that no one has heard from them for over sixteen hours now,' Patterson said. 'In normal circumstances that wouldn't be something to get excited about. But it's a hell of a long time to be stuck out on the fells or moors in this weather.'

'You're not wrong,' James replied. 'Look, finish sorting the board and I'll get the team together for a briefing. We need to start planning the day ahead.'

Some of the team were on their phones so James went from desk to desk telling everyone who was free to assemble in front of the evidence board in five.

He was almost done when DC Foley entered the room. The colour had returned to her cheeks and her long reddish hair was back to how it had been before it was battered by the wind.

She was carrying two cups of coffee, and as she handed one to James, she said, 'Get that down you, guv. It'll help to defrost your insides.'

He felt a flush of guilt and replied, 'I'm so sorry, Caroline. I helped myself to one on the way up and didn't think to get one for you.'

Her face cracked a smile. 'You're forgiven so long as I get some brownie points.'

He grinned back. 'You can count on it. And you'll earn a few more if you take it upon yourself to write up the report on our visit to Kentmere.'

Her smile widened. 'It's a deal.'

When the briefing got under way the atmosphere in the room was charged even though most of the team were knackered. James hadn't seen them looking so tense and sombre since last New Year when they struggled to solve the gruesome murder of the maid-of-honour at a wedding on the banks of Lake Windermere.

He began by thanking those who should have knocked off hours ago for sticking with it.

'I really appreciate it and so will the families of the men who are missing,' he said.

He then ran through what they'd found at the farmhouse and the details of their conversations with Neil Hutchinson and Warren Spicer. Most of what he told them they already knew, but as they listened, they made notes and asked questions.

'I don't think I need to spell out to you that we're working against the clock on this one and it still isn't clear exactly what is going on,' he said. 'We have four men who've failed to return from a trail hunt that might actually have been an illegal fox hunt. We don't know if they're lost, stranded or even if they're victims of a crime. But one of the dogs that they took with them has been found with what looks like blood on its coat. At the same time, we have to find out who vandalised the farm they set out from this morning, along with the vehicles that were parked there.'

He pointed to the evidence board and the photo of the empty gun cupboard.

'We've been told by Mr Rycroft's employees that the cupboard contained five shotguns, plus boxes of ammunition. But they've all vanished.' He then put his finger on the picture which had the word *murderers* scrawled on it. 'Here's another thing to be concerned about. The huntsmen in this are too far away to be identified, so we don't know if the four missing men are among them. But the message strongly suggests that one or more anti-hunt activists were responsible for the damage. They could have descended on the farm because they knew that the owner, Mr Rycroft, would be going on a hunt with his pals, so we need to draw up a list of all the people who were aware that the hunt was taking place, including friends and family members. I suspect the hunters didn't want it to be common knowledge so the list might not be that long.

'We also need to eliminate everyone who had threatened, abused or attacked any of the four men in the past. I reckon this list will be much longer given that fox hunters attract lots of enemies. And it will include Neil Hutchinson and the Spicer brothers.'

This was Patterson's cue to tell James that DC Kevin Hall, who was sent to the home shared by the brothers in Kendal, had reported back to say that Liam Spicer wasn't there.

'Have you tried his phone?' James asked.

Patterson nodded. 'I called as soon as DC Foley passed the number on to me, but it appears to be switched off. I can tell you, though, that the guy has previous. Three years ago he was charged with common assault while protesting at a trail hunt near Ullswater and got a fine. Then he received another fine for threatening and abusive behaviour during a Boxing Day meet last year. He and his brother have a reputation for going to protests with the aim of escalating things.'

'Good to know. Have you checked out Johnny Elvin, the man who apparently pulled out of going on the hunt at the last minute?'

Patterson shook his head. 'It's next on my to-do list.'

The discussion moved on to the search operation and the officer liaising with Mountain Rescue told them that as soon as the weather improved helicopters and drones would be deployed. Several other rescue teams were also on standby to assist the one that had been sent to Kentmere.

Another evidence board was then set up and a map of the area was pinned to it. James pointed to the location of the

Rycroft farm and it was noted that the hunters could have gone off in any direction from there.

Patterson then confirmed that none of the family members he'd spoken to had known the route the group were planning to take.

They were still focused on the map when a support staffer who was sitting at her desk raised a hand to get James's attention.

'You need to check this out, sir,' she said, indicating her computer screen. 'The story is trending online and a war of words has broken out between those who support fox hunting and those who oppose it. There are a lot of vile comments. Some people are even saying that they hope the men are no longer alive.'

CHAPTER FOURTEEN

James paused the briefing in order to check out the furore that had erupted on social media.

He saw that the story had certainly triggered a flood of nasty comments across various online platforms including Facebook, Twitter and Instagram.

People on both sides of the fox hunting debate were making their feelings known through a range of hateful and offensive remarks.

Let's hope the killers have been killed. That would make my Christmas.

I don't believe those guys have been trail hunting. They've obviously come unstuck while running down and slaughtering innocent animals.

Why should anyone feel sorry for those missing blokes? What they do is cruel and barbaric.

These comments are a disgrace. If those men are hunting foxes then they're doing us all a favour because those animals need to be culled.

The usual hate-filled rants from those who care more about pests than people.

James was appalled, but not surprised. For as long as he could remember the contentious issue had sparked ugly exchanges between hunt supporters and opponents.

'Most people thought that things would calm down after fox hunting was banned all those years ago, but it sometimes seems as though it's got worse,' he said to Foley who was looking over his shoulder at the computer screen.

'I know from first-hand experience how it can divide families,' she replied. 'My ex is a vet and for years has campaigned against what she calls "cruel blood sports". But her dad liked to hunt and they fell out over it. Then a couple of years ago they stopped talking to each other and her dad died of a heart attack shortly after.'

'That's sad,' James said. 'It makes you wonder how often such things happen.'

'All too often, I reckon. Although I had no idea how bad it was until my ex told me. The newspapers don't seem to pay much attention anymore. You have to go online to see what's going on.'

Her words prompted James to do just that out of interest, and what he came across within minutes he found quite shocking. There was video footage of raucous hunts where both hunters and protesters were seen being abused and assaulted. Several clips showed hounds savaging foxes, while others captured vehicles and property being vandalised. Plus, the online news and video feeds were full of distressing headlines going back just a few years.

Lone huntsman battered by a masked gang of protesters.

Disabled man hit by blood sport thugs.

Hunter beats protester with a whip.

Anti-hunt protester taken to hospital after Boxing Day clashes.

Footage captures moments armed police stop fox hunt saboteurs.

Police arrest six men over illegal fox hunting.

James mentioned some of the headlines when the briefing got under way again.

'I think they're an indication that we're likely to encounter a degree of resistance as the investigation progresses,' he said.

The briefing lasted another forty-five minutes, during which James assigned various tasks and roles. But it was still only just after 1 a.m. so he knew that some things would have to wait until later.

'We need to find out as much as we can about Rhys Hughes, Nigel Marr and Dylan Payne,' he said. 'Let's carry out background checks and check their digital footprints. And tell DC Hall to stay outside the Spicers' house. Plus, we need to arrange for the families of the missing men to come into the office so that we can talk them through what's happening and at the same time extract some information from them.

'Caroline, I need you to contact Rebecca Carter and Greg Pike to make sure they'll be on hand later to return to the farm. They're best placed to tell us more about Ted Rycroft since it appears he doesn't have any relatives. And I want them to go through the farmhouse with us to see if anything other than the shotguns has been taken.'

James also raised the prospect of staging a press conference later in the morning or early afternoon. Much depended on whether the four men turned up in the coming hours.

He ended the briefing by telling Patterson to send out an alert to the rest of the team, asking them to report for duty early.

His next job would be to contact the press office in Penrith and discuss with them what updated information to release. But first he needed more coffee to ease the dryness in his throat and something to eat to stop the grumbling in his stomach.

CHAPTER FIFTEEN

Christmas morning passed painfully slowly and concern for the missing men continued to grow.

There was still no word from them and the search remained on hold until the weather improved.

James ploughed on, noting every snippet of information that came across his desk while at the same time seeking to identify potential lines of inquiry.

Fatigue was making it hard for him to concentrate, but he was determined not to let it show. It was important to set an example for the rest of the team.

The mainstream news channels were running the story in their early bulletins and it was the lead on the BBC regional opt out covering Cumbria.

Most of the reports carried photos of the four huntsmen along with library footage and maps of the area they were believed to be missing in. This included Kentmere Valley, which was surrounded by high fells, and the remote Kentmere reservoir.

It was pointed out that the men set out from Ted Rycroft's farm but there was no mention of the damage that had been done to it, or of the dog that had been found.

At 5 a.m. James was informed that a press conference would take place at Constabulary headquarters in Penrith at mid-day. Superintendent Tanner had agreed to front it alongside a Mountain Rescue spokesperson. That suited James because fronting pressers was one of his pet hates.

At six o'clock the rest of the team started to arrive looking fresh and determined. First among them was James's right-hand man, Phil Stevens, who had moved up the ladder to replace him as detective inspector.

'And here I was naively believing that this Christmas would pass without another merry mystery for us to deal with,' Stevens said.

James was reassured by his presence. Stevens was a diligent, no-nonsense investigator who had proved himself to be a loyal number two. They'd got off to a rocky start three years ago after James was given the job of detective inspector that had been lined up for Stevens, but Phil soon got over it and now they had a good working relationship.

'You're right about this being a mystery,' James responded. 'And as it stands, we're a long way from solving it.'

'Well, it'll solve itself if those guys turn up and tell us that they spent the night in a bothy'

James nodded. 'That would most certainly bring some festive cheer. But there's still the mystery of who trashed the farm.'

He was still passing on what he knew to Stevens when another of his most highly valued team members entered the office.

Detective Sergeant Jessica Abbott also got a well-deserved promotion during the department shake-up back in the spring. James regarded her as one of the Constabulary's rising stars. Aged thirty-five and of Irish and East African descent, she had a sharp mind and a focused work ethic. James and his wife had been privileged to attend her wedding in the summer when she married her long-time paramedic boyfriend, Sean.

'I would have come in much sooner if I'd known what was going on,' she said. 'But Sean and I went to bed early because we spent the day at his sister's place and were shattered when we finally got home.'

'Well, you're here now and I have no doubt that you'll be shattered again by the end of today.'

The three of them then joined the rest of the team for another briefing at which James let them know about the forthcoming press conference. He also told those officers and support staffers who had worked through the night to go home and get some rest. But several of them, including DCs Patterson and Foley, said they wanted to remain on duty for at least a few more hours.

Patterson had a couple of updates to share, the first being that he had arranged a meeting with the families of the missing men.

'For various reasons the earliest we can get them here together is one o'clock. We'll have the wives of Dylan Payne and Nigel Marr, and Rhys Hughes's son, Owain, who lives with him. I've also spoken to the two people who work at Rycroft's farm, Greg Pike and Rebecca Carter. They've agreed to go there at three today and Tony Coppell says it won't be a problem to let them look around to check on what's been taken. I've also arranged for DC Isaac to take over from DC Sharma who's spent most of the night there.'

There was one piece of good news from the officer monitoring the weather and liaising with Mountain Rescue. Conditions had improved slightly and it was looking likely that the search could resume before sunset at around eight-thirty. To begin with, they would concentrate their efforts on the area where Pixie the dog was found.

They were still discussing the case and tossing ideas around when a call came in from DC Hall who had been stationed in an unmarked car outside the home of the Spicer brothers. He reported that Liam Spicer had just been dropped off by a taxi, but the detective was told not to approach him unless he came back out.

'I'll go straight there,' James said. 'Jessica, you'll be coming with me. Caroline, I need you to pull everything we have so far into a report and get it circulated.

'You'll be in charge here,' he said to Stevens. 'Can you get things ready to welcome the families and produce briefing notes on each of the men? I'd like to know if any of them have form and whether they've been targeted in the past by anti-hunt fanatics.'

He went to his office to get his coat and after shrugging himself into it, he called Superintendent Tanner to let him know what was happening.

'I've been told about the press conference, boss,' he said. 'I should be back by one and will update you before it begins.'

'Well, I have an unpleasant update for you, James,' Tanner said. 'I've just received word that at least one newspaper now knows about the vandalism at the Rycroft farm. It will no doubt spread like wildfire and add juice to the story.'

'Then we should view it as a positive, sir, and hope that it encourages anyone who suspects they know who did it to come forward. We could do with a few more suspects.'

As James hung up, he noticed that he'd just received a text message from Annie.

Merry Christmas my love. Hope all is well and that your night wasn't as bad as I fear it might have been.

Bella and me are fine. Call me when you can xxx

He resisted the temptation to call right away and instead responded to the text.

Morning to you, too. It was a cold night but I coped and I'm just about to go out again so will phone you later. I'm so sorry I can't be with you this morning of all days. Take some photos of Bella opening her presents, but hold some back for me to give her. All my love xxx

He was shoving his phone into his pocket when DS Abbott appeared in his office doorway.

'Are you ready to roll, guv?' she said. 'I've got the key to a pool car and Liam Spicer's address. It should only take us a few minutes to get there.'

'Then let's get going,' he said.

CHAPTER SIXTEEN

Liam and Warren Spicer lived in the southern section of town, out towards the Westmorland Hospital.

It was no longer snowing, but the drive there was still an unpleasant experience. The roads were dirty with slush, salt and grit, and there were some treacherous patches of ice.

DS Abbott, who was in the driving seat, spent most of the journey asking James questions about the investigation that he did not yet know the answers to. She also reminded him that she and her husband were keen hikers.

'I know that area pretty well,' she said. 'Sean and I walked the Kentmere Horseshoe a couple of years ago.'

'What's that?' James asked her.

'It's actually one of the longest and most remote walks in the Lake District and traverses all the fells bounding the upper valley and reservoir. I know there's a good chance that those four hunters headed in that direction from the farm, but they could also have gone east towards Sadgill or west towards Troutbeck. It's such a vast area and since the weather was pretty calm yesterday morning, apart from a few isolated rain showers, they probably covered quite a few miles before it turned nasty.'

'Which will make it harder for the rescue teams to find them.'

She nodded. 'Absolutely. But the more I think about it the more convinced I'm becoming that something serious must have happened to them and that they're not just lost or stranded. Those guys are far from amateurs when it comes to embarking on a trek or hunt. They'd have had their eyes on the weather and would have gone well equipped. And they'd have known that mobile phones can't be relied on in this part of the world.'

'Agreed. When a lone hiker goes missing it's easy to assume that he or she has had an accident or become trapped. But we're talking about four men and a bunch of dogs.'

Foley nodded. 'And there are the other factors that raise the level of concern. The damage to the farmhouse, that poor dog with what might be blood on its coat . . .'

'There's also the evidence that's pointing us towards anti-hunt activists,' James said. 'It's scary to think that a bunch of them might now be armed with five shotguns, complete with boxes of ammunition. Does it mean they intend to use them, and if so, on who?'

They were still trying to get their heads around it when they arrived at the Spicer home. It was in a row of squat, terraced houses with tiny front gardens.

Vehicles were parked along both sides of the street and it was Abbott who spotted DC Hall in the unmarked car close by. She pointed him out to James who then signalled for him to stay put.

It was approaching 7.30 a.m. when James rang the bell and they had to wait about half a minute before the door was opened by a short, squat man wearing a tracksuit.

James was reaching for his warrant card when the man let out a weighty sigh and said, 'There's no need to show your ID. You're coppers, right? I'd be able to tell from a mile off. Warren told me you'd probably be dropping by this morning. You're lucky to catch me in.'

'So, you're Mr Liam Spicer?' James said.

'That I am.'

'Then would you mind if we came in to have a word with you? I'm guessing your brother told you what it's about.'

He smiled then, cocky and confident, and gave a little shrug. 'I can give you half an hour at the most. There's a leaky pipe that needs my attention at a house over on Chapel Lane. I've agreed to repair it for the family so it doesn't ruin their Christmas.'

James smiled back and said, 'Then shall we get to it?'

They followed him into an untidy kitchen at the back of the house and he invited them to sit on one side of a large table while he sat facing them

James formally introduced himself and Abbott, and Liam listened in silence, his lips pressed together.

It struck James that he looked nothing like his younger brother. In contrast to Warren, Liam's hair was the colour of wet sand and he had a square, flat face.

'Can I start by asking if this is your house, Mr Spicer, or do you rent it?'

'Our parents gave it to us some years ago. They prefer to live in a bungalow by the sea in Whitehaven. It's suited me and Warren, but he wants to move in with Faye and as soon as he does, I'll put the place on the market. When it's sold we'll split the proceeds.'

'And when did you last speak to your brother?' James asked.

He shrugged. 'About half an hour ago, shortly after I got back here. You see, I went out last night and forgot to take my phone. Warren stayed the night with Faye so he couldn't get through to me.'

'And where did you spend the night, Mr Spicer?'

He stared at James, his eyes intent under dark brows. 'Not that it's any of your business, but I'm seeing a girl who has a flat near Gooseholme Park. I stayed there after we had a drink in the town centre. I'll be going straight back there after I've finished the job in Chapel Lane.'

'I see. According to your brother, you and he spent most of yesterday here. Is that correct?'

'It is, and I can save you both a lot of time by making it clear that neither of us had anything to do with wrecking Ted Rycroft's place. And we don't know why Rycroft and his mates are missing. It beggars fucking belief that we're in the frame.'

'Well, there are several reasons for that, Mr Spicer,' James said. 'We know that you and your brother have had run-ins with Mr Rycroft and threatened him on at least one occasion. Plus, you have form when it comes to acts of aggression against people who hunt foxes.'

Liam's face hardened and his eyes narrowed. 'I know that Warren has already told you that we've never threatened Rycroft. And if you reckon you've got proof showing that we have then I'd like to see it. And so would my lawyer. Look, I won't deny that in the past we tried to make things difficult for him and others like him when they went out slaughtering foxes. We've long been hunt saboteurs and we're proud of it, and until recently we didn't give a shit if we had to pay the occasional fine. But things are different now . . . we've settled down and our lasses don't want us mixed up in it anymore. And to be honest, they didn't have to tell us twice . . .'

'What do you mean by that?'

'Like I say, I'm proud of what we stand for but not everyone would agree. The publicity we've attracted has been bad for business. A number of people and companies have stopped using us. Some because they don't object to fox hunting and others because they don't want to give money to guys they believe to be trouble-makers.'

He sat back then, a defiant glint in his eyes.

'So, if it wasn't you and your brother who dropped in on Mr Rycroft's farm yesterday, then who do you think it was?' Abbott asked.

Liam glared at her with undisguised hostility. 'That bastard has more enemies than you will ever know. And not just because of the hunting. He's part of a clique of arrogant slimebags who think they're better than the rest of us.'

His face was contorted with anger now and James realised that he was going to be about as helpful as his brother had been.

'We will have to make further inquiries,' he said. 'And to that end, I'll need your girlfriend's name, address and phone number, plus your car registration.'

'The car's parked out front,' he said. 'The blue Ford Escort.'

He then provided them with his girlfriend's contact details, before adding, 'And for what it's worth, Inspector, I hope those guys turn up. I may well hate their guts, but I wouldn't want any real harm to come to them.'

James responded with a nod. He wanted to believe that the man was being sincere, but he couldn't be sure because his cold, grey eyes were devoid of compassion.

They showed themselves out and once back on the street, James took a photo of Liam Spicer's car. He then crossed the road and instructed DC Hall that he could return to headquarters.

'But first can you find out what cameras are in the area? If the brothers are lying about when they left here yesterday then traffic cam footage might help us prove it,' he said. He also gave him the details of Liam's girlfriend and asked him to pay her a visit to confirm Liam's story.

His phone rang then. It was DI Stevens.

'We've managed to contact Johnny Elvin, boss,' he said. 'He says he pulled out of the hunt at the last minute because he suffered a bout of food poisoning the day before and it laid him up. He claims he spent yesterday at home with his family but I've arranged for the guy to be brought to the office from his home in Shap so we can speak to him in person. He should be here in about forty minutes.'

CHAPTER SEVENTEEN

James put his phone on speaker as Abbott drove them back to headquarters. They both listened intently as DI Stevens summarised his short phone conversation with Johnny Elvin.

Elvin was married with a young daughter and was a dog breeder with his own kennels. He was a keen hunter and had been on quite a few trail hunts with Ted Rycroft and the others in the past. He was also a former county councillor and well known in the area.

It was coming up to 8.30 a.m. when James and Abbott walked back into the office.

'Those guys have been missing for over twenty-four hours now, guv,' Abbott said gravely.

'It might be time to prepare ourselves for the worst,' James said. 'Just as those families are going to have to.'

The team were still working flat out, speaking animatedly into phones and tapping at computer keyboards. It was a while since James had seen such frantic activity and it set his pulse racing.

'Let me know when Mr Elvin arrives,' James said to Stevens as he approached him. 'I'd like us both to talk to him.'

The DI gave a terse nod. 'Of course.'

'What was your impression of the guy, Phil?'

'The chat I had on the phone with him was brief, but he sounded genuine and appeared shocked. He'd heard his mates were missing when it came up on the news only minutes before I called him.'

'Have you run a check on him?'

'We have. He didn't come up on the database, but he does have a website that promotes his kennels.'

'Right. Anything else come in while we were gone?'

Stevens shook his head. 'Nothing worth bringing to your attention, boss. What did Liam Spicer have to say for himself?'

James relayed the conversation and said he wasn't convinced that Spicer had been honest with them.

'I've asked DC Hall to sus out CCTV in the area before visiting Spicer's girlfriend. Her name is Angela Beck and she lives and works here in town. I don't doubt that she'll confirm that he spent the night with her, but I'm more interested in where he spent the day.'

A patrol car with Johnny Elvin arrived at HQ sooner than expected and he was quickly shown up to the interview room where James and DI Stevens were waiting.

Elvin was a portly man tucked into an oversized winter coat that he shook himself free from as James did the introductions and thanked him for coming.

The man was bleary-eyed and unshaven, and he looked to be pushing forty. When he was seated opposite them James introduced himself and Stevens.

'Helen and me were having breakfast when it came up on the news that Ted and the others were missing,' he said, his voice gravel-edged. 'That was bad enough, but then we heard about what had been done to Ted's farm and I couldn't believe it.'

'I take it Helen is your wife,' James said.

'She is, and she's as worried as I am.'

'It's my understanding that you were planning to go out with them but couldn't because you were unwell,' James said.

Elvin nodded. 'It was food poisoning. No doubt about it. It hit me after I ate that bloody cake.'

'What cake?' Stevens asked.

Elvin shrugged. 'When I turned up at the kennels on Tuesday morning there was a box outside the door. Inside was a cake and a card wishing me a merry Christmas. There was no name and it just said it was "from a grateful customer".'

'So you don't know who it was?'

'Not a clue. Anyway, Ryan, my employee, was off that day so I scoffed the whole thing at lunchtime by myself. Whoever made it obviously knew I have a sweet tooth. But a couple of hours later I was spewing up my guts. I closed the kennels and went home, then spent all evening with diarrhoea and sickness. I had no choice but to tell Ted I'd join them for the hunt on Boxing Day instead'

'I take it you're better now,' James said.

'Much. By the time I woke up yesterday morning all I had were stomach cramps. But no way could I have gone out so I stayed home all day. I just wish I knew who made that cake because I'd love to know what muck they put in it.'

'Well, I'm glad you're okay now. But look, I need to ask you a question about what had been planned, Mr Elvin. And it's important that you provide me with an honest answer. Did the men intend to stick to the rules and embark on a legal trail hunt? Or were they going in search of foxes?'

Elvin opened his mouth to respond, but changed his mind and looked away, gnawing at his lower lip. After a couple of seconds, he drew in a long breath and turned back to James.

'We never play by the rules, Inspector,' he said sheepishly. 'Like a lot of hunters, we just pretend to. And one of the reasons we often go out on foot is that it's much easier to get away with it because we attract far less attention.'

'But you know yourself that most anti-hunt protesters and saboteurs are not fooled,' James said.

'That I do.'

'So, can you give me the names of any individuals who might have vandalised the farm?'

'I can point the finger at a few sabs who've caused problems for us, Ted's neighbour for one. His name is Neil Hutchinson and he's always slagging us off. And he's in cahoots with two of the county's most active sabs – Warren and Liam Spicer. Ted was threatened by one of them not long ago.'

'How do you know that?'

'Because I was there. It was Warren. The guy is a nutter and has a foul temper.'

'Can you tell us what happened?' James asked.

'It was about four months ago. Ted, Dylan, Rhys and me were on a night out here in Kendal. Nigel wasn't able to join us. We'd just left a restaurant and were heading for Dylan's car when we bumped into Warren and two of his mates. They'd clearly been drinking and Warren decided to call the four of us a bunch of animal killers. When Ted told him to piss off, Warren pushed him up against a wall and was about to lay into him but his mates pulled him back. As they led him away he yelled at Ted and said he was going to kick his head in when he got the chance.'

'And do you know if he carried out his threat?'

'Obviously he didn't, but then, it's common knowledge that the guy is all mouth. And his brother, who comes across as calmer and wiser, would probably have persuaded him not to do something so stupid.'

'How long have you been going on hunts with the group?'

'Those four have been hunting together since well before the ban came into force. I got to know them because they bought a few hounds from me. But it wasn't until about a year ago that I got invited onto a hunt and I saw it as a real privilege. I've been with them ever since. They're great guys.'

James thanked Elvin for coming and said that DI Stevens would arrange for him to be taken home.

Elvin got straight to his feet and said, 'Thank you, Inspector. But have you been totally honest with me? Do you really not have any idea what has happened to them?'

James shook his head. 'If we had I would tell you. But right now, it's a complete mystery.'

He'd already decided not to pass on the news about the dog and the shotguns taken from the farm.

'Well, I just pray that no harm has come to them,' Elvin replied. 'I can't help feeling guilty because it seems like I had a lucky escape by getting food poisoning. If I hadn't been left the cake, I'd now be with them.'

CHAPTER EIGHTEEN

James stepped out of the interview room with a dark unease twisting in his gut over the reason Elvin had given for not going on the hunt with his pals.

Food poisoning from a cake left by an anonymous customer seemed like an odd coincidence and therefore created a degree of suspicion.

But was it really possible that the man had made it up in order to give himself an excuse to stay at home on Christmas Eve? And if so, then was it because he'd known that something was going to happen?

These were questions he raised with the rest of the team when he passed on to them what Elvin had told them.

'I certainly think we should treat his story with a degree of caution,' he said. 'For one thing, it strikes me as slightly odd that someone would leave him a cake as a gift without saying who it's from. And it would have been relatively easy for him to pretend that he was unwell.'

'So, are you suggesting that he could have faked it because

he knew that his friends were going to get into difficulty?' DC Foley asked.

James nodded. 'We have to accept that it's possible even if it does seem unlikely.'

Foley pursed her lips. 'Then surely it means we can no longer assume that those men are missing because of the bad weather. We now have to consider third-party involvement in their disappearance.'

This prompted DC Patterson to say, 'Maybe they've actually been kidnapped and are being held somewhere.'

It was a terrifying thought, but the fact that the men had been missing for so long meant it could not be ruled out.

James said as much to Superintendent Tanner when he rang him ahead of the mid-day press conference.

'I think we should keep a lid on that line of inquiry for now until you've given it more consideration,' Tanner replied. 'And in the meantime, find out all you can about this Elvin bloke. Maybe he fell out with the others and did something to disrupt their Christmas Eve hunt. He might even have been responsible for trashing the farmhouse.'

'I'm still inclined to believe that was the work of anti-hunt activists,' James said. 'Elvin confirmed that Ted Rycroft was indeed threatened about four months ago by the younger Spicer brother. Both brothers insisted to me that it wasn't true, but Johnny Elvin claimed he was a witness. As such, it goes without saying that we should consider them as credible suspects, certainly in respect of the damage to the farmhouse and cars.'

* * *

97

Just before the press conference started news broke that the Mountain Rescue Teams had resumed their search thanks to a break in the weather. According to the forecasters it would be short-lived, but at least a helicopter was able to join in this time.

The presser was carried live on the news and James and the rest of the team watched it on the TV screens in the office.

Tanner sat beside a Mountain Rescue official and kicked off by stressing that every effort was being put into finding the missing men.

It wasn't long before a reporter asked about the vandalism at the farm and Tanner was forced to say that the police had no idea at this stage who was responsible. He chose not to mention the picture with the word *murderers* daubed on it, or the missing guns, but did say they were considering the possibility that the crime was carried out by anti-hunt activists.

In response to another question he said that as far as he was aware the men had set out on a legal trail hunt.

The Mountain Rescue official then described the difficulties and dangers faced by those taking part in the search before throwing back to Tanner to round things off. His voice was strong and authoritative as he spoke.

'We will work with the rescue services to do whatever it takes to find those men,' he said directly to the camera. 'And I appeal to anyone who has any information that might help us to come forward. If you think you saw them yesterday or this morning on the fells or moorland in the area around Kentmere then please don't hold back. Lives are at stake.'

* * *

After the press conference, James retreated to his office to make two quick phone calls. The first was to Annie who told him that she had been following the story of the missing hunters.

'My parents used to have a friend who lived on the edge of Kentmere village,' she said. 'I remember going there quite a few times. It's a lovely spot, but quite rugged and remote.'

'I've discovered that for myself,' he replied. 'And I have to go back there later.'

'But I take it you'll be coming home tonight.'

'Count on it. The only thing keeping me awake is adrenaline.'

He heard Bella making noises in the background and asked how she'd been.

'A bunch of energy as per usual,' she said. 'She loves all her presents and I've taken some photos and videos. I've decided to go over to Janet's for lunch now that I know you won't be here. It'll do Bella good to get out. And she'll enjoy a walk in the snow.'

Janet Dyer was Annie's best friend in Kirkby Abbey and had twin sons of her own. She was always on hand to babysit when James and Annie wanted or needed to go somewhere without their daughter.

'Did you catch the press conference that just took place?' he asked her. 'It was on the news.'

'No, I didn't. Have there been any developments?'

'A couple, but best not to talk about it over the phone. The most worrying thing is that those guys are still missing. And in a short while I'll be talking to their families.'

'I don't envy you that, James. This must all be so hard for them.'

'I'm sure it is. And once again I'm really sorry that I can't be there with you.'

His next call was to Tony Coppell who was still at the Rycroft farm.

The chief forensic officer said that his team would soon be wrapping up and returning to base with what they had collected.

'There's no evidence to indicate that anyone was attacked in the house and we haven't come across anything that offers up a clue to the route those men were planning on taking.'

'I half expected you to say that,' James said with a sigh.

'However, I did find something that might be of interest to you. It was a briefcase tucked under Mr Rycroft's bed. I suspect whoever trashed the place didn't know it was there. Anyway, it wasn't locked and inside was a bunch of documents such as insurance policies, bank accounts, pension information and Mr Rycroft's will.'

'Does anything stand out?'

'The contents of the will did cause me to raise an eyebrow because it was drawn up just two months ago.'

'He has no children or siblings so who benefits from it?'

'A chap named Gregory Pike. I gather he works for Mr Rycroft and you met him when you were here last night.'

'Exactly what is left to him in the event of Mr Rycroft's death?' he asked.

'The farm, along with all the man's possessions and any savings he has,' he said.

'That shouldn't be a surprise, I suppose, since the guy has worked on the farm for six years and it seems that Mr Rycroft hasn't got anyone else to leave it to,' James said. 'Still, we both know there's always cause to raise eyebrows when a person dies or goes missing shortly after they've drawn up or changed a will. We'll have to look into it.'

'I'll send the briefcase and its contents to Kendal then, along with the rest of the stuff we've bagged up.'

Speaking to the lawyer who drew up Ted Rycroft's will was one of the tasks James assigned when he had another catch-up with the team. By then DC Hall had arrived back to say that he'd spoken to Liam Spicer's girlfriend, Angela Beck, who had confirmed he'd spent last night with her. Surprise, surprise.

Hall had also made a note of the traffic and automatic number plate recognition cameras in the area and said he would arrange for footage from yesterday to be viewed.

'And check out all the cameras in and around Staveley,' James said. 'See if you can spot the cars belonging to the huntsmen heading through the village towards the farm.'

They were still discussing the various aspects of the investigation when the call came through that the families of the missing men were about to arrive.

'Have them taken to the conference room,' James said. 'And let's make them as comfortable as possible.'

CHAPTER NINETEEN

James returned to his office to collect his notebook and while there his phone rang. The caller was someone he hadn't heard from in quite a while.

'Morgan Garside,' he said when he answered it. 'How the hell are you?'

'I'm fine, James, thank you,' came the reply. 'I hope you're well too.'

'Can't complain. The family are doing great and the job is keeping me busy.'

'So I gather. Sounds like you have a real mystery on your hands with those missing huntsmen.'

'You're not wrong there, and it's getting more challenging by the hour. Is that why you're ringing me, by any chance?'

'No, it isn't,' Garside said. 'There's something I need to ask you. Have you got a minute?'

'Of course.'

James was intrigued. Morgan Garside was the Director General of the National Crime Agency, or NCA, which had been set up in 2013 to oversee the fight against serious and organised crime in the UK. It operated independently of the police and James had got to know Garside when he spent several years working there on secondment from the Met.

'You may have heard that Katie Brewer, our Director of Investigations, will soon be leaving on the grounds of ill-health,' Garside went on. 'Well, I'm keen to replace her with someone I know and trust, and naturally I thought of you.'

James felt his breathing stall and his skin prickle. This was indeed a bolt from the blue and he wasn't sure how to respond.

His silence prompted Garside to continue. 'I can appreciate that this has come as a shock, my friend. I'm sure that you're enjoying life up there in Cumbria, but I thought I would check to see if after three years you're ready for another challenge. This is a great opportunity. As you know, the director of investigations oversees the most high-profile cases as well as the various commands including International Corruption, Borders and Armed Operations.'

James was well aware of what the job entailed and it was most certainly something that appealed to him. But it would mean moving back to London and he'd been telling himself on an almost daily basis that he never would. And he was pretty sure that Annie would be horrified if he told her that he wanted to.

But at the same time, surely it wouldn't be sensible to dismiss it out of hand. After all, it was one of the most important law enforcement roles in the country and he had really enjoyed his secondment to the NCA – or 'Britain's FBI', as it was often called.

'You don't have to give me an answer today,' Garside said. 'All I need to know is whether or not you're interested.

Then you can give it plenty of thought and get back to me when you're ready. There's no great hurry.'

'Of course I'm interested,' James replied. 'What copper wouldn't be? And I feel honoured to be asked. But it's come out of nowhere so I need to get my head around it and run it past my wife.'

'That's exactly what I expected you to say, James, and I completely understand. It's a big decision to make, especially when you're heading up an all-consuming investigation. But hey, the job is yours if you want it. I've been given the go-ahead to appoint who I want and you're top of my list as I can't think of a better candidate given your experience and what I know about you. If you don't want it though that's absolutely fine. There are many others who will jump at the chance.'

'I'm sure there are, Morgan,' James said. 'So how long have I got to make up my mind?'

'Would a couple of weeks be okay?'

'Sure thing, but I doubt it will take me that long.'

CHAPTER TWENTY

James struggled to get his thoughts back on track as he headed for the conference room to meet the families of the missing men.

The job offer from Morgan Garside had thrown him and now his mind was veering in all directions. He was wondering why he hadn't turned it down outright and told Morgan that his focus now was on his family and not his career.

Was it because deep down he retained a sense of ambition and saw it as the opportunity of a lifetime that he'd be mad to pass up?

He supposed there was a small chance that Annie would tell him to go for it despite her misgivings. After all, they would almost certainly be able to rent a place in one of the safer parts of London. And of course they'd keep the cottage and still spend much of their time in Kirkby Abbey.

The timing of it wasn't good, though, what with another baby on the way and the fact that he had only been in his current job for nine months. Plus, the job offer was undoubtedly going to be an unwelcome distraction as he sought to get to the bottom of what had happened to the four huntsmen.

He got to the conference room before the families arrived. DC Foley was waiting for him and he was pleased to see that coffees and teas had been laid on and a support staffer was on hand to pour them.

The first to be brought in was Nigel Marr's wife Francesca, who was accompanied by their daughter Bridget, a pretty twenty-something with long, honey-blonde hair.

Her mother was in her fifties with a face that was washed out and pale. As James introduced himself, he could see the emotion shining in her eyes, and when she spoke the breath rattled hoarsely in her throat.

'Please tell me you have some good news for us,' she pleaded.

James felt a twinge of guilt and responded with a gentle shake of his head before waving her and her daughter towards chairs on one side of the table.

As they were sitting down, Rhys Hughes's son Owain appeared. He was in his late thirties, of average height and average build, and was wearing a grey suit that unfortunately looked too tight on him.

Last to arrive was Dylan Payne's wife Maria, with a woman she introduced as Kate, her friend and neighbour.

Maria was tall, late forties, with black hair tucked into a tight knot on top of her head. Her eyes were red and moist and her voice thin and scratchy.

Once they were all seated, James introduced Foley who sat with her notebook open, poised and ready. He then asked if any of them would like a hot drink. Owain was the only one who said yes.

As James took in their mournful expressions, compassion seized him. He wished he could give them hope but he knew that was going to prove extremely difficult, if not impossible.

'I'd like to begin by thanking you all for coming here,' he said. 'I know our officers have visited your homes and spoken to you, but I thought it sensible to bring you together so that I can update you and give you the opportunity to ask questions. I can only imagine how difficult this must be for you, not knowing what has happened to your loved ones. But we're doing all we can to find them and while that happens support and counselling will be made available to help you through it.'

'I just want to know if I'm ever going to see my husband again,' Maria Payne said in a small, pitiful voice. 'I begged him not to go yesterday morning because the weather forecast was so bad. But he wouldn't listen.'

'None of them ever do when it comes to going on hunts,' Francesca said. 'They all love it and have done so for years. And they know how to look after themselves, so they're rarely put off by rain, snow or high winds.'

'My dad has never got into difficulties before because of bad weather,' Owain chipped in. 'He's always been careful and the same goes for Nigel, Ted and Dylan. That's why all this other stuff has got me worried. The damage to the farmhouse and the cars that were left there. What the fuck is going on?'

'That's what we're trying to get to the bottom of,' James told him. 'The vandalism carried out on Mr Rycroft's farm is being thoroughly investigated and forensics officers have been there since last night. And I'm glad to say that the Mountain Rescue Teams have resumed their search. To begin with, they're returning to the area where one of your father's dogs

107

was found, Mr Hughes. As you know, she's unharmed and will be returned to you shortly. And we should regard it as an encouraging development.'

James saw no reason to tell them at this stage about the blood on the dog's coat. He also chose not to mention the missing shotguns when he switched the conversation back to the farm by asking if they had thoughts on who might be responsible for the damage.

Maria flicked her head in a small show of annoyance. 'You ought to be talking to those people who've been making life difficult for us for years,' she said. 'Dylan and the others have been threatened, abused and attacked by them so many times that we've all lost count. You probably know that Dylan and me run an outdoor clothing ship here in Kendal. Well, the front window has been smashed three times by those thugs.'

'Are you referring to anti-hunt activists, Mrs Payne?' James asked.

'Of course I am. We all live in fear of them. Why do you think I told the police that the lads were on a hike when I phoned you? I knew that if I said they were out trail hunting you'd assume they weren't abiding by the rules and so there wouldn't have been the same level of concern.'

'As a matter of fact, we've already questioned several individuals who identify as hunt protesters,' James said. 'They told us they were not responsible and their alibis have been corroborated. However, for a reason I'm about to explain to you, we will be talking to other activists who we deem to be potential suspects.'

He then told them about the fox hunting picture from Mr Rycroft's trophy room with the word *murderers* scrawled across it.

'Why has no one mentioned this before now?' Owain demanded to know. 'It's not been on the news and surely it proves that the animal rights lot are behind it.'

'We have to be careful not to make assumptions, Mr Hughes,' James said. 'You see, it could be that the damage was carried out by someone who wants us to believe the activists are responsible in order to stir up more controversy.'

'Oh, come off it, Inspector,' Francesca Marr said, her face intense. 'You know as well as we do that a state of war exists between the pro- and anti-hunt camps. Nothing changed after that stupid ban was introduced. It just made things more difficult for us and easier for them. I accept that most anti-hunt people don't resort to intimidation and violence, but some do, mostly the saboteurs in their black masks. And the same goes for a small number on our side. But Nigel and his mates get more than their fair share of harassment. And as Maria just said, it's been going on for a long time.'

'Is there a reason for that?' James asked.

'My dad reckons it's because over the years they've given as good as they got and stood up to the protesters,' Owain said. 'They've been involved in lots of confrontations and more than a few fights. The sabs have also tried to trash their reputations by accusing them of things they didn't do.'

'Such as?' James asked.

'Well, a protester once claimed that Nigel threatened him with a shotgun. Luckily my dad was filming the altercation on his phone and proved to the police that it was a lie. But even worse was the incident involving Ted's Jeep. It was after that they became prime targets for the sabs.'

'What incident was that?'

'It happened five years ago. The guys were in the Jeep when it struck a young woman after a hunt just south of Staveley. She was a protester who stepped in front of them holding up a banner. It was her own fault that she was hit but some guy who saw it claimed that Ted drove into her deliberately. He was a fellow protester, so he wasn't believed, thank God.'

'Was she badly hurt?' Foley asked.

'She suffered permanent brain damage and spent a lot of time in hospital. The anti-hunt brigade naturally made a big thing of it at the time.'

'But it was an accident,' Maria stressed, her voice raised. 'Dylan told me all about it. She tried to stop the Jeep because she knew who was inside.'

'Do you know what happened to her?' James said.

It was Owain who replied. 'As I recall, the girl's father died a couple of years later and her mum moved out of their home in Milnthorpe and took her to live somewhere else. But I don't know where.'

Owain and the two wives went on to reveal more examples of what they called a 'campaign of harassment' against the men. It included the time Owain's dad received a letter with a picture inside cut from a newspaper that showed a hunter lying on the ground covered in blood, having been attacked by sabs. The message with it said: *this will happen to you one day.*

And Francesca's husband Nigel was accused of stabbing a fox to death with a pitchfork, but again it was proved not to be true.

Talking about it eventually became too much for them all and Maria began to cry. James was then forced to concede

that given the unusual circumstances, they had to acknowledge the possibility that criminality was involved in the
mens' disappearance.

'Do you mean they might have been abducted and are
being held somewhere against their will?' Owain asked. 'Or
worse – that they were attacked and have been left to die out
there in the freezing cold?'

'I wish I could put your mind at rest,' James answered him.
'But I can't.'

As they stood to leave he asked them one last question.
'Before you go, do any of you know why Johnny Elvin pulled
out of the hunt at the last minute?'

'Yeah, we were told about the food poisoning,' Maria
answered. 'It's a shame he didn't share that flipping cake with
the rest of them.'

CHAPTER TWENTY-ONE

The first thing James wanted to know when he returned to the office was whether the Mountain Rescue Teams had found anything. But it came as little surprise when he was told that they hadn't, even though crews from other parts of the county along with specialist police units had joined in.

There was some unsettling news, though. A rescuer had been injured after being blown over in the high winds. He dislocated his shoulder when he toppled down a snow-covered hill into a tree.

Thankfully he was now on his way to hospital and the search was continuing. But more blizzard conditions were being forecast and the Met Office had even issued a 'risk to life' warning for parts of northern England, including Cumbria.

James consulted his watch and saw that it was almost time to head back to Ted Rycroft's farm. But first he needed to make his team aware of what the families had told them.

'The missing men have apparently been targeted by anti-hunt activists for years,' he said before asking Foley to read from her notes the examples they were given, including the claim that Ted Rycroft deliberately drove into a young female protester.

'I actually remember that incident,' DC Elizabeth Booth said. 'Nothing came of it because it couldn't be proved that it was anything other than an accident.'

'And that's probably what it was,' James responded. 'But dig out whatever exists on the database and see what you can find online.'

Two officers were then tasked with looking back over the other incidents that were mentioned involving threats and violence against the men.

James shared about the briefcase found under Mr Rycroft's bed at the farm.

'When it's brought back here, I'd like someone to go through the contents,' he said. 'The will is of particular interest so we need to make contact with the lawyer who put it together and pick their brain. I'd like to know why it was drawn up only a couple of months ago and if there was an earlier version. I'll be going to see Greg Pike, the beneficiary, in a short while and intend to raise it with him. But when I spoke to him last night, he didn't give me any reason to suspect him of anything untoward. He came across as a loyal employee, as did Rebecca Carter, his colleague at the farm.'

Before bringing the meeting to a close, he told DCs Patterson and Foley to go home and get some rest.

'I'll return here after I've been to the farm with DS Abbott, but I won't be staying for long,' he said. 'By then I'll need to take some time out as well. So, let's make sure we're well covered overnight. And if that means drafting in more officers from elsewhere, then so be it.'

* * *

PC Malek was among the officers who still hadn't knocked off so he drove James and Abbott to the Rycroft farm.

The sky was heavy and grey and the gusty wind continued to batter the landscape.

The thought that it would soon start to get dark filled James with dread because he knew it would further hamper the search. And the longer it went on the harder it was to remain positive. He was now wondering what the odds were on them still being alive. And if they were, would they manage to survive another freezing night?

As they arrived at the farm the scene was very different to the night before. They could now see the grassy slopes and windswept fell tops in the distance. And daylight showed them just how remote the location was.

A cordon had been set up across the approach lane to stop any unauthorised vehicles getting through. But leading up to it there were several parked along the grass verge, including a TV news satellite truck.

They saw several people wandering across nearby fields and since at least one of them appeared to be taking photographs, it seemed obvious that they were part of the press pack.

An officer in a fluorescent yellow jacket waved them through the gate and several more were milling around the yard.

The farmhouse itself looked rather shabby now that it wasn't cloaked in darkness. It didn't help that the glass in the windows had been replaced by a hotchpotch of different materials.

The forensics team were still at it and a large marquee had been set up in front of the barn for them to use.

PC Malek parked next to it and when James and Abbott got out Detective Constable Dawn Isaac greeted them. She'd taken over from DC Sharma earlier in the day and had been keeping them informed of what was going on at the farm.

'It took me a couple of seconds to realise it was you,' James said. 'I can barely see your face.'

She was wearing a woollen hat over her head and ears and a thick scarf that covered her chin.

'That's because it's so frigging cold up here,' she replied, and shivered theatrically. 'I'm not used to it.'

He grinned and patted her arm. Isaac was a canny Scottish lass who he regarded as another solid and dependable detective. She was also fun to be around, with a wicked sense of humour and a contagious smile.

'I take it Mr Pike and Miss Carter aren't here yet,' he said.

A shake of the head. 'The office checked though and they're on their way.'

'Then while we wait you can fill us in on how things are going.'

As they walked towards the house Isaac told them that she'd been in touch by radio with the Mountain Rescue Teams and the news wasn't good.

'They haven't found anything,' she said. 'No tracks, no equipment, no more dogs, and no clues as to where those men are. The team that went west from here is now heading back because conditions are deteriorating and – as you know – one of them had an accident.'

'Have they covered a lot of ground?'

'Not as much as they would have if the weather had been better. It doesn't help that we don't know in which direction they went or how far the dog walked to get to the bothy where she was discovered. The area is vast and strong crosswinds have delayed the deployment of drones.'

They entered the house, which was now looking much tidier. The floors had been cleared of most of the objects that had been strewn across them and the broken glass had been swept into small piles.

A couple of white-suited SOCOs were still taking photos and making notes, but it was clear that most of their work had been carried out.

'Tony left about half an hour ago,' Isaac said. 'He told me he was going to pop home before driving to HQ and he left me with a list of all the items that have been removed.'

'And have the media mob given you any problems?' Abbott asked. 'We saw them outside.'

'We've had to stop them coming onto the property, but they've been fairly well behaved considering this is a case that it seems everyone is talking about. I've managed not to answer any of the questions that have been thrown at me, but they've been taking lots of pictures and videos around the farm.'

Isaac took them on a tour of the house for Abbott's benefit and pointed out that many of the damaged items were on their way to the lab to be examined.

They were looking around the upstairs trophy room when a uniformed officer came bounding up the stairs to inform them that Mr Rycroft's two employees had just arrived.

'But there seems to be a problem, sir,' the officer said to James. 'Miss Carter is quite distressed because on the way here she received an anonymous message on her phone from someone saying they hope her boss turns up dead.'

CHAPTER TWENTY-TWO

James spotted Rebecca Carter as soon as he stepped outside. She was wearing the fur-trimmed jacket she'd had on the previous evening and standing next to Greg Pike in front of the marquee.

James offered his thanks to them for coming and saw immediately the taut expression on Rebecca's face.

'Are you all right, Miss Carter?' he asked.

She blew out her cheeks. 'I think so. Just a bit shocked.'

'Well, let's get you both inside the house,' he said. 'You can tell us about the message you've just received and we'll look into it for you. We'd also like you to take a look around and let us know if any of Mr Rycroft's possessions are missing that we haven't taken away ourselves for further investigation. We have a list of those objects for you to consult.'

He led them into the living room where Abbott and Isaac were waiting, but Rebecca and Greg appeared not to even notice them as their wide, startled eyes took in the smashed TV screen, the broken bottles from the drinks cabinet, the pictures that had been ripped from the walls, and the upended Christmas tree.

Greg just shook his head, speechless, but Rebecca let out a strangled sob and covered her mouth with her hand.

'We still don't know who was responsible,' James said. 'But I'm confident that it's only a matter of time before we find out.'

Rebecca lowered her hand from her mouth and turned to him, her eyes brimming with tears.

'First you need to find out where Ted is,' she said, phlegm rattling at the back of her throat. 'There's only so long we can hold on to the hope that no news is good news.'

James got them to sit side by side on the sofa and said, 'So, let's start with this text message that's been sent to you, Miss Carter. My officer told me you found it quite upsetting.'

She unzipped her jacket and reached inside for her phone.

'It came through as we were driving here,' she said. 'I have no idea who sent it because there's no name or number.'

She brought up her messages before handing the phone to James, who read the text out loud.

'"We don't know each other, Rebecca, but someone told me that you work for that scumbag Ted Rycroft. You should be fucking ashamed of yourself. I'm glad he's missing and I hope he turns up dead along with those other cowards who kill foxes for fun." Have you been sent anything like this before?' he asked.

She shook her head. 'No. And it's not as if I've ever condoned what Ted does. I just help organise the quad rides and hikes. I don't support fox hunting, but I know a lot of people do so I decided a long time ago that it was best not to get involved or take part in any public debate.'

'I've had a few such messages sent to me since I started

working at the farm,' Greg said. 'Ted once told me that it goes with the territory. I feel very much as Rebecca does about it though. I've never known an issue to stir up so much hatred.'

James turned to Rebecca. 'Would you mind if we take your phone back to the station so we can get our technical people to see if there's any way to find out who sent the message? It won't take long and if you're prepared to wait, we can give it straight back to you.'

'Of course. It's not as if we have anything else to do.'

There was a lot to touch on with the two of them so James asked Rebecca if she was okay to continue. When she told him she was, he told them he'd spoken to Neil Hutchinson and the Spicer brothers.

'They all deny having anything to do with what happened here and they have alibis for Christmas Eve,' he said. 'And though both brothers deny that they had ever threatened Mr Rycroft, we spoke to Mr Elvin who said he witnessed Warren saying he was going to hurt him.'

'That's right. It happened one night here in Kendal,' Greg said.

James nodded. 'We intend to have another conversation with the brothers about that. Mr Elvin also let it be known that the men were not intending to go on a trail hunt. It was just what they wanted people to believe. They were going in search of foxes.'

Greg clicked his tongue against the back of his teeth. 'Look, neither of us were told even though we both suspected as much. But the thing is they sometimes do stick to the rules and follow a scent instead of a fox. I know that for a fact because on a couple of occasions I was asked to lay the scent for them.'

'That's true,' Rebecca said. 'It's happened at least once since I've been working here.'

James decided it was time Rycroft's employees had a look around the house and he and Abbott accompanied them. The pair didn't find it easy, though, and each room they entered caused them to express their shock and dismay.

When Rebecca saw the state of the office that she spent a lot of her time in she struggled to hold in her emotions.

She picked up a small photo with a cracked frame that lay on top of the desk. In the image she was posing with a small group of people.

'Ted allowed me to personalise this room so that I'd be comfortable in it,' she said. 'These were my colleagues at the office I worked at in Windermere before I came here. I was ready for a change, you see, and I wanted a part-time job so I could have more time for the book I'm trying to write. My ambition is to be an author.'

She wiped her eyes with her sleeve as she looked in the drawers and cupboards, but said that nothing appeared to be missing. More shocks were in store for them in the trophy room.

'Have you found the shotguns and ammunition yet?' Greg asked James.

'No, we haven't,' he replied. 'What can you tell us about them?'

'Not much, really,' Greg said. 'Ted hasn't used them in quite a while. But I do know that two of them are semi-automatics and can carry as many as twelve shells in the magazines.'

It was a painful process for both of them and at the end of it – and after looking over the list of objects that had been taken away for further investigation – they said they believed that only the shotguns and ammunition had been taken.

James was trying to work out how to separate them when Greg solved the problem for him by asking if he could go and check on the sheep.

'I'll come with you,' James said and told Abbott to rustle up a hot drink for Rebecca.

Greg needn't have worried. The sheep were well fed and watered as it turned out that the officers on site had been keeping an eye on them.

While in the barn James raised the subject of Ted Rycroft's will.

'It was in a briefcase under his bed with various other documents,' he said.

James was well aware that he might be about to betray Rycroft's confidence if he hadn't already told Greg that he was the beneficiary. But he felt that, in the circumstances, breaching such an ethical boundary was acceptable.

In the event he needn't have worried.

'I think I know where you're going with this,' Greg responded. 'You obviously know that he's leaving his entire estate to me and you want to know why.'

'I wasn't sure you knew,' James said.

Greg nodded. 'Ted told me before he did it. He said I'd been like a son to him and he had no one else to leave it to.'

'So why was the will drawn up just two months ago?'

Greg tugged at his bottom lip with his teeth and tears gathered in his eyes.

'Because three months ago he was diagnosed with terminal colon cancer,' he said. 'He reckons he has about a year if he's lucky. He made me promise not to tell anyone and plans to make it known himself only when it gets to the point where he needs to go into hospital.'

CHAPTER TWENTY-THREE

James had no reason to disbelieve what Greg had told him about Ted Rycroft's terminal illness. The man would know that it'd be easy to check by obtaining his boss's medical records.

He assured Greg that he wouldn't make it public so long as there was no evidence to suggest that Mr Rycroft was no longer alive.

He shared the news with Abbott though, of course, as they drove back to Kendal. Greg followed in his Ford Escort with Rebecca as his passenger. She would stay at the station while a quick check was carried out on her phone, but James thought it unlikely that whoever sent her that nasty text message could be traced.

'Did he tell you how Mr Rycroft had managed to keep his illness secret from everyone else?' Abbott asked.

'The diagnosis came out of the blue apparently, as it often does with colon cancer,' James said. 'By the time the symptoms started to appear it had spread through his body and was deemed to be incurable. He doesn't want others knowing because he doesn't want them to feel sorry for him.'

When they arrived at headquarters Abbott took charge of sorting Rebecca's phone while James went straight to the office. As soon as he entered, he was given the bad news by DI Stevens that the Mountain Rescue Teams had again called off the search because of the weather.

There were no other significant developments, but Stevens told him that all lines of inquiry were being actively followed up. They included checking the CCTV footage between Kendal and the home belonging to the Spicer brothers and making sure that Johnny Elvin hadn't lied when he said that he didn't leave his house on Christmas Eve.

'Someone needs to drop in on him on the pretext of getting more information on his pals,' James said to the team. 'And I want whoever goes to speak to the wife and see what she has to say.'

Tony Coppell was on hand to provide a forensic update, which didn't really amount to much. He stressed that they hadn't found any blood stains in the farmhouse or on the vandalised vehicles and that they had yet to determine whether it was definitely blood on the dog and if so, whether it was animal or human. Various objects, including the defaced hunting picture, were being analysed in the lab.

James filled the team in on his latest visit to the farm. He told them about the anonymous message sent to Rebecca and what Greg had said about his boss's cancer.

'I'm convinced he's telling the truth, but we need to access Mr Rycroft's medical records to be sure,' he said. 'And let's run a background check on Mr Pike because at the end of the day he will benefit if anything bad happens, or has happened, to his employer.'

By now James was drained of energy, his eyes squinting

with tiredness. The evening was fast closing in and if he didn't get some sleep soon, he'd be incapable of doing his job properly.

All the same he couldn't help but feel guilty when he left the building an hour later. Those four men were still missing and their families and friends were going through hell on Christmas Day. It just didn't seem right that he should take time out to recharge his batteries.

But he knew that he had no choice.

It took him longer than usual to cover the twenty-five miles from Kendal to Kirkby Abbey in his Audi. Snow, wind and ice forced him to drive slowly and with extra care, and this stopped his mind switching feverishly between the investigation and the job he'd been offered at the National Crime Agency.

He reached the village just after six, by which time his eyes were heavy and he could feel one of his dreaded tension headaches brewing.

Bright festive lights adorned most of the buildings and it wouldn't have surprised him if the huge Christmas tree in the market square was visible from outer space.

The village, with its population of only about seven hundred, always made an effort to fully embrace the season of goodwill. It was one of the many things he loved about the place and why even a job as prestigious as Director of Investigations at the NCA might not be enough to lure him back to London.

He no longer missed the never-ending beat of the big city where he had spent most of his life. And surely it would be good for his children to grow up surrounded by mountains, lakes and moors rather than tower blocks and jam-packed roads?

Kirkby Abbey and the surrounding countryside had won him over and before the call from Morgan Garside it was where he was sure he'd be spending the rest of his life. But now a seed of doubt had been planted and it was set to stir up a range of unsettling issues.

Their four-bedroom cottage was within a short walk of the school where Annie used to work as a teacher. It was a quiet location that offered them spectacular views of the fells from the upstairs windows.

He'd sent a message to Annie before leaving the office and so the front door was pulled open just before he reached it and there she stood with Bella in her arms.

The sight of them lifted his spirits and sent a rush of warm blood through his veins.

'Merry Christmas to you both,' he said. 'Getting back here wasn't easy and at one point I thought I might have to turn back.'

'Well, we're both pleased that you didn't, aren't we, Bella?' Annie replied, and he watched his daughter's adorable face break into a smile.

But as he smiled back, she looked past him, raised an arm and pointed.

'Snow,' she muttered. 'Snow.'

Annie laughed. 'Don't take it personally, Daddy. I'm sure she's pleased to see you.'

After stepping inside and closing the door behind him, he kissed his wife and swapped his briefcase for his daughter.

The first thing Bella did was wrap her arms around his neck and push her face against his. It was just what he needed and his heart swelled in his chest.

The weight of the pressure he'd been under soon began to

lift and he managed to keep the headache at bay with a couple of paracetamols and a glass of whisky.

Annie asked him about the investigation and said she had continued to follow it throughout the day. The shock registered on her face when he made her aware of the aspects of the case that hadn't been made public.

Afterwards he messed around with Bella and her new toys for a while and he and Annie exchanged gifts. He gave her the new laptop she'd been hinting at and she gave him two bottles of his favourite Scotch whisky. They then played on the floor with Bella until she fell asleep on his lap. After putting her to bed, he was finally able to switch his full attention to his wife who dished up the beef casserole she'd prepared the day before.

As always, she made him realise how lucky he was to have her in his life. To him, she was still as beautiful as when they'd first met, with her delicate features, bright blue eyes and long, shiny black hair. If it wasn't for the small baby bump, he doubted that anyone would notice that she was five months pregnant.

He was aiming to mention the job he'd been offered over dinner, but before he got around to it Annie brought up the subject of her uncle Bill, and as she spoke her face clouded over. 'I tried to get through to him this afternoon to wish him a merry Christmas,' she said, 'but he wouldn't come to the phone. He told one of his carers that he didn't know who I was and wasn't prepared to talk to a . . . a stranger.'

'Christ, Annie, I'm so sorry.'

Bill Cardwell, her late mother's brother, was suffering from severe dementia and it got so bad six months ago that he'd had to go into a care home in Penrith.

James could tell that she was upset, but she was managing to hold back the tears.

'I was expecting this day to come because his condition has been deteriorating rapidly of late, but it's still a blow,' she said. 'I'll pay Bill a visit as soon as I can. I'm hoping that when he sees me, he'll remember who I am, but I'm not counting on it. The last time I saw him I had to keep reminding him that I'm a relative.'

James decided that it wouldn't be fair to mention the job offer. He didn't want to give her something else to worry about.

After the meal, they sat cuddled up on the living room sofa and watched the story of the missing huntsmen play out on the television news. There was video footage of the Rycroft farm taken from a distance, photos of the four missing men, and interviews with pro- and anti-hunt extremists who blamed each other for the fresh war of words that the case had sparked on social media.

James was too tired to stay up late and before they went up to bed he rang the office to see if there had been any further developments. There hadn't.

Even though he was exhausted, sleep did not come easily as the events of the day played heavily on his mind and he couldn't shake the feeling that tomorrow was going to bring with it more bad news for those desperate families.

CHAPTER TWENTY-FOUR

Day Three
Boxing Day

James had set the alarm for six but Bella had them up at five. She was an early riser most mornings and when she woke, she wanted the world to know it.

He'd had an unsettled night and probably managed only about four hours of sleep. Despite that, he found he felt rested and ready to face whatever challenges the new day thrust upon him. Annie had also struggled to drop off, no doubt because she was worried about her uncle.

Before getting out of bed, James checked his phone but there were no messages, which told him that it had been an uneventful night for the staff who were on night shift. But what of the four huntsmen? How had they coped? Had they even managed to survive the night? The thought of it sent another wave of guilt crashing through him. He just hoped that today he and the team would make more progress and that the weather would be kinder.

He showered and dressed while Annie served Bella her breakfast, and was pleased to find that she had coffee and toast on the table for him when he entered the kitchen.

He made a point of sitting next to Bella's high chair while she stuffed her face with fruit and yoghurt, his gaze switching between her messy antics and the wall-mounted TV.

'I think it was another rough night out there. Those poor men,' Annie said.

The TV was tuned to Sky News and it was their lead story. Updates included the fact that one of the dogs had been found alive and James suspected that the information had been leaked by the families as they were the only ones outside the department who knew. There were also short interview clips with Dylan Payne's wife Maria, and Nigel Marr's daughter Bridget. They both appealed for anyone who had information on the missing men to contact the police.

'It's got to the point where we no longer believe they're just lost or trapped somewhere by the weather,' Maria said, her voice thick with emotion. 'Even the police now suspect that there's more to it, especially as Ted Rycroft's farm was vandalised soon after they set out.'

A media liaison officer at Constabulary HQ wouldn't be drawn on any of the speculation, insisting that there was still no evidence of third-party involvement in the disappearances.

He did say that Mountain Rescue Teams were hoping to resume the search in the coming hours, once the weather improved.

'You told me last night that you're working on the assumption that they're alive,' Annie said as she sipped her coffee. 'Do you still believe that, bearing in mind that no one has heard from them for over forty-eight hours?'

'The truth is I don't know what to believe,' James admitted. 'This whole thing is as puzzling as it is disturbing. It's got everyone confused.'

The drive to Kendal wasn't as bad as James had feared it would be. The overnight snow showers had been fairly light and gritters and salt spreaders had been deployed since the early hours. It helped too that halfway through the journey the wind dropped significantly.

He was in the office by seven and within half an hour he was joined by the rest of the team. They all looked tired, especially DC Foley whose bloodshot eyes were set back in their sockets.

'I had a terrible night,' she said. 'I didn't drop off until eleven o'clock and then I was awake at four and couldn't get back to sleep.'

'Well, you did better than me,' DC Patterson said. 'I slept for three hours at the most because the neighbour's dog didn't stop barking.'

The briefing got under way at eight and officers reported back on various lines of inquiry.

Ted Rycroft's medical records had been obtained and it was confirmed that he had indeed recently been diagnosed with colon cancer. So, Greg Pike had told the truth but he remained a person of interest because he was the sole beneficiary of Mr Rycroft's will.

DC Hall confirmed that he had viewed some of the Christmas Eve traffic and CCTV footage from cameras between Kentmere and the home of the Spicer brothers, but so far, their cars had not shown up. However, he had spotted those vehicles belonging to Dylan Payne, Rhys Hughes and Nigel Marr.

'They were heading towards Kentmere around seven on Christmas Eve morning,' he said. 'The cameras picked up a few other cars but the lighting was poor and not all of the number plates are clear enough to identify. And later in the day the weather was too bad to identify any cars.'

The digital data specialists had been unable to trace whoever had sent the text message to Rebecca Carter.

'This isn't unexpected since these days there are a number of methods people can employ to conceal their identities when sending texts and emails,' one of the techies said. 'Burner phones can be used and it can be done through special apps and what's known as "virtual private networks".'

James was aware of such methods, which were becoming increasingly sophisticated. They were of growing concern to governments and law enforcement agencies the world over.

The next item on the agenda were the inquiries being made into the various anti-hunt protesters. But just as DC Booth began to tell the meeting what she'd come up with, one of the support staff members came rushing into the room and started waving at James to seize his attention.

The room fell silent as the man hurried up to where James was standing in front of the evidence board.

'There's someone downstairs I think you'll want to see as a matter of urgency, sir,' he said, his voice loud and excited. 'It's Gordon Carver, the reporter with the *Cumbria Gazette*, and he's got something he says he needs to show you.'

'Do you know what it is?' James asked.

The man nodded. 'He claims his paper has been sent an email with a photograph attached. And it apparently shows one of the missing huntsmen lying dead in the snow.'

CHAPTER TWENTY-FIVE

James was waiting with DS Abbott when Gordon Carver was brought up to his office.

The reporter was one of the few hacks the team trusted and they had a constructive quid pro quo relationship with him.

James could see the tension in the man's neck the moment he walked through the door. He pinched his face into a tight smile as he acknowledged Abbott, but when he looked at James the smile vanished and his eyebrows drew together.

'The photo was sent to the *Gazette*'s news email address two hours ago,' he said. 'My editor forwarded it to me as soon as it was noticed and told me to bring it straight to you.'

'And you're sure it's not a prank?' James asked.

Carver shook his head as he snatched his phone from his pocket.

'We don't think so and you'll see why when you read the message that came with it. But it's clearly from a fake address. The account name is all gibberish and you can't respond to it.'

He opened up the phone, tapped the email icon, and passed it to James.

'If it's genuine then it takes the story to a whole new level,' Carver said. 'We're already poised to run with it in our online feed.'

James read the message first and the words filled him with a heart-stopping dread.

The real hunt has begun.

He then opened the full colour photo and a cold chill swept over him.

It showed a man lying on snow-covered ground with his head and shoulders propped up against a dry-stone wall. His face was clearly visible – eyes closed, mouth open – and the snow that rested on top of him, covering most of his clothes, was stained with what looked like blood.

'We've compared the image with the photos that have been released of the missing men and we're convinced it's Nigel Marr,' Carver said.

And so was James. He recognised the bald head and crooked nose, and he assumed that whoever took the picture had positioned the body in such a way so that there wouldn't be any doubt that he was one of the four missing huntsmen.

James handed the phone to Abbott who reacted to what she saw by inhaling a loud shaky breath. She went to speak but the words wouldn't come out.

'You need to send the email to us so that we can have it analysed,' James said. 'If it is real then we'll have to get to his wife before it's out there.'

'I can appreciate that, but this is big, James,' Carver said.

'It appears to be proof that Nigel Marr has been murdered. And it begs the question of what has happened to the other three.'

Just then the office door was pushed open and DC Patterson appeared, a grave expression on his face.

'We've got a problem, guv,' he said. 'The email you're discussing, along with the attached photo, has also been sent to at least three other news outlets – the *Daily Mail*, *The Sun* and the BBC. The press office has taken calls from each of them.'

Within seconds, James received a call from the Chief Constable's office.

While he waited to be put through to the man himself, he told Abbott to take Carver outside and have the photo and email transferred to the system.

'Print off copies of both for the team and set things up for a briefing as soon as I've finished here,' he said. Then to Carver, he added, 'Thanks for bringing this to us, Gordon. You'll have to bear with me while the powers that be decide how to respond.'

Carver wasn't given a chance to reply because James turned away when Chief Constable Roger Casey came on the line.

'I take it that you've been made aware of what has happened?' Casey said.

'Only just, sir. A *Cumbria Gazette* reporter came here in person to show us the email and photo. And then we were told that it has also been sent to the Beeb and two national tabloids.'

'Well, it was brought to my attention just over fifteen minutes ago. I've just spoken to Superintendent Tanner and we agree that we have to take it seriously and work on the assumption that it's not a hoax. And there's no way the media will hold back from running with it even if we ask them to.'

'I agree, sir. As far as they're concerned, this is a story that just keeps on giving.'

'I've asked Tanner to oversee the response from this end. He's taken the email and photo to the Digital Crime Unit. He'll also beef up the search by involving our own teams. We need to check out every inch of dry-stone wall in that part of the county while continuing to look for those other three men.'

'We also need to consider that the bodies of the other three men might also be lying out there somewhere, waiting to be discovered.'

'It just doesn't bear thinking about,' Casey said. 'But look, wherever this investigation goes from here we need to prepare ourselves for a surge in the number of incidents involving pro- and anti-hunt activists. The online abuse is pretty sickening already and tension between the two sides is likely to reach boiling point when this gets out. The email makes it clear what the motive is and the aim is surely to stir up more trouble.'

'It might be an idea to try to put a stop to hunts that are due to take place over the coming days or weeks,' James said. 'It's obviously too late to stop those happening today, but there are bound to be a few scheduled for the weekend and New Year's Day. If they go ahead, things could get out of hand.'

'That is certainly a thought, but I'm not sure if it'll be possible. Let me look into it. Meanwhile, how does this impact on things at your end?'

'I'll go and see Mr Marr's wife right away,' James said. 'She needs to see the picture. It's not something I would normally contemplate, but I don't want her to get wind of it from some reporter. And for all we know, she may have also been sent a copy. Either way, we'll start treating this as a possible murder investigation and try to work out how to link all the threads together.'

'Good. If you need more people and resources just ask Tanner to sort it. I'll rubber stamp whatever you request.'

After saying goodbye, James phoned the Super who told him that another national newspaper, *The Daily Mirror*, had also received the same email.

'What a nice start to Boxing Day,' Tanner said. 'This case has got more fucking layers than a wedding cake.'

They briefly discussed what steps would need to be taken and Tanner gave James the news that Mountain Rescue Teams had just resumed the search.

'They've been told to pay particular attention to dry-stone walls, even though they run for hundreds of miles over the area,' he said. 'It's just a shame the photo doesn't show even a glimpse of the landscape in the background. But I'm guessing that was deliberate.'

Tanner went on to reveal that this latest, startling development had sent a shockwave through the Constabulary and that a sense of panic had seized every department from the top down.

'You don't need me to tell you that most of the pressure will fall on you as the senior investigating officer, James,' he said. 'But I know you'll do whatever it takes to get to the bottom of this and you can rest assured that I'll have your back the whole way.'

CHAPTER TWENTY-SIX

As James addressed the team, he managed to keep his voice low and measured despite the ugly fear that was spreading through him.

Fortified by a strong coffee, he stood in front of the evidence board, which Foley had updated. It now had pinned to it printouts of the photo and email, plus the message sent to Rebecca Carter.

He began by telling DC Foley that he wanted her to go with him to Francesca Marr's home near the village of Selside, just about six miles north of Kendal.

'We have no choice but to make her aware of the photograph before it's splashed all over the papers and online,' he told her. 'And for all we know, the sadistic bastard could have sent the email to Mrs Marr as well. Before we set off though, can you contact her daughter, Bridget? If she's not with her mum then I'm sure she'll want to be. And we should also send uniforms to speak to Maria Payne and Rhys Hughes's son, Owain. They're going to be in a right state when they hear about it.'

He then passed onto the team the headline points from his conversations with Superintendent Tanner and the Chief Constable.

'Like me, they don't believe that the photo is a mock-up,' he said. 'But we won't know for sure until Mr Marr's body is found or he turns up alive.'

DS Abbott returned to the room then, having escorted Gordon Carver out of the building.

'He says he'll check in with us later, guv,' she said. 'He rang and told his editor that the *Gazette* wasn't alone in receiving the photo. They now want to run the story as soon as possible to try and pip their competitors, but won't do so without informing us in advance.'

'We have to accept that it won't be long before it's plastered all over the front pages,' James said, 'which is why the pressure on us will soon be off the scale. The search for the men is being ramped up, but we can't be sure that the weather won't take another turn for the worse and cause more problems.'

He pointed to the evidence board and drew attention to the list of questions written on it in black marker.

'"Who vandalised the farmhouse and cars, and defaced the picture with the word *murderers*?"' he read aloud. '"Did that person or persons go on to hunt down the hunters, then either abduct or kill them?"'

James then asked the team to tell him what progress had been made with the various lines of inquiry. This prompted DC Booth to raise a hand.

'I've been looking into those claims by the families that the men have been targeted over the years by activists,' she said. 'And it's unquestionably true. We got involved on various occasions when they were threatened and even assaulted. Just ten months ago a saboteur threw a tin of paint over Nigel Marr during a hunt and six months before that we investigated a claim that Dylan Payne had spat on a female protester, but it turned out not to be true.'

Booth then opened her notebook and began reading from it. 'The group started to attract attention after the incident where the protester was struck by Ted Rycroft's Jeep,' she went on. 'It was five years ago and guess what? That also took place on Christmas Eve.'

'What more can you tell us about it?' James asked.

'Well, the guys were on a hunt near Staveley and a mob of sabs turned up to disrupt it. There were scuffles, but nothing serious. They didn't take horses so Mr Rycroft drove them there in his Jeep and they put three or four dogs in the rear. But afterwards, on the way back to his farm, they were driving along a lane when this girl apparently stepped out in front of them waving an anti-hunt banner. Mr Rycroft tried to avoid her but he couldn't. He hit her and she fell backwards, smashing her head on a rock lying below the hedge.'

'What happened next?'

'They stopped and got out to see if she was okay, but she was bleeding and unconscious so they called for an ambulance. Another protester came forward after and claimed he'd witnessed it. He told the attending officers that she didn't step in front of it. He said she stayed close to the hedge, but the Jeep swerved into her on purpose. Obviously, he couldn't prove it and it was his word against theirs. But her fellow sabs refused to believe it was an accident and used it as part of their propaganda. Given the timing, I suppose it's possible that someone could have decided to mark the fifth anniversary by making them pay.'

'It's an interesting theory, but we'll need more to go on than just the Christmas Eve link,' James said. 'What else did you find out?'

'The girl's name is Joanna Grey,' Booth said. 'She was just twenty-one at the time and was living with her parents in Milnthorpe. I trawled the internet and found a photo of her, which I'll print off in a bit. But looking back I discovered that the family were also the targets of a great deal of online abuse from pro-hunt activists who insisted that what happened to her was her own fault.'

'That can't have been pleasant,' Abbott commented.

'I'm sure it wasn't. Anyway, I managed to dredge up quite a few nasty comments and accusations from various online platforms. Joanna was called all kinds of names and the guy who claimed he'd witnessed what happened received a couple of phone calls from people who threatened to harm him if he didn't retract what he'd told the police about it not being an accident.'

'Have you got a name and address for him?' James asked.

'I have. It was in the file. He's Karl Kramer and he lives in Windermere, or he did back then. But that's as much as I know. I'll try to contact him today.'

'What about Joanna's family? Owain Hughes said the father died from a stroke about a year after the incident and his widow moved away with Joanna.'

'They did. I'm still trying to find out where they went and what's happened to them.'

'Then keep at it and let me know if they've got any thoughts on who might be behind this.'

'There's something else that you should know, sir,' Booth said. 'Following the incident involving Joanna, one of the most vocal critics of Ted Rycroft and his group was a man named Shane Logan, an anti-hunt activist living in Burneside, who has the privilege of being on the database. Ten months ago he was fined for smashing the windows of a house in Carlisle owned by a prominent fox hunter. Plus, he was ordered to pay compensation. He was also behind a bunch of vile online posts saying that the men who were in the Jeep that knocked Joanna down should be in prison.'

'What else do we know about the guy?' James said.

'I found a photo of him with two of his mates taken when they were protesting at yet another hunt last Boxing Day. And I got a surprise when I saw that the two mates were none other than Liam and Warren Spicer.'

James felt a muscle twitch in his jaw at the mention of the Spicer brothers. He asked Booth to forward the photo to him and the rest of the team, and seconds later it came through on their phones. It had been downloaded from one of the many anti-hunting websites in the UK and showed the three men standing in a field holding a banner between them that read: *Killing foxes is not a sport.*

Shane Logan was in the middle, a heavy set man who looked to be in his forties, with a beard and hardly any hair.

'He's got previous for committing an act of vandalism against a fox hunter's property and he sounds like a right nutter,' Booth observed.

'We should have a word with him,' James said. 'Have you got his address?'

'Not yet, sir, but I'll get right on it.'

'You do that and I'll go and see him. We know that he and the Spicer brothers had it in for Ted Rycroft and his pals, so

141

maybe they got together and paid a visit to the farm on Christmas Eve. Then, after trashing the place, they could have gone hunting for the hunters.'

CHAPTER TWENTY-SEVEN

James's head was reeling under a jumble of thoughts after the briefing. The lack of any witnesses and firm forensic evidence was making it difficult to pull the various strands together, which was exactly what he told Superintendent Tanner when he called to update him.

After running through the latest developments, he added, 'I think it's time we scaled up the search, sir. I'm sure the teams have been checking out all the abandoned properties and farms across the area. But we should start looking inside those that are occupied as well. The teams can ask for permission and if it's refused we can go there with a warrant.'

'And this is because you reckon it's possible those men are being held somewhere against their will?' Tanner responded.

'It's something we have to seriously consider. If they took shelter in a place of their own choosing then I'm convinced we would have heard from them by now. And that photo, if genuine, is clear evidence of third-party involvement.

I'm going to see Mrs Marr now to show it to her. It's not something I'm looking forward to, but it has to be done.'

'I agree. While I have you, I've just received some early feedback from the experts. They don't believe that the image has been manipulated. So, unless Mr Marr is pretending to be dead, then it's his body lying out there.'

'And that raises several more questions,' James said. 'Did he die at that spot next to the wall or was he killed elsewhere and moved there? And where the hell are the other three?'

'I'll speak to the Chief about gaining access to occupied properties,' Tanner said. 'Meanwhile, I gather a freezing mist has descended on the landscape west of the Rycroft farm and it's apparently severely restricting visibility.'

'That's all we need,' James said. 'Nature seems determined to make this hard for us.'

After coming off the phone, James returned to the evidence board, scanning it for inspiration. DC Booth had pinned a photo of Joanna Grey to it. The picture was taken while she protested at the trail hunt near Staveley before she was hit by Ted Rycroft's Jeep. She was carrying a banner that read: *For Fox Sake, Stop Hunting.*

James thought she looked more like a teenager than a twenty-one-year-old. She had a mop of curly brown hair that kissed her shoulders and a pleasant, oval-shaped face.

His eyes then moved from her to the photo of the body in the snow. This was much larger, printed on an A4 sheet of paper, and it sent a shudder down his spine.

The man's pale, stiff features looked as though they were frozen in place and James was sure he could see snowflakes in his open mouth.

The last thing he wanted to do was show the picture to Mrs Marr, but he feared it would soon be out there for all to see. It might be possible to get the BBC and the national newspapers to hold back on going with it for a couple of days, but there was every chance the photo had been sent to other, less reputable news outlets as well. Or perhaps it would be posted online and spread like wildfire on social media.

Foley broke into his thoughts just then.

'Guv, I've phoned Bridget Marr and she's still at her mother's house near Selside,' she said. 'She got really anxious when I told her we were coming to see her. She asked if we'd found her dad, which suggests the photo hasn't been sent to them yet, and I said we hadn't, but there was something we needed to show her.'

'And how did she react?'

'She just fell silent. I said we'd be there in under half an hour.'

James checked his watch. 10.15 a.m. 'Then let's get going,' he said.

CHAPTER TWENTY-EIGHT

Foley took the wheel of a pool car for the drive to Selside. The Marr family ran a farm about a mile from the village and according to the satnav it was just off the A6.

The road was pretty clear of traffic and thankfully it wasn't snowing so it was a fairly easy ride. The worst of the weather was currently to the west of them, over the Kentmere Valley, and dark clouds hung above the fells. James wondered how difficult it was proving to be for the rescue teams.

'This is going to be a first for me,' Abbott said, as she tapped her fingers on the steering wheel. 'I've never shown someone a photo of what's believed to be the dead body of their loved one.'

'That makes two of us,' James said. 'I wish we didn't have to do it. But it's clear that the bastard who took it wants it to cause even more friction between those who support fox hunting and those who oppose it. I'm betting it'll be the major media talking point within hours, especially with all the hunts that are taking place across the country today. It will be impossible to keep a lid on something as shocking and sensational as that wretched picture. Not to mention the message that was sent with it.'

'Do you think that whoever wrote that message also wrote the message that was left on the picture of the hunters at the Rycroft farm?'

'That scenario is definitely one we need to give serious consideration to,' James said. 'The problem is that forensics haven't turned up any evidence of anyone being attacked at the farm. That would suggest those men set out on their hunt before the place was trashed. Yes, they could have done it themselves – either on purpose for an unknown reason or accidentally because they were off their heads on booze or something else – but I don't think it's a serious possibility anymore given this new development. So, maybe they were followed from there and then attacked or abducted later in the morning or afternoon. Alternatively, two groups of anti-hunt activists might have been working in tandem. One group did the business at the farm while the other group laid a trap for the men.'

Foley bit down on her bottom lip as she considered it. After a moment, she said, 'This case has got to be the strangest one I've ever worked on, guv. I'm still not sure exactly what we're dealing with and it'll be even more disturbing if forensics find that the blood on the dog's coat is human.'

'I know what you mean, Caroline. Hopefully the test result will come through soon. The process is always slower over Christmas.'

*　*　*

The Marr farm was a sprawling affair nestled between two low hills and James was surprised to see a 'For Sale' sign as they approached the entrance. It made him realise that there was still a lot he didn't know about the four missing huntsmen.

The yard was large and empty, except for two cars that were parked in front of a smart, detached stone farmhouse.

To the left of it was a stone barn and to the right a tall, steel storage building.

The place was surrounded by grazing land but there were no animals to be seen wandering across the snow.

It was Marr's daughter Bridget who opened the front door to them. When James last saw her, she had been wearing a thick winter coat and jeans. Now she had on jogging bottoms and a T-shirt.

'Hello again, detectives,' she said, her voice thin and stretched. 'Mum's waiting for you inside.'

They followed her along the hallway and into a spacious dining room where Francesca was sitting at the table with her fists clenched on top of it.

It looked to James as though she was bracing herself for bad news. Her face was bare of make-up and her eyes were heavy and red, indicating that she'd been crying.

'Please take a seat and tell me what this is all about,' she said.

They did as she asked while Bridget went and sat next to her mother.

James could feel the muscles knotting in his stomach and he was suddenly having second thoughts about showing her the picture of the man who was believed to be her husband. A voice inside was telling him that it would be too cruel, but another, louder voice was insisting it would be far more painful for her to see it for the first time on TV or the front page of a newspaper.

Foley must have sensed his hesitation because she leaned forward and said, 'We didn't realise you were selling the farm, Mrs Marr. Has it been on the market for long?'

Before replying, Francesca took a deep breath through her nose, which inflated her chest.

'Only about three months. We've already had an offer from a company that wants to turn it into a caravan park with a bed and breakfast. The contracts are being drawn up and we plan to take the sign down when the deal is done.'

'Do you mind me asking why you're selling up?' James asked.

'To be honest with you, Inspector, farming isn't what it used to be. For the past couple of years we've struggled to make ends meet,' she said. 'We sold our livestock six months ago and have been living off the money we made.'

'Will you be moving away from the area?'

She shook her head. 'We own a holiday cottage in Keswick and if all goes well with the sale we'll have enough to retire on and live there full time. Nigel says we should make the most of . . .'

The mention of her husband's name proved too much. She gulped in a deep breath and squeezed her eyes shut. When she opened them again, they were wet with tears.

'Please get to the point,' she sobbed. 'It's killing me not knowing if I'm ever going to see him again. We've got so much to look forward to and now . . .'

Her daughter put an arm around her and James saw that she too was on the verge of crying.

He felt a tightening in his chest as he reached into his pocket and pulled out the photo.

'There's something you both need to know,' he said. 'A photo has been sent anonymously to several media outlets and it purports to show Mr Marr.'

Francesca stared at him across the table, a deep frown creasing her forehead.

'There's a good chance it will soon be in the public domain so I feel compelled to give you the option as to whether or not you want to see it now. But I must warn you that you'll find it very upsetting.'

'I need to see it,' Francesca said.

'So do I,' echoed her daughter.

James passed the photo across the table and Francesca picked it up.

'We believe that to be your husband, Mrs Marr,' he went on. 'It will be music to our ears if you tell us that you don't think it is.'

As soon as Francesca looked at the image her lips parted in shock and a choking sound rushed out of her mouth. She held it close to her face for several seconds, while pain and confusion distorted her features.

'I . . . I'm sure it's him,' she murmured, her bottom lip quivering. 'But that doesn't have to mean he's dead. He could be alive. He might be sleeping. He's not . . .'

The desperation in her voice made the hairs on James's head bristle.

Bridget snatched the photo from her mother and stared at it, eyes wide, jaw agape.

'Oh, my lord, that *is* him,' she wailed. 'What sicko would have done this?'

As she turned to her mother her face looked as though the blood had been sucked out of it. Francesca reached out and pulled her daughter close and they both broke down.

James didn't know how to respond so he chose not to. Instead, he and Foley sat there in awkward silence as mother and daughter clung to each other while their tears gushed out.

CHAPTER TWENTY-NINE

It was several minutes before Francesca and her daughter managed to regain control of their emotions. By then James was riddled with guilt for having delivered such a crushing blow.

They both wore tortured expressions, their faces pale with shock and drained of blood.

James coughed at the dryness in his throat before he began to tell them what he knew.

'I'm really sorry you had to see that,' he said. 'We know that it was sent to the BBC, the *Cumbria Gazette* and at least three national newspapers. But it's likely that other newspapers and online platforms also received a copy. And I'm sorry to say that it will be impossible for us to stop it being published or aired.'

'Did Maria and Owain also receive a copy?' Francesca asked as she started playing with her wedding ring.

'Not as far as I know. But we will be bringing it to their attention.'

'And you say it was attached to an email?'

James nodded. 'Yes, it was. But it came from a fake account and it's very unlikely that we'll be able to trace the sender.'

'And was there a message with it?'

'There was.'

'Then we'd like to see it.'

Once again, he felt he had no choice since it was possible that she would be sent a copy anyway.

He took out his phone, but instead of showing them the email he read out the message.

'It says: "The real hunt has begun".'

Francesca's hands flew up to her face in horror and she started to sob again. Her daughter swallowed hard, her chest jerking, but this time she managed to hold in the tears.

James shifted uneasily on his chair and said, 'I want you to know that we've scaled up the search and that everything possible is being done to find your husband and the others. Unfortunately, we're not able to pinpoint the location where the photo was taken.'

Francesca removed her hands from her face and squinted at James as tears continued to make tracks down her cheeks.

'I'm sure that Nigel's anti-hunt enemies are going to enjoy hearing about th-this,' she spluttered. 'And that photo will make their day.'

'And not just them,' Bridget said with a sharp edge to her voice. 'My dad will lap it up too, I bet.'

Her words took James by surprise and he exchanged an anxious look with Foley who lifted her brows.

'I'm sorry, but you've confused us with that remark,' James said to Bridget. 'Should we take it to mean that Mr Marr is not your father?'

She set her lips into a thin line and gave a brisk shake of the head.

'I wish he was but no, he isn't. My real dad is a piece of shit who made Mum's life a misery for years.'

Francesca reached out and placed a hand on her daughter's arm. Then to James, she said, 'I was married for ten years to a man named Aaron Drax. I suspect you've heard of him, Inspector, because he served over eight years in prison for dealing drugs and possessing a gun.'

'I'm sorry, the name is not familiar to me, Mrs Marr,' James said.

'Well, it is to a lot of people in the area, or it used to be. He was a violent man who was abusive to me and our daughter. I divorced him nine years ago. Then, three years later, I married Nigel and moved onto the farm. It was the best thing I ever did. My ex wasn't happy, of course, because he hated the thought that I'd fallen in love with someone else. He was in prison by then and sent abusive messages to me and Nigel from his cell before the authorities managed to stop him.'

'And is he still locked up?'

'I'm afraid not. He was released five weeks ago and is back here in Cumbria.'

'How do you know?'

'Because he walked into a pub in Kendal three weeks ago and Nigel was there with Ted and Dylan. When he spotted my husband, he went over to him and told him he wanted Bridget to contact him. He tried to give Nigel his phone number, but Nigel refused to take it.'

'Did it kick off?'

'Almost. He swore at Nigel and said that Bridget was his

daughter and if he tried to stop him seeing her, he'd regret it. Then he rushed out.'

'I wouldn't have called him anyway,' Bridget said. 'I just wish he'd been kept in prison for the rest of his life. It's where he belongs.'

James turned back to Francesca. 'Why didn't you tell us about this when we spoke yesterday, Mrs Marr?'

'I didn't think it was relevant. You gave the clear impression that Ted's farm was vandalised by anti-hunt activists. And Aaron is himself a keen hunter. Always has been.'

'Still, I think we should speak to Mr Drax, if only to eliminate him from our inquiries. Do you know where he's living?'

'No. Why would I?'

'It's not a problem. I'm sure we can easily find out.'

James saw her jaw set with tension. 'Do you actually believe that he could be involved in what has happened?' she said.

'There's no evidence at present to indicate that,' he replied. 'But we can't ignore the fact that after his recent release from prison he came into contact with your husband and two of his fellow huntsmen.'

James could see from their faces that they were both struggling to take it in, but as far as he was concerned, Aaron Drax was the latest name to be added to their list of potential suspects.

'Before we go, do you have any further questions? I'll answer them if I can,' James offered, kindly.

Both Francesca and her daughter shook their heads and shrank back into themselves.

'I'm going to arrange for a family liaison officer to come here,' he said, as he picked up the photo from the table and returned it to his pocket. 'They'll stay as long as you want them to and can act as a barrier between you and any reporters who turn up to try to get an interview. I promise to let you know as soon as there are any further developments and please don't hesitate to contact me if you need to. You have my mobile number. And once again, I'm really sorry that I was forced to bring the picture and the message to your notice.'

They showed themselves out and as they walked along the hall to the front door, they heard both women break down in tears.

CHAPTER THIRTY

As soon as they drove away from the farm James rang the office and asked to be put through to DC Booth.

'First I need to know if you have an address for Shane Logan,' he said when the detective came on. 'We're just leaving Mrs Marr's place.'

'I have, guv, and it's on the Burneside Road,' she replied. 'I'll text you the details, but as yet I don't have his phone number.'

'What else have you found out about him?'

'According to his Facebook page, he's married to someone named Sonia and works as a farm machinery mechanic. His conviction for smashing the window of the hunt supporter's home in Carlisle is the only one on record. But he's been prolific when it comes to spreading bile online. Just a week ago, on his Twitter page, he posted a photo of himself at a recent trail hunt holding a poster that read: *only scum kill for fun.*'

'We'll go straight to his home before returning to head-quarters,' James said. 'Meanwhile, I want you to see what we have on a guy named Aaron Drax. He's Francesca Marr's first husband and he's just come out of prison after doing an eight-year stretch for dealing drugs and possession of a weapon.'

'Is he considered a suspect?' Booth asked.

'Most definitely. Dig out his picture and add it to the evidence board. At the next briefing we'll go through what we have and where we go from here. I take it there's nothing new on the search?'

'Only that the weather is still shit and causing problems. The chopper has been grounded already and in some parts of the Kentmere area the mist has reduced visibility to just a few yards.'

'Well, there's not much we can do about the weather other than pray that it'll improve,' James said. Before ending the call, he asked Booth to send a family liaison officer to Mrs Marr's home.

Seconds later a text came through with Shane Logan's full address and mobile phone number.

'I've just had a thought, guv,' Foley said, as she steered a course towards Burneside. 'Ted Rycroft's farmhand, Greg Pike, is the one who told us about the Spicer brothers. I wonder if it might be worth finding out if he has any useful goss on this Logan character as well.'

'That's actually a good call,' James said. 'Luckily I made a note of his number.'

Greg was surprised to hear from the police and mistakenly assumed he was going to be told that his boss had been found.

'I wish that were the case, Mr Pike,' James said. 'But sadly, it isn't. The search is ongoing and we're still trying to find out who paid an unwelcome visit to the farm.'

'Then what can I do for you, Inspector?'

'I want to pick your brain about a man who has been brought to our attention. His name is Shane Logan and we understand he's a friend of Liam and Warren Spicer.'

'That he is,' Greg said. 'And he's just as disruptive as they are.'

'We've been told that he started targeting Mr Rycroft and the others following an incident five years ago when a young woman protester was hit by Mr Rycroft's Jeep.'

'That's right. It was an accident, but a bunch of sabs refused to believe it and to this day they still go on about it.'

'Do you know if Mr Rycroft has had any run-ins with Logan?'

'Plenty of times. He frequently turns up at trail hunts to hurl abuse at Ted and accuse him of breaking the law. Once he even turned up at the farm with a group of sabs and they videoed themselves singing the Manfred Mann classic *Fox on the Run*.'

'So, is he always hanging around with the Spicer brothers?'

'A lot of the time, yeah. They often get together at Neil Hutchinson's farm to plan what mischief they're gonna get up to.'

'Then Logan is also a friend of Hutchinson?'

'More than a friend. He's Hutch's nephew, the only son of his sister who lives in Spain with her husband. And there's no doubt in my mind that he would have helped them trash Ted's place.'

'As I've already told you, Mr Pike, Neil Hutchinson and the brothers deny being responsible.'

'And you believe them?' He sounded incredulous.

'We'll have to accept their word for it until there's evidence to the contrary,' James said. 'Now, can I also ask you if you know a man named Aaron Drax?'

After a pause, Greg said, 'I've never met him, but I know he used to be married to Nigel Marr's wife. After they separated, he got banged up for drug dealing and some other stuff.'

'Well, he's now out of prison and back here in Cumbria. Has Mr Rycroft mentioned bumping into him recently?'

'Not to me he hasn't.'

'Okay. One last question. How is Miss Carter? I know that the message she received made her quite anxious.'

'I spoke to Rebecca earlier and she's still pretty shaken by it. But thankfully she hasn't had any more.'

'That's good. I'll make a point of calling her to check in.'

'Have you any idea when we can go back to the farm?' Greg asked.

'Not yet, but I'm hoping we'll be finished up there soon. And rest assured the sheep are being looked after.'

CHAPTER THIRTY-ONE

Shane Logan and his wife lived on the road that ran between Kendal and Burneside. It took James and Foley just over fifteen minutes to get there.

It was a detached house with grey brick walls and a short driveway on which was parked a black Vauxhall Corsa.

The woman who answered the door to them was in her early thirties and of medium height. She had fine black hair cut straight in a boyish style, and was wearing a high-necked lambswool sweater over tight slacks.

'Are you Mrs Logan?' James asked. 'Mrs Sonia Logan?'

She screwed up her brow and nodded. 'Yes, that's me. What can I do for you?'

They both whipped out their warrant cards and held them up for her to see.

'We're police officers, Mrs Logan,' James said. 'I'm Detective Chief Inspector Walker and this is Detective Constable Foley. We would . . .'

Alarm shivered behind her eyes and she responded with,

'Oh no, please don't tell me that Shane has been involved in an accident. Is that why I can't get him on his phone?'

'That's not why we're here,' James said quickly. 'I'm sure that your husband is fine. In fact, the purpose of our visit is to have a word with him.'

She breathed a sigh of relief. 'You gave me a scare.'

James pushed out a smile. 'Then please accept my apology. But do you know where we can reach Mr Logan?'

'He's doing a job over in Cockermouth. He left early this morning and I've been calling to find out when I can expect him home. But I can't get through. He warned me that might happen though as the farm he's at is in an area with a poor mobile signal.'

'And would I be right in assuming that you don't have an address or contact details for this property?' James asked.

'Yes, you would, because he keeps all that stuff on his phone. But look, you're starting to worry me. What's all this about? Why do you want to speak to Shane?'

'I suspect you've heard about the four men who've been missing since they set out on a Christmas Eve trail hunt from a farm near Kentmere?' James said. 'A farm owned by Mr Ted Rycroft, a man your husband is all too familiar with.'

She hesitated before responding. 'We both saw it on the news last night, but I still don't see why—'

'We're trying to find out what has happened to them, Mrs Logan. And we're also investigating criminal damage that was carried out at the farm in question.'

Her expression showed irritation. 'I get it now. You think that Shane has been up to his old tricks. Well, I can tell you that he hasn't. He made a big mistake ten months ago when he smashed those windows in Carlisle. But he promised me he wouldn't do anything like that again and I know he hasn't.'

'That's good to hear,' James said. 'But I should point out that there's evidence to indicate that the damage to the farm was carried out by someone who opposes fox hunting. As part of our enquiries, we're contacting anti-hunt protesters who've made their feelings known to Mr Rycroft and his fellow huntsmen. Your husband is among them as the many belligerent comments he's posted online have been brought to our attention.'

'But he's allowed to express his opinions and concerns,' she responded. 'This is a free country and like millions of other people he feels strongly about fox hunting. And I don't blame him. It's barbaric.'

James took out his notebook. 'Would you mind giving me his mobile number? I'll try calling him myself.'

Her eyes flashed with impatience. 'I'll need to get my phone. It's in the kitchen. If you wait here, I'll—'

'Actually, we'd like to ask you a couple of questions, if that's okay,' James interrupted. 'If you can answer them for us, it might not be necessary to contact Mr Logan.'

There was another brief moment of hesitation before she waved them inside.

They followed her into the kitchen, which was all granite and beech and matching appliances.

She picked up her phone from the worktop, opened it, and read out the number.

'Let me see if I can get him,' she said. 'I'd rather you put your questions to him.'

But the call failed to go through and disappointment clouded her features.

'This happens a lot and it's so bloody frustrating,' she said.

'It's one of the few downsides of living in this part of the country,' James responded.

After replacing the phone on the worktop, she looked at her watch and said, 'So, come on then. What is it you want to ask me? I need to leave for work. I'm already running late.'

'Do you have far to go?' Foley asked her.

'A pub in Staveley. I serve behind the bar.'

'And your husband is a farm machinery mechanic. Is that correct?' James said.

'It is. He's been doing it for years.'

'Just as he's been protesting against fox hunting for years.'

She shrugged. 'He wouldn't have to do it if the ban was properly enforced. But it isn't. You know that as well as I do. Fox hunting still goes on all over the country.'

James cleared his throat and said, 'There was a road accident not far from here five years ago in which an anti-hunt protester named Joanna Grey was seriously injured.'

'Yes, I know about that.'

'And was your husband acquainted with Miss Grey?'

'He knew her, yes. And I'm sure you're aware that Shane does not believe it was an accident. And neither do I. Ted Rycroft should have been prosecuted because he drove into that poor young woman on purpose. There was a witness who saw it happen, but your lot chose not to believe his account.'

'And ever since then your husband has targeted Mr Rycroft and his associates with insults and accusations online. That's right, isn't it?'

Her eyebrows slid upwards and she jammed her tongue into the inside of her cheek.

'When are you going to ask me a question that you don't already know the answer to, Inspector?' she said.

James gave a nod. 'Fair enough. In that case I'd like you to tell us if you can account for Mr Logan's movements on Christmas Eve. Did you spend it together?'

'In actual fact, we didn't,' she replied. 'I spent it with my parents who live in Ravenstonedale.'

'And your husband?'

She tutted. 'Well, I'm going to have to disappoint you there. You see, he was with his best pals all day. They went out protesting at a fox hunt. I'm not sure where, but I think that it was near Ambleside. Afterwards they went for lunch and had a few drinks, but he was home by six. So, if you want to confirm that he has an alibi for when the Rycroft farm was damaged then you only have to talk to them.'

'And who are they?' James asked.

'They're brothers and their names are Liam and Warren Spicer. They live in Kendal.'

CHAPTER THIRTY-TWO

'Well, that was a result,' Foley said as they climbed back into the pool car. 'Either that woman just told us an outright lie or the Spicer brothers did.'

'It could be that Mrs Logan was lied to by her husband,' James replied.

'Then if so, we need to find out why.'

James had chosen not to let on that they had already spoken to Liam and Warren Spicer and that the pair had claimed they spent Christmas Eve at home with each other. So was it true or not? It was a question he needed to put to them as soon as possible.

'It also strikes me as a tad suspicious that she can't reach her husband on his phone,' Foley said. 'Makes me wonder if he's not really doing a job near Cockermouth. He just wants her to think he is.'

'Then where else would he be?' James said.

Foley shrugged. 'Who knows? If our four huntsmen were abducted and he was involved then perhaps he's with the three we hope and believe to be still alive.'

James played the conversation with Sonia Logan over in his mind. His gut was telling him that she hadn't lied to them, that she'd told them what she believed to be the truth. And if that was so then a dark cloud of suspicion now hung over her husband.

James called the office to let the team know that they were on their way back. He was informed that the mist over the Kentmere area was gradually lifting and it was hoped the chopper would soon be airborne again.

He was also told that the Digital Crime Unit had not been able to trace the origins of the email that had the photo of the body attached to it.

'Whoever sent it is obviously tech savvy,' James said to Foley.

'It's really not that difficult these days to hide your identity online or when using a mobile phone,' she replied. 'It's why hackers and scammers are raking in such vast sums. They know how hard it is for us to catch them.'

It was an area of crime that James wasn't an expert in. He knew about the online trolls and cyber stalkers, and how they seemed to operate with impunity. And he was well aware of the sheer amount of explicit, offensive and threatening material that was posted every single day across the internet. And that was why he feared the photo of the body would soon be unleashed on an unsuspecting public, causing outrage and division on a massive scale.

Back at HQ the team were still beavering away. Before he began the briefing, James downed a strong coffee and got stuck into a cheese sandwich. He was still chewing on it as he listened to what the team had to tell him.

DI Stevens said that a family liaison officer was on her way to Mrs Marr's home and that uniforms had spoken to Maria Payne and Owain Hughes about the photo.

'They're both convinced it's a genuine picture of Nigel Marr,' Stevens said. 'And naturally they're now dreading what might follow it.'

Next up was DC Booth who said she had an address for Francesca Marr's first husband, Aaron Drax.

'I also dug out the file on him, sir,' she said. 'As you know, he recently came out of prison after serving eight years and six months for conspiracy to supply Class A and B drugs, money laundering and being in possession of a handgun. He was actually sentenced to eleven years but was released early on licence. At the time of his arrest, he was living in Manchester, where he moved soon after his divorce from Mrs Marr. Organised crime officers found five one-kilo blocks of cocaine hidden in bags in his bedroom, along with the handgun and five rounds of ammunition.

'He'd earned himself a reputation as a violent, short-tempered villain and he was up to no good when he lived here in Cumbria. But his criminal career took off after the divorce. And it's noted in the file that his ex-wife claimed he'd been physically and emotionally abusive to her during their marriage.'

'This is significant because according to Mrs Marr he walked into a pub three weeks ago and saw Nigel Marr, Ted Rycroft and Dylan Payne,' James added. 'He asked Mr Marr to pass on his phone number to his daughter, Bridget, presumably because he wanted to rekindle whatever relationship they once had. Marr refused and Drax swore at him and said he'd regret it if he tried to get in the way of him seeing his daughter. We have to consider the possibility that Drax decided to get his revenge.'

'He's currently living just south of here with his widowed father, in Oxenholme,' Booth said. 'I've spoken to his supervising officer who says that as far as he knows the man has been adhering to all his licence conditions and keeping a low profile. You just need to give the word, sir, and we can haul him in.'

'What about the family of Joanna Grey, the young woman hit by Ted Rycroft's car?' James said. 'Have you managed to locate them?'

'That's still a work in progress, sir.'

James gestured to the photos on the evidence board. 'These guys are now persons of interest to us. Warren and Liam Spicer, Neil Hutchinson and Shane Logan are all anti-hunt activists. Aaron Drax is the exception. His wife told me he's a keen hunter himself, or was before he got banged up. But that doesn't mean he's any less of a suspect. It just means that if he's in any way involved then it's for a different reason.'

He went on to list the tasks he wanted carried out immediately, including locating and interviewing Shane Logan, bringing the Spicer brothers in for a formal interview, and establishing where Aaron Drax was on Christmas Eve.

He then asked DI Stevens for an update on Johnny Elvin.

'Uniform dropped in on him,' Stevens said. 'He stuck by his story and his wife confirmed that he never left the house on Christmas Eve. According to her he stayed in bed most of the morning and was pretty rough.'

As James started to assign tasks his phone began vibrating in his pocket. At the same time at least three of the desk phones began to ring, which usually signalled that something was up.

James pulled out his phone and saw that it was Superintendent Tanner who was calling.

'What's up, boss?' he said when he answered.

'We need to prepare ourselves for a shitstorm, James,' Tanner said. 'The photo of the body in the snow, along with the email message that came with it, has appeared online. And it's already going viral.'

CHAPTER THIRTY-THREE

The photo had been posted on one of the more extreme hunt saboteur websites. Above it was the headline: *Look what someone sent us!*

The post included a brief report explaining that the man in the picture was Nigel Marr, one of the four huntsmen who had gone missing, and naming the other three.

By the time James laid eyes on it the photo was popping up all over the internet. Some of the sites took a more cautious approach by blotting out the face of the man propped up against the dry-stone wall. But several didn't bother disguising him.

Within half an hour the mainstream media were going with the story. The BBC and Sky News were leading their bulletins with it, but ensuring that the face was covered and the blood on his chest blotched out, and it was being added to the online news feeds.

Gordon Carver called James to tell him that they were going to have to go with it on the *Cumbria Gazette* website.

'Can you give me a quote, James?' Carver asked.

'What are the press liaison people saying?' James replied.

'I'm still waiting for them to get back to me. I'm guessing they're overwhelmed.'

'Well, you can say that an unnamed source within the force confirmed that an investigation is under way to try to establish the source of the email and that Mr Marr's wife has been spoken to. And stress that the search for the missing men has been scaled up.'

'Is that all you want to say?'

'For now, yes. But you'll no doubt get an official statement before long. Are you going to publish the picture?'

'We are, but we won't show the face. It's a tricky one, I know, and I'm sure it won't go down well with some of our readers. But it's a big story and we can't ignore it now that it's out there and creating such a stir.'

Even within the office the publication of the photo was causing a high level of disquiet. James's team members were used to dealing with shocking events, but this was something different and it had touched a nerve.

'I was hoping that it'd be considered too sensitive to make public,' DS Abbott said. 'But I should have known that in this day and age the more horrific something is, the more exposure it will get.'

James told DC Foley to make Mrs Marr aware of what had happened.

'And let's ensure that she's well protected from the press who are bound to descend on her home like vultures,' he added.

It had only just turned mid-day and the story was already provoking a fierce reaction. Disgraceful comments were appearing across social media and several notorious hunt saboteurs even claimed that Nigel Marr had got what he deserved.

On BBC News a prominent hunt supporter called for calm and said, 'This is the work of a psychopath who wants to create even more unrest and hostility between the two sides. We can't allow them to succeed.'

At 1.30 p.m. the Chief Constable fronted an impromptu press conference in Penrith. He made it clear that every effort was being made to find out who had taken and distributed the photo.

'It's still undergoing forensic analysis and so we can't say with certainty if it has been doctored in any way,' he said. 'I would ask that reporters refrain from contacting Mr Marr's family and the families of the other missing huntsmen. This is a very upsetting time for them and unwelcome intrusion by the media will serve only to intensify their suffering.'

James eventually managed to return his attention to the briefing that had been put on hold, and he called everyone together with the aim of dishing out the various tasks.

But even before he started speaking there came another interruption, this time from DC Patterson who shouted from across the room for everyone to be quiet.

Then, in a voice that was clipped and urgent, he said, 'I just took a call from Control, guv. Mountain Rescue have been in touch. They've found a body.'

CHAPTER THIRTY-FOUR

The news that a body had been discovered sent a cold, crawling sensation down James's spine. He'd been expecting it, of course, but that did not lessen the impact.

Within minutes he learned that it was found a few miles north-east of Kentmere village, close to the River Kent.

A narrow lane took vehicles to within about five hundred yards of it and from there it could be reached via a rough bridleway.

James also received confirmation that it appeared to be the body of Nigel Marr. The rescue team leader took a photo on his phone and sent it to Control, and it was almost identical to the one that was all over the news.

Word came through that scene of crime officers, under the supervision of chief forensic officer Tony Coppell, were already on their way there, along with half a dozen uniforms. And so too was forensic pathologist Dr Pam Flint.

'It won't be an easy job processing the scene in these conditions,' James said, as he addressed the team again before departing for the location himself.

'At least it's not snowing there at the moment,' DC Patterson pointed out. 'The mist has lifted and that particular area is enjoying a period of relative calm. That's why they got lucky and stumbled on the body. But according to the forecast it's not likely to last.'

James had told DS Abbott and DC Sharma they would be accompanying him to the scene and he instructed DI Stevens to follow through on the points they had discussed earlier.

'It won't be long before the media mob are tipped off about this and they'll be clamouring to update the story,' he went on. 'So, we need to be prepared to react. I don't think there is any doubt now that Nigel Marr was murdered and all we can do is hope and pray that his pals haven't met the same fate.'

James, Abbott and Sharma set off from headquarters in a Land Rover driven by PC Malek, headed along the now familiar route towards Kentmere village.

It wasn't long before they drove past Ted Rycroft's farm where a small police presence remained.

Beyond it, the narrow lane twisted its way through the rugged, whitewashed landscape. The hills on either side were shrouded in low grey clouds that threatened more snow.

At one point they saw the distinctive red jackets of the Mountain Rescuers in the far distance. They were little more than dots, which was a sobering reminder to James of just how big an area they were having to cover.

He realised they had reached their destination when the road ahead of them was blocked by a patrol car. An officer waved them through a gap in the hedge on one side of the lane.

'You need to park in the field, sir,' he said. 'And then go the rest of the way on foot. Forensics and the pathologist arrived a short time ago.'

After parking between two more patrol cars, they all climbed out of the Land Rover and James cursed as his shoes sank into the bitter snow.

'I keep a pair of wellies in my car boot,' he said. 'But I stupidly forgot to put them on.'

James felt a tightening in his stomach and a fierce apprehension as he led the way along the lane to the start of the bridleway. That was where the Mountain Rescue Team had retreated to. There were eight of them and they looked tired and shell-shocked.

James paused briefly to thank them and their leader explained that they were now going to continue the search for the other three huntsmen.

'I don't know how long it'll be before we have to call it quits, though,' he said. 'It looks set to be another wretched night.'

The bridleway was about twelve feet wide and bordered by low, uneven dry-stone walls. Stones crunched under their feet as they made their way along it, passing through a small patch of woodland before reaching the crime scene.

There were groups of uniforms and white-suited SOCOs dotted about, most of them on the bridleway, while some stood on the other side of the wall to the right.

James was rigid with tension as he approached the spot and the breath whistled out of his nose.

The first person he recognised was Tony Coppell, who hadn't yet slipped on his face mask. When he saw James, he raised an arm and gave him a thumbs up.

One of the uniforms then stepped forward and made the group aware of three cantilevered stone steps in the wall, and they used these to climb over it.

As soon as James reached the other side, he saw the body propped up against the wall and his heart jumped a beat.

There was a figure kneeling over it and even though her hair and most of her face were covered, he knew immediately that it was Dr Pam Flint. The forensic pathologist had wasted no time getting to work.

James stepped forward while Abbott, Sharma and PC Malek hung back.

'How's it looking?' he said to Coppell, who wrested his eyes away from the notepad he'd been scribbling in.

'Too soon to know if we'll find much,' Coppell answered. 'The scene has been seriously contaminated by the weather and we haven't even begun to find out what's under the snow. Pam got here just after we did and I thought it best to leave her to examine the body first. As you can see, the photo that was emailed to the papers was unfortunately not a fake.'

Coppell reached down into a leather case that lay open on the ground next to him, pulling out a clear evidence bag containing a wallet, which he held up.

'She checked his pockets first and found this,' he said. 'Inside are credit cards and a driving licence in the name of Nigel Marr.'

James clenched his jaw as an image of the man's wife flickered in his mind.

'I wonder what the odds are now of finding the other three alive,' Coppell said.

Dr Flint looked up suddenly and waved them both over. She had brushed the snow from on top of the body and James could see that she had also opened up the man's jacket, revealing a blood-stained shirt beneath.

'Brace yourselves for a surprise, chaps,' she said. 'I can already tell you with a hundred per cent degree of certainty how this poor fellow died.' She placed a gloved hand close to a huge, ugly hole in his chest. 'This is a shotgun wound and I'm confident that what's left of the shell will still be inside him.'

CHAPTER THIRTY-FIVE

James flinched as his gaze swept over the corpse of Nigel Marr. The face was like an ice sculpture, the skin rigid and translucent.

The rest of his body was as stiff as a board and as Dr Flint brushed away more snow from around it, several blood stains could be seen on the frozen ground.

James was struggling to take in the fact that the man had been shot. What had started out as a group of trail hunters going missing during a Christmas Eve meet had become a murder investigation involving a firearm. And he couldn't help wondering if the weapon was one of those taken from the Rycroft farm.

This was another completely unforeseen development. Although gun crime in Cumbria had increased in recent years, it was still relatively rare compared with other parts of the UK. And it was a clear and disturbing indication that those responsible for this murder were resourceful as well as ruthless.

'It appears he has a number of injuries beneath his clothes,' Dr Flint said without looking up. 'Blood has soaked through at several points, including his left shoulder and right knee. There's severe bruising on his left hand and he has various broken bones, including two fingers and his right arm.'

'What does that tell you?' James asked.

She turned towards him. 'I believe it means he was dragged here after he was killed and in the process his body was battered by rocks, gravel and rough foliage. His jacket and trousers are badly torn in places and there's severe grazing on the areas of skin that have been exposed. I'm sure I'll discover more of what I'm convinced are post-mortem injuries once he's unclothed and on the examination table.'

'So, you don't think he was shot here.'

She shook her head. 'The blood stains would be more extensive, I'm sure, and the rest of his body would be in better shape. These wounds are not consistent with a beating, and as you can see, there are no marks on his face.'

'Was he dragged far from where he was killed?'

'It's impossible to give you a definitive answer to that question, James. It would depend on whether he was pulled across smooth, grassy fields as well as rough terrain. And any tracks that might have helped us have been wiped out by the snow, the wind and the Mountain Rescue Team.'

'What about time of death?' James asked.

'I think it's safe to say that he died on the day he disappeared. And he was probably brought to this spot within hours, or perhaps early the next morning. From the look of him, he's most certainly been exposed to the elements for quite a while. And it's worth noting that the freezing weather would have slowed the process of decomposition.'

Dr Flint turned back to the body and asked one of the SOCOs to take some close-up photographs.

James stood watching them for a few minutes with a grim, tight expression on his face. Around him the other SOCOs searched carefully for anything that could be construed as evidence.

Abbott, Sharma and PC Malek had set off to explore the field on this side of the wall. It sloped down towards a large area of woodland and beyond that were cloud-covered hills. The area was rural and remote, with no properties in sight.

James was still trying to marshal his thoughts when Coppell stepped up beside him and said, 'It wouldn't have been that difficult to have brought the body here, James. The Mountain Rescue guy told me that this field is easy to access from all directions. There are tracks and bridleways and a footpath runs through the woods to a lane that carries traffic. Plus, there are more than a few openings in the dry-stone walls. The body could have been hauled here after being tied or chained to some kind of farm utility vehicle, such as a small tractor.'

A thought crashed into James's mind and he said, 'What about a quad bike?'

Coppell cocked his head to one side and frowned. 'Like the quad bikes at Mr Rycroft's farm?'

'Exactly. He rents them out. Maybe one of the guys rode one on the hunt.'

'That wouldn't be so unusual. Quads have been an integral part of hunting for years. They carry the person whose main role is to dig and flush out foxes and to block up dens. And there have been quite a few news stories about pro-hunt supporters ramming bikes into saboteurs during hunts.'

'I seem to recall there were four in the Rycroft stable,' James said. 'Rebecca Carter was in charge of renting them out. I'll need to ask her if any are missing. Can you arrange for one or more of your team to examine the quads that are still at the Rycroft farm?'

'Of course.'

'Meanwhile, I reckon it'll make sense for the search for the others to focus on this area. Say a three-to-four-mile radius to begin with.'

Coppell flicked his head towards the sky. 'I wouldn't bank on much more being achieved today. It will soon be dark and if I'm not mistaken those are nimbostratus clouds up there. So, we need to process this scene and remove the body before they offload another pile of snow on us.'

CHAPTER THIRTY-SIX

While a forensic tent was being hastily erected over the body, James made some calls.

He spoke first to Superintendent Tanner and told him that Nigel Marr had almost certainly died from a shotgun wound to the chest.

'I know there will have to be a formal identification, but there's no doubt that it's him,' he said. 'He was carrying his wallet with ID. And it appears he was shot elsewhere and dragged to this spot.'

He passed on the information that Pam Flint had provided and suggested the search for the other three men be narrowed down to this particular area.

'And if the weather permits, we should draft in a dog unit,' he added. 'There's an outside chance the killer left a track that can be traced. They might also pick up the scent of the other three hounds.'

'I'll liaise with Mountain Rescue and our own teams on that,' Tanner said. 'Good shout. Meanwhile, the Chief has given the nod for them to search occupied properties and farms if they get permission. If not, we'll go in with a warrant.'

'That's good to know, sir.'

'And will you sort things in respect of Mr Marr's wife and daughter?'

'That will be my next call,' James said.

'Then keep me posted. I'll draw up a statement for the press office to release.'

James then phoned DI Stevens and filled him in.

'You need to send someone to break the news to Mrs Marr right away,' he said. 'I suggest Caroline since she went there with me earlier. And Maria Payne and Owain Hughes also have to be told.'

'Consider it done, guv.'

'Have you made any progress?'

'Some. I spoke to Liam Spicer about ten minutes ago and he and his brother have agreed to come in at six, and they're bringing a lawyer with them. I told them we have some follow-up questions, but kept it vague.'

'Okay. And Shane Logan?'

'His phone still appears to be switched off and we don't know where he's supposed to be working over near Cockermouth. We'll keep on it though.'

'What about Aaron Drax?'

'I got his supervising officer to talk to him. The guy says he was at home with his father throughout Christmas Eve and the dad's prepared to corroborate that.'

'We should bring him in just the same given his background in organised crime and his recent encounter with three of the huntsmen. I'll be returning to headquarters myself shortly and the team should be warned that they'll likely be working well into the evening – again.'

James pocketed his phone and blew warm air into his cupped hands. The temperature was dropping and the wind was picking up. Soon the SOCOs would be struggling to do their job.

Abbott, Sharma and PC Malek came back from their exploration of the surrounding area, saying they'd found nothing of interest. No tracks in the snow. No discarded items. No sign that anyone had been in the field in the recent past.

James told them what Dr Flint had said about the injuries to the body and how she believed Nigel Marr was shot elsewhere and dragged here.

'Ahmed, I'd like you to remain at the scene until the body is removed. Jessica, Seth, we'll head back to HQ.'

By this time much of the snow around the body had been swept aside in the hope that there would be pieces of potential evidence underneath. But so far nothing had turned up.

'He would almost certainly have had a backpack with him along with his phone,' Coppell said when James asked him what they were hoping to find. 'But I'm assuming his belongings were left at the murder scene – probably deliberately – by his killer. His wallet, on the other hand, could have been left in his pocket so we'd have no trouble identifying him.'

James went on to snap a few photos on his phone of Mr Marr's body and the area around it. By now the blood was beating in his ears and he felt cold right through his bones.

He sent PC Malek off to get the Land Rover warmed up and went to touch base with Dr Flint before returning to Kendal.

She was standing over the body now and dictating notes into her phone.

'You're off then, are you?' she said as she looked up and regarded him with those intelligent brown eyes of hers.

'Back to the office,' he said. 'There's a lot to get done.'

She'd removed her mask and pulled down her hood, and as always, her expression gave nothing away. He was glad she had been on call for this one, and not only because they had a good working relationship. She was in her late forties now, but for the past decade she'd been regarded as one of the best forensic pathologists in the north of England.

'I've completed my initial examination,' she said. 'The van is on its way to pick up the body and I'll crack on with the post-mortem first thing in the morning. But I really don't expect any surprises. From what I've seen so far, I believe Mr Marr was shot at mid to close range.'

'I take it you know that his three friends are still missing?' James said.

She nodded. 'I'm well aware of that. Do you think they're still alive?'

'I want to believe they are, but anything is possible. For all we know, they could be being held against their will and the intention is to kill them one at a time and then dump their bodies somewhere for us to find.'

'But what would be the purpose of that?'

James gave a small shrug. 'I can only think of one reason. The sickos behind this want to drag it out to ensure that it attracts as much publicity as possible. And if it is all about their opposition to fox hunting, as we think it could be, then it's a sure way of instilling fear in all those people they regard as their enemies.'

CHAPTER THIRTY-SEVEN

It started to get dark as they drove away from the scene. James's eyes were dry and gritty and it felt like his mind was overloaded.

He could tell that Abbott was also feeling the weight of the day's events. She sat next to him grinding her teeth and her breath was coming in short, unsteady gasps. He wasn't surprised. This was a tough case for all of them and it was easy to believe that the horror show had only just begun.

'What are you thinking, Jessica?' he asked her.

She turned to him, her face pinched and tense. 'That there could be three more bodies out there in the wilderness and someone has taken photos of them. Photos that will soon be emailed to loads more papers and websites.'

James nodded. 'That's occurred to me as well. For Mrs Marr and her daughter, it's going to be like having their hearts broken twice over.'

'I just wish I could make sense of it, guv. There surely has to be more to it that a deranged hatred towards people who hunt foxes.'

'Not necessarily. Terrorists kill people in order to bring about change. We call it "ideologically motivated violence". Maybe that's what this is all about.'

'I suppose so,' Abbott said. 'It would explain the message in the email. And the word *murderers* scrawled on the picture in Ted Rycroft's trophy room.'

Even before they arrived back at the station, the media had learned about the discovery of Nigel Marr's body.

James answered a call on his mobile from Gordon Carver at the *Cumbria Gazette*.

'All we've been told is that it was found north of Kentmere,' Carver said. 'Can you confirm for me, James, that the photo that was sent to us was of him?'

'There will have to be a formal identification process before we can confirm either way,' he said.

'But can you at least tell me how he died? Was he murdered?'

'That still has to be determined, but we don't believe it was an accident. The details will be forthcoming. And before you ask, there's nothing new to report on the other three men.'

'Do you think they're still alive?'

'The off-the-record answer to that, Gordon, is that I'm really not sure. We hope you can appeal to your readers for information.'

'We've already done that and no one has come forward with any. If they had I would have told you.'

'It's different now there's a body. That usually makes people think twice about holding stuff back.'

As they turned into the police station car park, James decided to cut the conversation short, but not before telling

Carver that he wanted to be the first to know if the *Gazette* received a second email with another gruesome photo attached.

The sense of anticipation in the office was palpable. DI Stevens had already briefed the team, but everyone wanted to hear James and Abbott give their first-hand account of what they had seen.

Before he began, James transferred the photos he'd taken at the scene from his phone onto the system so they could be viewed on the screens.

He then referred to his notes as he ran through everything that Dr Flint and Tony Coppell had told him. He was onto the subject of how the body might have been transported to the spot against the dry-stone wall when someone drew his attention to a news report on the TV.

The room fell silent as a BBC presenter stopped mid-way through a link into a sport story so that she could deliver some breaking news.

'Police searching for the four men who went missing while trail hunting in Cumbria on Christmas Eve have confirmed that a body has been found.

'It's believed to be that of Mr Nigel Marr, who was one of the four. According to a Constabulary spokesperson, foul play is suspected. Mr Marr's wife and daughter have been informed.

'Meanwhile, the whereabouts of the other three men is still not known.

'The grim discovery, several miles from the Lake District village of Kentmere, comes just hours after a photograph purporting to show Mr Marr lying dead in the snow was sent *anonymously to various media outlets. Police have so far been unable to determine who sent it.*

'The email contained a message which read: The real hunt has begun.

'This has led police to believe that the sender could be an extreme anti-hunt activist. It was also confirmed earlier that the farm belonging to another of the men, Mr Ted Rycroft, was vandalised on Christmas Eve. The farm, also close to Kentmere, is where the men set out from on their trail hunt. Vehicles belonging to them were also damaged.

'What has happened has turned the spotlight once again onto the controversial subject of fox hunting, which still continues even though it was banned years ago. It's been suggested that Mr Marr's group were taking part in an illegal fox hunt, and although this has not been verified, it has led to growing friction between pro- and anti-hunt groups who are trading insults and accusations across social media.

'Cumbria Police are expected to release a more detailed statement later this evening and when they do, we'll bring it to you.'

James pulled his gaze away from the screen and checked the time on the wall clock. It was coming up to five-thirty and he reminded the team that the Spicer brothers were due to arrive in half an hour.

They already knew what Sonia Logan had said about her husband spending Christmas Eve out protesting with them.

'Someone isn't telling the truth and we need to get to the bottom of it,' he said. 'Jessica and I will interview them separately. They're bringing their own solicitor so that should save us some time.'

He then returned to the subject of how Mr Marr's body might have been transported to the spot where it was found.

'One thought is that a small utility vehicle such as a tractor or a quad bike might have been used. We know that there are four quad bikes parked at the Rycroft farm and that he rents them out,' he said. Pointing to DC Isaac, he added, 'I'd like you to call Rebecca Carter, Dawn. See if any are missing and if she knows whether the group took one or more with them on the hunt.'

James turned to DC Hall, who was perched on the edge of his desk. 'Kevin, have you had any success with traffic cameras between the Spicer home and Kentmere on Christmas Eve?'

'Warren Spicer's car was picked up heading that way, but that was just before six, when he drove to Neil Hutchinson's farm to pick up his fiancée,' Hall replied. 'No sign of it earlier in the day.'

James murmured a curse under his breath and said, 'That doesn't mean they didn't venture out earlier. They could have travelled in another car. In fact, find out what vehicle Shane Logan drives. He might have picked them up. Although, I'm sure there are various routes they could have taken to avoid being spotted.'

They only had time to cover a few more topics before word came that the Spicer brothers had arrived.

'One final point,' James said to Stevens. 'Be ready to apply for a warrant to search their home and take possession of their digital devices. I'll want to move quickly if they fail to convince me that they haven't lied to us through their teeth.'

CHAPTER THIRTY-EIGHT

James hurried to reception to greet the Spicers while DS Abbott prepared two of the interview rooms.

The brothers hadn't bothered to dress up for the occasion. Liam was wearing a dishevelled tracksuit and Warren had on a grubby cagoule and faded denim jeans.

By contrast, their lawyer, a man James had never met before, wore a blue fitted business suit beneath a smart black overcoat. He introduced himself as Ralph Arkin and was in his forties with bushy dark hair peppered with grey.

James thanked them for coming and explained that the intention was to interview Liam and Warren separately.

'Are you happy to move between the two rooms, Mr Arkin? If not, we can provide a duty solicitor.'

'No, it's fine. I'm not expecting this to take long, so let's get on with it.'

'We're curious to know why you want to talk to us again,' Liam said. 'There's nothing we can add to what we told you before. And believe me, the news about Nigel Marr's body being found has shocked us as much as it has everyone else. But we honestly don't know anything about it.'

'We felt it necessary to have another conversation with each of you because of certain things that have come to light,' James said.

'Would I be right in assuming that this is now a murder investigation, Detective Chief Inspector?' Arkin said.

James gave a solemn nod. 'You would. I'm not in a position to provide you with details of Mr Marr's injuries, but I can confirm that he was the victim of foul play.'

'And what about those men he was with?'

'They're still unaccounted for, I'm afraid. And as I'm sure you can appreciate, concern for them is growing by the minute.'

James showed them to the interview rooms. A uniformed officer had been positioned between them outside in the corridor.

'Can I go first?' Warren said. 'I'm gagging for a fag so the sooner it's done the sooner I can go outside and light up.'

Liam rolled his eyes and shrugged. 'Suits me. Just be careful what you say and don't let the buggers stitch you up.'

'I'm not stupid, bruv.'

Abbott was on hand to show Warren and his lawyer inside the first room while James opened the door to the room next to it.

'There's coffee, tea and biscuits, Mr Spicer,' he said to Liam. 'Make yourself comfortable. An officer will be outside if there's anything you need.'

Once Warren and his lawyer were seated at the table, James thanked them again for coming and got straight down to business.

'When we spoke to you at Neil Hutchinson's farm on

Christmas Eve, I asked you certain questions to which you gave answers that I now have reason to believe were not true.'

Warren's mouth tightened and his nostrils flared. He fixed James with a cold stare and said, 'I remember exactly what I told you and I didn't lie.'

James placed his notebook on the table, flipped over a page, and read from it.

'You told me that you'd been in verbal scraps with Ted Rycroft while protesting against hunts he was taking part in. But you insisted that you never actually threatened him.'

A shrug. 'That's right. And it's the truth.'

'Well, I've spoken to someone who disputes that. This person witnessed you pinning Mr Rycroft up against a wall about four months ago. Your friends had to pull you off him. You then threatened to kick his head in.'

Warren gave a frosty smile. 'And I suppose your witness is that bastard Johnny Elvin. It has to be him since the others who were there are missing. Well, he would say that, wouldn't he? But all I did was call the four of them a bunch of scumbags for breaking the law by hunting foxes. That was all. It didn't get physical.'

Arkin cleared his throat and said, 'Is that all you have, Inspector? Surely if it did happen as Mr Elvin says it did, then a formal complaint would have been made at the time.'

It was the answer James had expected so he moved quickly on to question number two.

'Is it true that you are close friends with a man named Shane Logan, Mr Spicer?'

'Sure. So what? Have you got him in your sights as well?'

'We haven't spoken to him yet,' James said. 'But we did speak to his wife earlier today and she told us that he spent

194

Christmas Eve with you and your brother, and that the three of you went to protest at a trail hunt before going for lunch and a drink.'

His jaw hardened. 'But that's bollocks. I told you that me and Liam stayed home. We didn't go out until early evening.'

'I know that's what you said, but we now have to wonder if you lied to us. And that the truth is the three of you went to Mr Rycroft's farm and then followed him and the others into the valley.'

Warren leaned on the table and his face took on a fierce intensity.

'This is fucking ridiculous,' he fumed. 'We've both told you we had nothing to do with what's happened and I don't know why Sonia told you that Shane spent that day with us. I haven't seen him in over a week. Ask him yourself. He'll tell you.'

'We haven't been able to contact him and neither has his wife,' James said. 'He's working over near Cockermouth apparently.'

'Well, that's not unusual. He does jobs all over the county.'

He was shaking now and fury lit up his eyes, but just as he was about to continue his rant, his lawyer placed a hand on his arm and told him to cool it.

Then to James, Arkin said, 'I can understand why my client is angry and upset, Inspector. He has made it clear to you where he was on Christmas Eve and unless you have irrefutable evidence to the contrary, I see no point in continuing this interview.'

Unsurprisingly, the interview with Liam went much the same way, except that he kept his cool and his face remained poker straight throughout.

He claimed the last time he saw Shane Logan was when he had a drink with him over a week ago.

'We never made arrangements to meet up on Christmas Eve,' he said. 'We've already told you that we'd pulled back from protesting because it became too risky. In fact, I'm sure Shane told me he was going to have to work that day. I can't imagine why he would have told Sonia something different.'

James asked Liam if he was aware that Logan was fined ten months ago for smashing the windows of a house owned by a prominent hunt supporter in Carlisle.

'It's common knowledge,' he answered. 'He got done for it.'

'And I take it you also know that he has targeted Mr Rycroft with a number of vile social media posts because of something that happened five years ago when his—'

'There's no need to spell it out for me,' Liam snapped. 'I know all about how Rycroft smashed his Jeep into that poor girl. He got away with it and it angered a lot of people. Not just Shane. The prick deserved all the flak that came his way. And so did the others because they were in the Jeep with him and helped to cover it up.'

'Did you know the girl in question, Mr Spicer? Her name was Joanna Grey.'

He shook his head. 'I think I might have met her, but I'm not sure. All I know is that her father died and the family moved away from the area. I've no idea where they are now.'

James ended the interview there. He decided not to mention the search warrant he was going to obtain because he wasn't sure now that there were reasonable grounds.

Instead, he thanked them yet again for coming in and asked Abbott to show them out of the building to where Warren Spicer was filling his lungs with cigarette smoke.

CHAPTER THIRTY-NINE

As soon as James returned to the office, he was given the news that the search for the three other huntsmen had been called off for the night.

Snow was again pelting down across the whole of the Kentmere Valley and beyond, and strong winds were making conditions dangerous for the rescue teams.

Luckily Nigel Marr's body was able to be removed before the weather deteriorated.

DC Sharma was now on his way back to headquarters and Tony Coppell had let it be known that his SOCOs hadn't found any useful items of forensic evidence at the scene. He was planning to visit the Rycroft farm to examine the quad bikes before returning to Kendal.

'But I have got one piece of good news to impart,' Sharma said. 'I've heard back from the lab and you'll be glad to know that it was animal blood on the dog's coat. Not human.'

'That's a relief,' James said. 'I suppose we have to assume that it could have come from one of the other dogs, or perhaps another creature it came into contact with while in the bothy.'

'I'm not sure we'll ever get to know the answer to that.'

James could feel the frustration growing inside him as he called the team together and told them the Spicers were sticking to the story despite what Sonia Logan had claimed.

'It means that several serious questions remain unanswered,' he said. 'Are the pair of them lying, or is she? Or did her husband lie to her about meeting up with the Spicer brothers on Christmas Eve? And where the hell is he and why can't he be contacted?'

'Do you think it's possible that the pair have done something to him, guv?' DC Patterson said. 'What if all three of them did trash the farm and then went after the huntsmen with the intention of killing them? But then later Logan decided he couldn't live with himself and threatened to come to us. So, they put him out of harm's way. I know it's a bit of a leap, but everything about this case stretches the imagination.'

'You're spot on there, Colin,' James said. 'Which is why it's a theory we need to seriously consider.'

'Can I suggest a variation on that, guv?' DC Isaac chipped in. 'Suppose they did vandalise the farm and then go after the group, but their aim wasn't to kill them – it was to rough them up. But then things went too far and one of the men died so they felt they had no choice but to kill them all. And once they'd done that, they thought it would be a good idea to make the most of it by moving the bodies and posting pictures. But that proved too much for Shane Logan and so he had to be taken out of the picture.'

Various other ideas and theories were thrown into the mix and before long James's head was spinning with them.

'I was beginning to have second thoughts about obtaining a warrant to search the Spicer home and access their devices,' he said. 'But now I'm convinced we should pursue it. At the same time let's check traffic cameras again, this time to see where the two of them went yesterday and today.'

As the briefing continued, James updated the team on the blood found on the dog's coat and learned that DC Isaac had called Rebecca Carter about the quad bikes at the farm.

'She told me her boss only has four so none are missing,' she said. 'And she reckons that the group sometimes take one on trail hunts, but only when they go out on horses. And Mr Rycroft usually rides on it.'

James looked again at the wall clock. It was already gone seven and he decided it was time to tell those who'd been in since early this morning to go home. The late shift officers were already in and would keep on top of things during the night.

But just then DC Hall came off his phone and said, 'I've got news on Shane Logan, guv. I was looking for his car registration when Control flagged that his name was entered into the system a couple of hours ago. Earlier today his car was involved in a serious crash on the A66 just north of Keswick. He was rushed by ambulance to Penrith Hospital. That's where he is now. I've just spoken to the emergency department who told me he's still unconscious, but stable. And his wife has just arrived there.'

James asked Hall to contact Penrith station and get them to send someone straight to the hospital.

'Fill them in and tell them that Logan is a potential suspect in the murder of Nigel Marr,' he said. 'But I also want someone to go from here to interview the wife and find out what the hell is going on. I'm assuming he was on his way back home from Cockermouth when this happened, which is why she couldn't get through to him on his phone.'

'I can go,' Patterson offered. 'I live near Penrith so it makes sense.'

James thanked him and added, 'You also need to ask her what the truth is about where her husband was on Christmas Eve. And fingers crossed he comes to and recovers so that we can question him as well.'

'At least it puts paid to speculation that the Spicer brothers did something to him,' Stevens said.

James agreed. 'But that doesn't mean he's not up to his neck in what's happened or that he doesn't know the whereabouts of Dylan Payne, Rhys Hughes and Ted Rycroft.'

CHAPTER FORTY

They were coming to the end of another day that would dwell in James's mind for years to come. A day blighted by murder, grief and cruelty.

The photo of Nigel Marr lying dead on the snow. The pain etched into the face of his wife when she saw it. The repulsive message in the email that was sent to the papers. And then the hole in the man's chest, put there by a merciless killer who surely craved attention.

As he sat at his desk typing up his report of the day's events, James's thoughts kept drifting to Maria Payne and Owain Hughes. They would no doubt be living in fear of what the next day was going to bring.

Would a photo of Maria's dead husband emerge? Or would it be one showing Owain's dead father?

James wanted to believe that he could still save those men and spare Maria and Owain the anguish that now consumed Francesca Marr. And if they were indeed still alive then he was determined to find them.

A lump formed in his throat and he realised for the first

time just how much this case was getting to him. It was proving to be one of the most challenging of his police career and he didn't believe he was close to solving it.

There were so many disturbing factors to take into account. So many chilling elements to grapple with.

As his fingers flew over the keyboard, his phone buzzed with an incoming text. It was Annie responding to a message he'd sent earlier telling her he'd be late home again.

Drive carefully, my love. I've just put Bella to bed and there's a ready meal for you if you want it xxx

He couldn't wait to get home, but he suspected he would struggle to get a good night's sleep.

Most of the team had left the office, but he'd decided to get the paperwork out of the way so that he'd be ready to crack on first thing in the morning.

He'd told them all to report for duty at 6 a.m. and be prepared to come in earlier if the need arose.

He was expecting it to be another eventful day and he'd already drawn up a list of action points.

- GET AN UPDATE ON SHANE LOGAN AND HIS ACCIDENT.

- ESTABLISH A HIERARCHY OF SUSPICION – WHO OF THE INDIVIDUALS IN THE FRAME IS THE MOST LIKELY SUSPECT?

- INSTRUCT SEARCH TEAMS TO CHECK INSIDE OCCUPIED PROPERTIES AND FARMS.

- SPEAK TO TANNER ABOUT ANOTHER PUBLIC APPEAL FOR INFO.

- BE READY FOR MORE PHOTOS AND MORE BODIES TO TURN UP.

By the time he finished the report his eyes were heavy and he had to will his woozy brain to sharpen up.

Before leaving the office, he checked with Control to see if anything new had come in. It hadn't. Finally, he put in a call to DC Patterson who had sent a text half an hour ago to say he had arrived at Penrith Hospital.

'I was about to ring you, guv,' Patterson said. 'I've spoken to the medics and had a quick chat with Sonia Logan.'

'I take it her husband is alive?'

'He is, but he remains unconscious. He suffered head and chest injuries when he was thrown through his car window. The doctors are confident he'll pull through, though, but they can't say how long he'll be in a coma.'

'And how did it happen?'

'He apparently skidded on a patch of ice and lost control. Then his car ploughed into the side of a parked lorry.'

'Was he on his way home?'

'It would appear so, but his wife doesn't understand why he didn't call her before leaving Cockermouth. I'm wondering if he was planning to go somewhere else before returning home.'

'Is she still there?'

'Yes, she is, and I expect she'll stay all night. She's informed his parents, who live in Spain. As you know, the mother is Neil Hutchinson's sister. They're looking to fly over as soon as they can.'

'Have you asked her about Christmas Eve?'

'I have, and she still insists that her husband told her that he spent it with the Spicer brothers. I didn't tell her that they were claiming it wasn't true.'

'I think that was sensible. Best we talk to him first. Have you got his phone? I'm hoping that will tell us something.'

'It wasn't with him when he was put into the ambulance so it must be in his car, which was towed from the scene. I've asked one of the local uniforms to recover his stuff and let us see it. Another local officer will be staying here through the night to keep an eye on things. If it's okay with you, guv, I'll make my way home now and come back first thing.'

'You do that, Colin. And thanks for going there.'

On the way home James listened to the news on the radio. It continued to be dominated by what one reporter dubbed *'The Lake District Murder Mystery'*.

No doubt with the blessing of the Chief Constable, the Constabulary press office had provided confirmation that Nigel Marr had been shot. This had heightened the level of interest in the story and even the local MP had condemned the killing and expressed deep concern for the three men who were still missing.

James was surprised to hear a clip of an interview with Greg Pike.

'I knew Nigel and he was a good man,' Greg said. *'What's happened to him is tragic and undeserved. And I'm praying that no harm will come to the others. I've worked for Ted Rycroft for six years and he's like a father to me. Sure, he likes to go trail hunting, but he never breaks the law. I urge anyone who knows who is behind this to contact the police.'*

James got a mention then as the detective in charge of the investigation.

'*DCI Walker moved to Cumbria three years ago having served twenty years in London with the Metropolitan Police,*' the newsreader said. '*He's already been involved in three high-profile cases, which have all taken place during the Christmas period in recent years.*'

By the time James arrived in Kirkby Abbey his body was stiff and heavy with exhaustion. He had already decided that it was too late to raise the subject of the job offer with Annie. He didn't want to be talking about it into the early hours.

As he walked through the front door she was there to greet him with a hug and a kiss.

'You don't need to tell me what kind of day you've had,' she said. 'I can imagine. I've been following the news and it's been like binge-watching a horror series.'

It was almost ten o'clock now and he couldn't face the ready meal so Annie filled a bowl with crisps and he started nibbling on those as he downed a large, belly warming whisky.

She told him she had arranged to go and see her uncle in the care home later in the week and planned to take Bella with her.

'He did take my call this time but got really upset because he couldn't remember me,' she said. 'He even apologised and told me that he believed me. It was really strange and hard not to cry. I then had a brief conversation with one of the carers who reckons his condition is declining rapidly.'

James was updating her on the case when his phone rang ten minutes later. It was DC Booth and she began with an apology for calling him so late.

'I checked with the office first, sir, and they told me when you left there. I figured you would still be up.'

'You figured right,' he replied. 'So, what's up?'

'You tasked me with contacting Karl Kramer, the guy who witnessed Ted Rycroft driving his Jeep into Joanna Grey five years ago, and I've finally managed to track him down. Turns out the address on the system was out of date and he moved from Windermere to Kendal a year ago. I plan to drop in on him first thing in the morning, and that's why I decided to ring you. I reckon you'll probably want to go with me when you hear what I've found out about him.'

James experienced a rush of adrenaline and sat up straight on the sofa.

'Go on then,' he said. 'I'm listening.'

'Well, when the incident occurred five years ago, Kramer was a soldier serving in the military. He worked as an armourer, which meant he helped repair, maintain and adapt small arms and weapons, including shotguns. But two years ago, he was medically discharged. Apparently he became deeply depressed as a result of all the abuse he received for claiming that Miss Grey was driven into deliberately. He started drinking more than was good for him and got into several fights in public.'

'This sounds like a breakthrough of sorts to me,' James said. 'You were right to call me and I'll most definitely come along with you to speak to him.'

'But there's more, sir,' she replied. 'Mr Kramer is also a very committed anti-hunt activist and has posted numerous angry posts on social media, some directed at Mr Rycroft and those others who are missing. The latest appeared this morning on a hunt saboteur Facebook page. And it struck me as quite alarming.'

'What does it say?'

'I printed it off so I'll read it to you. It says: "On Christmas Eve five years ago, I witnessed those four missing huntsmen commit a heinous crime when they callously drove into a young woman and caused her serious injury. At last God has seen fit to inflict on them a just punishment."'

James released a thin whistle from between his teeth. 'I agree with you that it's deeply alarming, Elizabeth,' he said. 'Do you know if he's on the criminal records database?'

'He isn't. I checked.'

'Even so, it goes without saying that he should be added to our list of suspects in this case. What else do you know about him?'

'He's aged thirty-two and single. I haven't come across any mention of children. He describes himself as a web designer and I get the impression he works from home.'

'Meet me in the office at six tomorrow. We'll brief the others and then pay him an early visit. Oh, and well done, Elizabeth. You've done a great job.'

CHAPTER FORTY-ONE

Day Four

James had set the alarm for five and when it went off, he had to force himself out of bed.

He was still dog-tired after another restless night during which he got very little sleep. Every time he closed his eyes, he saw Nigel Marr's blood-soaked body and heard his devastated wife crying her heart out.

When he did drop off, he dreamt of finding other bodies on the windswept moors and even saw a hooded figure trudging through the deep snow armed with a shotgun.

The alarm woke Annie too and as he was pulling on his dressing gown, she offered to make him some breakfast.

'No, you stay put,' he said. 'I'll get showered and be on my way. Bella is still sleeping for a change so make the most of it.'

The first thing he did was to peer out of the window to check on the weather. It was still dark, but he could see that it was looking relatively calm.

He couldn't resist checking the forecast on his phone and

was relieved to see that although more snow was predicted, there was going to be less of it.

He moved quickly on to his messages but there was nothing fresh to get him excited. Next, he brought up the BBC News feed and although they were still leading with the story, it hadn't been updated. The top line was that the search would continue today for the three missing trail hunters while police investigated the murder of Nigel Marr.

It didn't take him long to shower and get dressed. Before setting off, he made Annie a cup of tea, gave her a kiss, and had a peek at Bella who was fast asleep with her mouth wide open. He couldn't resist giving her a peck on the forehead even though he risked waking her.

Once he was on the road his pulse jumped up a notch as he focused on the day ahead. Two significant developments had given rise to a degree of optimism.

The first was the mystery surrounding Shane Logan. Did he or didn't he spend Christmas Eve with the Spicer brothers? And if he didn't, then why did he tell his wife that he did?

But even more encouraging was the emergence of Karl Kramer as a potential suspect. An ex-soldier who spent time working with weapons and harboured a serious grudge against Ted Rycroft and his fellow huntsmen.

He'd said that God had seen fit to inflict a just punishment on the men for what had happened to Joanna Grey five years ago. But perhaps the truth was that he was the one who'd decided that it was time they were made to suffer.

*   *   *

209

As soon as he arrived at headquarters, he got himself a coffee and a bacon sandwich.

He was behind his desk by six, making calls and preparing for the morning debrief.

The rest of the team drifted in over the next twenty minutes, by which time he was ready to roll.

Top of the agenda was Karl Kramer and he credited DC Booth with tracking him down.

'Elizabeth and I will be going to see him straight after this briefing,' he said. 'And while we're gone, I'd like you all to plough on with everything else.'

He also told them he had spoken to DC Patterson who had informed him that Shane Logan hadn't yet regained consciousness. In the meantime, his mobile phone had been recovered from his wrecked car and though it was damaged, it had been delivered to the digital forensics team.

'His wife is still insisting that he spent Christmas Eve out protesting with Warren and Liam Spicer, but they're adamant that he didn't,' James said. 'It's our top priority to get to the truth as soon as we can.'

He went on to tell them that the search for the three missing men was about to resume. 'Almost a hundred police officers, along with sniffer dogs, have been drafted in to assist. DC Sharma, I'd like you to be the one liaising with the search teams. And since they now have the go-ahead to check out occupied properties, I want you to get them to visit Neil Hutchinson's farm,' he said. 'As far as I'm concerned he's still in the frame for three reasons: he's close to the Spicer brothers, Shane Logan is his nephew, and he's had a long-running feud with Ted Rycroft. And speaking of the Spicers, let's try to secure that search warrant.'

James read out his list of action points, which included sounding out Francesca Marr's first husband Aaron Drax, and having another conversation with Johnny Elvin.

'Finally, we need to be ready to respond if the killer or killers send out another photo of a dead body.'

CHAPTER FORTY-TWO

Karl Kramer lived on the other side of the town near Sandlands Park and James drove himself and DC Booth there in a pool car. It was a straightforward journey along the A6 and across the River Kent.

They pulled up outside the modest end-of-terrace house in a nondescript street after only ten minutes. It was 7.30 a.m. and still dark, but a downstairs light was on inside.

Just as they were about to get out of the car, Booth's phone pinged. It was resting on her lap so she picked it up, noted who the message was from, and said apologetically, 'D'you mind if I quickly reply to this, guv? It's my husband. He's supposed to be doing a shop today but I forgot to leave him a list, which means he's utterly clueless.'

James grinned and told her to go ahead. At fifty-six, Elizabeth Booth was the oldest member of the team and she was married to a former police officer who had retired a year ago. She'd elected to join him and so was retiring herself in just over a month's time. She was one of the most experienced members of the team and James knew that she was going to be greatly missed.

'All done,' she said after less than a minute. 'That's one of the reasons I'm bailing out early. He needs someone around to help him cope with not being a copper anymore.'

'I expect I'll be much the same when it comes to packing it in,' James said jokingly.

There was a tiny, neglected front garden with weeds sprouting up through the pathway paving slabs. And the rendered walls of the house were in desperate need of a fresh coat of white paint.

After they rang the bell, the door was promptly opened by a tall man who was wearing pyjama bottoms and a vest that showed firm muscles bunched beneath it.

'Mr Kramer?' James asked him.

He nodded without speaking and a deep frown settled across his face.

'We're sorry to bother you so early,' James continued as he held up his warrant card. 'I'm Detective Chief Inspector Walker and my colleague is Detective Constable Booth. We need to speak to you and so would it be possible to come inside?'

Kramer stared at James for a few moments before producing a tepid smile.

'Let me guess. This is about my Facebook post, isn't it? Some snowflake has made a complaint and you're looking into it because you've got nothing better to do.'

'No one has complained as far as I'm aware, Mr Kramer, but it is one of the things we want to discuss. You see, we're investigating the murder of Nigel Marr and the disappearance of his three fellow huntsmen. And we know that you are one of a number of people who feel the men deserve to have bad things happen to them.'

His jaw set. 'Are you telling me I'm a suspect?'

James shook his head. 'At this stage, we just have some exploratory questions and we'd very much appreciate it if you would agree to answer them.'

Kramer turned down the corners of his mouth and shrugged. 'Very well. Come inside. But you'll have to take me as you find me. I've only just hauled myself out of bed and the place is a mess.'

The interior wasn't as messy as James expected it to be, given the warning, but it was gloomy, cramped and somewhat run-down.

'I just rent this house and it's cheap,' Kramer said because he obviously felt the need to explain. 'If it was mine, I'd do it up. And I don't plan to be here much longer anyway. I've got my eyes on a place in Sedbergh. It's quieter there.'

'How long have you been here?' James asked as they followed him into the kitchen where the light was on and the kettle was boiling.

'About a year,' he replied. 'I got fed up living in a tiny flat in Windermere and being surrounded all the time by hordes of tourists and day-trippers. A couple of pals from my army days live here so when this place came up, I went for it. But it's not been as comfortable as I'd hoped it would be.'

He waved them towards the table and asked if they wanted a tea or coffee. They both opted for coffee and James took a moment to get the measure of the man.

He had a mop of unruly dark hair and a hard, unhealthy looking face pitted with grey stubble, which made James suspect he might still have a drink problem.

He waited until the coffees were poured before he began.

'You actually came to our attention before you posted that message on Facebook yesterday, Mr Kramer,' he said. 'When Ted Rycroft and the others went missing on Christmas Eve we started looking into their backgrounds and that was when we were told about your encounter with them five years ago.'

Kramer didn't seem surprised that James had brought it up. He stood with his back against the sink, arms folded.

'I assume you didn't leave it at that,' he said, his voice strong and steady. 'What else have you found out about me?'

James gestured for his colleague to answer.

Booth took out her notebook and read from it.

'At the time you were serving in the military as an armourer,' she said. 'It was while you were home on leave that you joined a trail hunt protest near Staveley. You'd been an anti-hunt activist for some years before then though. Anyway, when the hunt was over you were heading home when you saw the accident involving Joanna Grey.'

He gave her a narrow look. 'It wasn't an accident. I was standing barely thirty yards away. Ted Rycroft steered his Jeep into her. She was close to the hedge and she wasn't standing there holding up a banner like they said. She was just holding it while walking. When I confronted Rycroft, he didn't seem too concerned about her even though she was unconscious. All four of them then turned on me and got really aggressive. When the police arrived, they claimed that I was making it up because I'd failed to stop their hunt from going ahead.'

'And that wasn't true.'

'Of course not. I know what I saw. But the police took their words for it and for months I was bombarded with abusive messages and phone calls. It was horrendous and really got to me. But it was worse for Joanna's family. They suffered more than I did and things went from bad to worse for them.'

'Did you know the family?' James asked.

He shook his head. 'Not back then. I'd met Joanna a couple of times at protests. She was really nice. She was also committed to the cause and not afraid to make her voice heard. But she never recovered from what happened. Her brain was damaged and she could barely communicate afterwards. I made a point of introducing myself to her parents and together we campaigned to get the police to arrest those men. But it didn't happen because it was the words of four against one. Then, not long after Joanna came out of hospital, her dad died. Living here got too much for her mum so she moved the two of them away.'

'Did you stay in touch?' Booth asked.

'For a while.'

'So you know where they went?'

'Whitby. It was where the parents lived before moving to Cumbria. Her mum, Alice, became Joanna's carer. Joanna has an older sister, Kerry, but she was living in America with her boyfriend when the incident happened. As far as I know she's still there. Mrs Grey was the person I used to ring, but only occasionally, and usually to tell her what Rycroft and the rest of the bunch had been getting up to. Then, about a year ago, something must have happened because my calls stopped going through and I haven't heard from her since.'

'Did you try to find out what had happened to them?' James asked.

'No, I didn't. We weren't close, after all, and it occurred to me that they might have decided to sever contact because I was a painful reminder of what had happened to Joanna.'

'So, you don't know how Mrs Grey can be contacted.'

'Not anymore.'

James could tell from his face that just talking about it had stirred his emotions.

'I'd like to come back to you now, Mr Kramer,' he said. 'I gather you struggled with dealing with it all and that was why you were medically discharged from the army.'

'I got depressed and turned to the booze,' he responded. 'It was stupid of me, but I couldn't help it. It's still hard to believe that my life got fucked up because of what I witnessed that day.'

'I'm sure there are some people who would take the view that you had every right to get revenge against the men you hold responsible,' James said.

The remark was intended to get a reaction and it did. His chin jutted forward and he uncrossed his arms.

'Then you lied to me when you said I'm not a suspect,' he snapped. 'You do think I shot Nigel Marr and have done something to the others.'

'Well, did you?'

'Of course I fucking well didn't. Even during ten years in the army I never shed anyone's blood. That doesn't mean I'm not glad that Marr is dead, though. That bastard was in the Jeep that day and it was either him or one of the others who called me from a burner phone and threatened to hurt me if I didn't stop talking about it. But for me it's been enough to attack them on social media. It's satisfying, it pisses them off, and I've never got into serious trouble because of it. And if you must know, I've not been in contact with any of them for years.'

'Then you're telling us that you didn't pay them a visit on Christmas Eve?'

'That's exactly what I'm telling you. I didn't go out because I had a bloody hangover. I stayed in the night before and got pissed. I felt so bad in the morning that I couldn't get out of bed.'

'Can someone corroborate that?'

'I don't see how. I live here by myself and as usual no one came to spend Christmas with me. I didn't surface until the middle of the afternoon.'

'Do you have a car, Mr Kramer?' Booth asked him.

'No. I ride a bike. A Honda Hornet. It's around the back.'

'Then I assume you won't have a problem with us making a note of the number plate.'

He shrugged. 'Doesn't worry me. I've got nothing to hide. You can see it through the window over there.'

As Booth moved to snap a photo of it on her phone, James felt uncertainty beat inside him. He wasn't sure where to take it from here. The man had answered their questions and if he was lying about a Christmas Eve hangover then the onus was on them to prove it. He quickly decided that it was probably best to leave it at that for now and come back if and when they came up with something that would cast doubt on what he'd told them.

'We'll probably want to speak to you again, Mr Kramer,' he said. 'But before we go, it's worth saying that there are certain individuals who feel the same way you do about Mr Rycroft and his friends. Their names are Neil Hutchinson, Shane Logan and Warren and Liam Spicer. Can you tell me if you're acquainted with them and if so when you last saw them?'

He didn't have to think about it.

'Yes, I know them all. We've met up at hunt protests over the years. But it's been weeks since I last saw any of them.'

CHAPTER FORTY-THREE

'I really don't know what to make of him, guv,' Booth said as they drove back to headquarters. 'I veered between sympathy and suspicion. What was your take?'

'Much the same, actually,' James replied. 'He made no secret of the fact that he holds an all-consuming grudge against Ted Rycroft and co, and I believed him when he said the fall-out from his encounter with them has buggered up his life. But I'm not convinced that he would only seek to get his own back by slagging them off on social media. He might not have killed anyone during his time in the army, but he sure as hell would have learned how to. And also how to hurt and entrap people.'

Booth nodded. 'Plus, he's a big bloke and pretty strong, I reckon. He wouldn't have had to exert much effort to trash the farm and move a body from one location to another.'

'We also need to take into account the job he did in the army,' James said. 'He specialised in weapons, including small arms.'

'Should we seek a warrant to search his house?'

'I'm not sure it would be granted since we don't have anything on him other than a vague suspicion. We have to do some more digging. His alibi for Christmas Eve sounds plausible given that he's had problems with drink, but he's got no one to back it up. So, let's start by trawling road cameras and CCTV, see if he was out and about on his bike. DC Hall can help you there since he's already pulled footage in.'

'And are you still keen for me to track down Joanna Grey and her mother? Thanks to what he just told us about them moving to Whitby I've got more to go on.'

'Yep, keep it up,' James said. 'It's a long shot, for sure, but we can't ignore the fact that Joanna's mother won't be shedding tears over Ted Rycroft and the others. And who's to say that she didn't encourage, or even pay, someone to get even with them for what she believes was done to her daughter?'

It was still quite early when they got back to the office so not much progress had been made.

DC Patterson called from Penrith Hospital to tell James that Shane Logan was still out cold so he couldn't be interviewed.

James instructed him to stay there and to use the time to chase up digital forensics to see if they'd managed to get into the man's mobile phone.

He then passed on to the team what Karl Kramer had said and explained why he wanted DC Booth to make contact with Joanna Grey's mother.

DC Sharma's update on the search for the missing men wasn't very encouraging. Even though teams had poured into the fields and woodlands surrounding the location where

Nigel Marr's body was dumped, they'd had no success in finding anyone.

'Our own officers will be going to Neil Hutchinson's farm soon and they'll ask for permission to search inside the buildings,' Sharma said. 'If it's not granted, they'll call me and I'll try to get a search warrant.'

The story was still playing out on the news and one segment on the BBC caught James's eye. It was a studio interview with a hunt saboteur and a hunt supporter, and for a change they weren't at each other's throats. Instead, they both called on people on either side of the argument to tone down the explosive rhetoric.

'*I am appalled at what I'm seeing across social media,*' *the hunt sab said.* '*It just isn't right to post such vile comments that are designed to stir up trouble. For one thing, it hasn't been established that those men have been targeted because of their views on hunting. And if it is the case, then it should be made clear that the vast majority of people who oppose hunting would never do anything other than peacefully protest.*'

The hunt supporter responded with, '*And most of the pro-hunters I know are fully aware of that, which is why we should not allow this situation to get out of control and cause even more distress.*'

DI Stevens, who had also been watching the interview, said, 'I fear it might be too late for that. From what I've seen things are already completely crazy on social media. I've never known a situation to create such a storm.'

Stevens made the team aware of an online forum on which hunt supporters were openly discussing ways to seek revenge on behalf of Nigel Marr and his pals. One contributor urged his co-conspirators to vandalise the homes of prominent anti-hunt activists. Another called on them to *physically attack the bastards and put as many as you can in hospital'*.

'This is only one example of what's going on out there,' Stevens said. 'On the dark web it's apparently even worse. There are dozens of anonymous posts from people claiming that they attacked the men and intend to kill all four of them.'

James was about to respond when a support officer approached him to say that a young woman named Rebecca Carter had arrived in the building and wanted to talk to him.

'She's told reception that she's employed by Ted Rycroft and that you've spoken to her a couple of times,' the officer said.

'That's right, I have. Do you know what she wants?'

'She's apparently received another message on her phone and she wants to show it to you.'

James sucked in a breath as unease swell in his chest. 'Go and bring her straight to my office,' he said.

Minutes later Rebecca appeared, clearly shaken. Her face was tense, jaw locked, and when she spoke, her voice was laced with despair.

'Thank you for seeing me, Inspector,' she said.

'It's no trouble, Miss Carter. Please take a seat and tell me about this message you've received.'

'It was sent during the night and I saw it this morning when I got up and turned my phone on.'

As she sat down, she took her phone out of her handbag and unlocked it.

'After I read it I knew I had to show you and so I came straight here. But just like the other one I got I don't know who sent it because there's no name or number.'

She brought up the message and passed the phone across the desk. As James read it, the blood stiffened in his veins.

One down and three to go. Will your shameful boss be next?

CHAPTER FORTY-FOUR

James felt his stomach clench into a hard ball as he read the message again.

'I don't understand why it was sent to me,' Rebecca said.

He looked up at her. She was blinking furiously and her anxiety was tangible.

'It could simply be because you work for Mr Rycroft,' he said.

'Do you think it means that Ted is dead, like Nigel? That someone has shot him as well?'

'I can't answer that, Miss Carter, because I simply don't know. This message could be from someone who is also completely in the dark as to what is going to happen, but for some reason wants to upset you.'

'Are you any closer to finding them?'

'Again, I don't know. Hundreds of people are out there searching and all we can do is hope that they're still alive.'

'And what about Nigel's killer? Do you have any clue as to who it could be?'

'We're following several lines of inquiry and we're inter-viewing individuals who are known to have criticised, threatened or attacked any or all of the four men in the past. But it's taking time because there are quite a lot of them, as you know yourself.'

'Will you want to check my phone again?'

'Yes, please. I'll have the technicians look at it.'

'Does that mean you've managed to trace the sender of the first message? If so, then that person could have sent this one.'

'We haven't, I'm afraid, so we don't know if it is the same person. Can you think of anyone who would want to give you a hard time? And not just because you're employed by Mr Rycroft.'

She shook her head. 'I've racked my brain and I can't. Besides, that first message said we didn't know each other, so I'm assuming it was from a complete stranger.'

'I need to get this message copied and have the technicians take a look at it,' he said. 'Would you bear with me while I go and get it sorted?'

'No problem.'

He abruptly left the office and crossed the room to where DI Stevens was updating the evidence board.

'Take a look at this, Phil,' he said. 'It was sent to Rebecca Carter last night.'

As Stevens read the message, his eyes grew large in their sockets.

'Holy fuck. Could this be from someone who is actually involved? The same person who sent out the email with the photo?'

'Possibly. I want you to get it circulated to the rest of the team and take the phone to see if the techies can trace the sender. If not, can they at least tell us if it came from the same account as the first message she received?'

'I'll do it right away, boss.'

'I want to ask Miss Carter a few questions so can you also bring it to the attention of Superintendent Tanner?'

Back in his office, James asked Rebecca if she wanted a hot drink. She opted for a coffee and so he nipped out and got her one from the vending machine.

When he was seated again, he asked, 'Do you know if your colleague Greg has also received any anonymous messages?'

'No, he hasn't,' she replied. 'I phoned him on the way here to check.'

As she sipped her coffee, James noticed that the mug was shaking slightly.

'How are you coping with all this, Miss Carter?' he asked. 'It can't be easy for you.'

She placed the mug on the desk and pushed her fringe out of her eyes. 'It's like a never-ending nightmare,' she said. 'In my mind's eye I keep seeing the damage that was done to the farm and I can't help thinking that Ted won't be coming back. I couldn't stop crying after I saw the photo of Nigel on the news and when I opened that message today, I actually threw up. It doesn't help that I'm single and live by myself. I've got friends, but my closest pal went away for Christmas and isn't due back until the new year.'

'What will you do if, God forbid, Mr Rycroft doesn't return to the farm?'

'I have no idea. I suppose I'll have to look for another job. I don't think Greg will want to keep the farm going even though I know that Ted has left it to him in his will. I expect he'll sell up and do something else.'

James raised his brow. 'Mr Pike told you about that?'

A shake of the head. 'It was meant to be their secret but I overheard them talking about it a month or so ago, along with Ted's cancer diagnosis. It upset me, of course, but I didn't tell either of them that I knew because I didn't want to disrespect Ted's wishes. I assumed they would break the news to me eventually.'

By now her voice had dropped to a whisper and it looked as though she was struggling to hold it together.

'I really appreciate you coming straight here with the message,' he said. 'If you need to leave, I can arrange for your phone to be delivered to your home.'

'I'll wait for it if that's all right. I've got nowhere to go.'

'Then would you mind if I ask you one last question?'

'Of course not. Anything to help.'

'Great. Well, we've been made aware of two individuals who have frequently condemned Mr Rycroft and his friends on social media. Their names are Karl Kramer and Shane Logan. Do you know them?'

'I know *of* them,' she replied. 'Ted has mentioned them a few times and has made it clear that he doesn't like what they write about him. I've seen him get really angry.'

'Have they ever come to the farm or threatened Mr Rycroft?'

'Not that I'm aware of. But I'm only there three days a week and spend most of the time in the office and talking to the people who arrive to ride the quad bikes and go hiking with Ted. Greg might be of more help on that.'

James needed to get back to the team so he thanked Rebecca again and arranged for a support staff member to take her to the canteen.

'She'll stay with you until your phone has been checked and you can be on your way,' he said.

CHAPTER FORTY-FIVE

The latest message to Rebecca Carter was yet another shocking development in a case that James and his colleagues were struggling to get their heads around.

They now had to prepare themselves for a second body to turn up and with it would come more pressure, more publicity and more grief.

But Ted Rycroft wasn't the only one of the Christmas Eve hunters who were still missing. There was also Dylan Payne and Rhys Hughes. So how long would it be before they too were the subjects of anonymous messages?

'Should we now expect a photo of Ted Rycroft to be emailed to the media?' DS Abbott asked, and James knew it was a question that was on everyone's mind.

'We need to be ready for that,' he responded. 'I don't think there is any doubt now that we're seeing a carefully constructed plan being played out step by agonising step. A plan aimed at causing as much anger and upset as possible on a grand scale. Why else would whoever is behind it be stretching it out for so long?'

The first thing he'd done after his conversation with Rebecca Carter had been to ask DC Foley to produce a single sheet of paper listing the various messages that had become vital pieces of forensic evidence. Once he'd read it, he'd asked her to print off copies for everyone.

Now he instructed her to hand them out so that he could call attention to how significant he regarded them.

'Take a moment to reacquaint yourselves with the messages,' he said. 'With so much going on it's easy to forget the details and we can't let that happen here.'

The list was in order of when each message was received, and as James read it though again a shudder rippled through him.

1st text message sent to Rebecca Carter:
We don't know each other, Rebecca, but someone told me that you work for that scumbag Ted Rycroft. You should be fucking ashamed of yourself. I'm glad he's missing and I hope he turns up dead along with those other cowards who kill foxes for fun.

Email sent to papers with photo attached:
The real hunt has begun.

2nd text message sent to Rebecca:
One down and three to go. Will your shameful boss be next?

'So, let's start with that first message to Rebecca Carter,' James said. 'It appears to be from some random stranger who was reacting to the news that Mr Rycroft was missing. But why pick on Rebecca? Why not her colleague, Greg Pike? And can it really be that Rebecca and the sender of the message don't know each other?'

'That wouldn't surprise me, guv,' DC Abbott said. 'It's probably generally assumed that because she works at the farm, she's a hunt supporter. And in the eyes of the more extreme anti-hunt brigade that would make her a legitimate target regardless of whether they've ever met her.'

It was a fair point and several others agreed with it. Next James read out the message contained in the email sent to the media.

'This one speaks for itself,' he said. 'It's from a fake account, no doubt set up for this very purpose. What we may never know is whether the person who wrote it also carried out the killing.'

'What's the thinking on that, sir?' DC Isaac said. 'Are we assuming that it's all the work of a single perp, or several?'

'Instinct tells me that more than one person carried out the damage to the Rycroft farm,' James answered. 'And then a trap must have been laid for the huntsmen, and it's hard to believe that one individual could have pulled that off alone. Next comes the moving of the body, which also would have been hard for someone operating alone. I could be wrong on all counts but we'll only know when we solve the case.'

James moved to the final message, and after reading it out, said, 'Rebecca Carter opened this one this morning and brought it straight to my attention. It could conceivably have come from any of the men on our list of suspects.'

'Does that include Shane Logan, guv, even though he was in hospital when it was sent?' Stevens asked.

James shrugged. 'It is possible that he set it to be sent automatically on a timer. Although I do accept that it's extremely unlikely given that he didn't know he was going to crash his car.'

James went on to press home the point that the messages needed to be subjected to a considerable amount of thought and forensic analysis.

'Even if we're unable to trace where they came from there are potential clues in the wording,' he said. 'For instance, the claim in the first message to Rebecca that "we don't know each other" might be a way of diverting attention from the fact that they do. So, let's spend some time looking for messages beyond the messages, if that makes sense.'

James doubted that it did make sense to every member of the team, but he was sure that it would at least concentrate their minds, which might be enough to prompt one of them to see something that wasn't immediately obvious.

He spent the next fifteen minutes prioritising actions in respect of social media monitoring, securing search warrants, interviewing Francesca Marr's ex-husband, Aaron Drax, and viewing more road traffic footage.

The office TV monitors were on throughout and tuned to the rolling news channels. Nigel Marr's murder was still the lead story, coupled with the search for the other missing huntsmen.

But there was also news of a major outbreak of violence at a trail hunt taking place this morning near Troutbeck, where two hunt saboteurs had been badly beaten by a group of masked hunt supporters and had been taken to hospital with serious injuries.

James was watching the footage of what looked like a mini riot when his phone rang.

It was Gordon Carver at the *Cumbria Gazette* and what he had to say hit the DCI like a sharp blow to the gut.

'We've just received another email with a photo attached,' Carver said. 'It's similar to the first one but the body appears to be that of Ted Rycroft.'

CHAPTER FORTY-SIX

James had to wait almost a minute for Gordon Carver to forward the latest email to him, and by then news had come through that it had been sent to other media outlets.

Once again it contained a message that was dark and deeply disturbing.

Well done, hunters – another pest put down.

The attached photo showed a grey-haired man who was clearly Ted Rycroft sitting on snow-covered ground with his back against the trunk of a tree. His chin was resting on his chest and part of his face was missing. Where his left cheek should have been there was a large black hole and beneath it his shirt collar was stained with blood.

It looked to James as though the man had been shot in the head and the image caused everything inside him to turn cold.

He handed his phone to Stevens, and, fighting to keep his

voice steady, said, 'This has got to be the sickest and most bizarre case I've ever been involved with.'

Stevens looked at the photo and grimaced. But then he drew it closer to his face and frowned.

'Hang on a sec,' he said. 'This might actually help us find him.'

'What do you mean?'

He passed the phone back to James, adding, 'On the right, you can see a small part of the landscape beyond the tree.'

James stared again at the image and saw what his DI was referring to.

'You're right. I didn't take that in because I was entirely focused on the body.'

It was a narrow view of fields, woodland, a few remote stone buildings, and in the distance the slopes of Harter Fell.

'Anyone familiar with the area might be able to work out where the picture was taken,' Stevens said.

'Then let's send it to the rescue teams and anyone within the Constabulary who professes to know every nook and cranny of the Lake District,' James replied.

The first step was to put the photo onto the system so that it could be viewed on the monitors and the desktop computers. While that was being done, James touched base with Control and Superintendent Tanner.

He learned that the photo had been sent to the same media outlets as the first one had – the *Cumbria Gazette*, the BBC, and three national newspapers. But no one doubted that it had also been dropped like a bomb on the internet.

The level of excitement in the office once again reached fever pitch as the team discussed how to respond to this latest development. Even though it hadn't been entirely unexpected, the shock factor was significant.

Virtually everyone involved in the investigation was present, including forensic pathologist Dr Pam Flint, who had carried out the post-mortem on Nigel Marr and had arrived to present her findings.

'We have to react swiftly to this on several fronts,' James told his colleagues. 'He has no next of kin but Mr Rycroft's employees, Rebecca Carter and Greg Pike, must be told asap. And tell the FLOs who are with Maria Payne and Owain Hughes to pass the news on to them. Let's also commit more resources to keeping track of what appears on TV and the web. This second photo will cause mass hysteria in the media and whip up more discord between the pro- and anti-hunt factions.'

Before assigning tasks, James asked Dr Flint to present her report. Reading from her post-mortem notes, she confirmed that Mr Marr had died from a shotgun wound to the heart.

'The shot was probably fired from only a matter of yards away,' she said. 'The twelve gauge shell passed between his ribs, went straight through his heart, and got lodged in the intercostal muscle. I believe he would have died immediately or within minutes. The other injuries he sustained are consistent with being dragged over rugged terrain. A number of bones are broken and there are numerous bruises and cuts.'

Dr Flint rounded off her report by saying that arrangements would now have to be made for Mrs Marr or her daughter to formally identify the body.

The following hour up to lunchtime was manic. The photo purporting to show a dead Ted Rycroft, plus the message in the email, became the hottest topic of the day and started to appear all over the internet alongside the one of Nigel Marr. As before, most of the mainstream media covered up the face, but the more questionable internet sites didn't bother to.

A distressed Rebecca Carter phoned James after being told about it and asked if he was able to confirm that it was definitely her boss in the picture. When he said he wouldn't know for sure until the body was recovered, she broke down and couldn't carry on speaking.

He took another call minutes later from the Chief Constable who expressed concern that the investigation appeared not to be making much progress.

'This has turned into a fucking horrorfest,' he complained. 'If the aim of those responsible is to grab the headlines, then they've achieved that twice over. You need to up your game and bring this to an end.'

James briefed him on where they were at and the difficulties they faced. After the call ended, he swore out loud. It was always the bloody same with the top dogs when they started to feel pressured by bad publicity. They felt the need to apply pressure themselves even though they knew full well that it was never helpful.

Armed with the photograph, the search teams were able to concentrate on a smaller area. And even among James's colleagues there was one support officer who was convinced he knew roughly where the body was located and pointed to it on the wall map.

Thankfully the snow held off and the wind dropped, but it wasn't until two o'clock in the afternoon that James was informed that a second body had been found.

CHAPTER FORTY-SEVEN

A small fleet of vehicles headed towards the location of the second body.

A patrol car took the lead followed by James and DS Abbott in the Land Rover, being driven once again by PC Malek. Behind them was Tony Coppell and his team in two forensic vans, and bringing up the rear was Dr Flint in a pool car.

The location was about half a mile east of where Nigel Marr was found. It was on the edge of a wood close to a rough path that was frequently used by hikers and horse riders.

A police search team had come across the body soon after one of its officers was shown the photo and recognised the view of the landscape. It had quickly been established that the body was the one in the photo, complete with a fatal wound to the left side of the head.

James remained silent for most of the journey as dark thoughts chased through his mind. The pace at which events were taking place was unnerving. Christmas Eve had been on Sunday and since then four men had gone missing, a farm had been trashed, and two dead bodies had turned up. Not to mention the sinister messages and horrific photos that had been sent out to cause alarm and disgust.

They drove through Staveley and Kentmere, but this time the route they took did not pass Ted Rycroft's farm.

The nearer they got to the location the more formidable the clouds above became and it seemed very much as though a blizzard was brewing.

The sight and sound of a police helicopter greeted them as they approached the scene along a quiet lane banked by thick hedgerows. It was hovering over to their right above dense woodland.

The lane was just wide enough for two vehicles to pass each other so they were able to park along one side. Within minutes James and the others were making their way along the path through the wood, the crunch of snow beneath their feet.

It was Tony Coppell who put into words what everyone was thinking as he laboured under the weight of two heavy forensic cases.

'I want to believe that we won't be coming back this way tomorrow and the day after,' he said. 'But I have an awful feeling in my gut that we will.'

They had to leave the path and trudge across several yards of ankle-deep snow to get to the body, which was surrounded by officers in hi-vis jackets. When James saw it, he felt the acid lodge in his throat.

'We searched all the pockets and found a bunch of keys and a wallet,' one of the officers said. 'The name on his various cards is Ted Rycroft.'

As Dr Flint and the SOCOs pulled on their forensic suits, James knelt down beside the dead farmer and studied the corpse as dispassionately as he could.

The face wound was extremely gory, exposing frozen lumps of flesh and raw bone inside the large hole.

'I'm guessing he was dumped here,' he said, loud enough for the others to hear. Flicking his head towards the path, he added, 'It'd be a fairly easy spot to reach on a quad bike or small tractor.'

Rycroft had been placed with his back against a tall oak tree that was one of several along the edge of the wood. Beyond them a field rolled down towards a narrow, winding stream. Darkness was encroaching, but James could still see Harter Fell in the distance.

He got to his feet and realised he was standing where the person who took the photo must have stood. The mere thought of it snatched his breath away.

'Okay, out of the way James,' Dr Flint said. 'Let me get on with my job and tell you what you need to know. Then I can arrange for the body to be moved before the weather closes in.'

He stepped back as she began her examination. At the same time Tony Coppell and his SOCOs got to work processing the scene. But James didn't expect them to find much in the way of forensic evidence if this wasn't where the murder was committed.

He and Abbott took some photos on their phones and then joined the uniforms who were looking around the immediate area. The spot was fairly remote and at this time of year it would not have attracted many visitors.

The two detectives paused to look out across the field and

James pointed to the west, saying, 'Nigel Marr's body was dumped about half a mile in that direction. So, you have to wonder where both bodies came from and over what distance they were carried or dragged.'

'If we assume the mode of transport was a quad bike or small tractor then those things can move like lightning across really rough ground, as well as up and down steep hills,' Abbott replied. 'It means Ted Rycroft could have been killed several miles from here. If his body was moved before the weather turned bad on Christmas Eve then they could have covered a hell of a lot of ground in a fairly short time.'

James nodded. 'And I suppose it's possible that more than one quad or tractor was used and the bodies taken in different directions.'

They talked about the case and where they might go from here as they waited for Dr Flint to complete her initial examination. It was only another twenty minutes or so before she beckoned them over.

'He was killed by a shotgun shell to the head just above the left cheekbone,' she said. 'He would have died instantly and you should work on the basis that it happened on Christmas Eve at about the same time as Mr Marr was killed. And just as with Mr Marr, I believe he was dragged across rugged ground. There are numerous tears in his clothes, mostly on the back, and various cuts and bruises on his exposed flesh. Plus, I can already see that a number of his bones are broken. I don't think there's any doubt that he was murdered somewhere else and brought here.'

'I agree,' Tony Coppell said. James hadn't realised that the chief forensic officer was standing close behind him. 'There's no blood on the tree or on the ground beneath the snow around him. It's basically the same MO as the murder of Nigel Marr.'

James was making a note of what he'd been told when his phone went off. It was DI Stevens.

'Hi, Phil,' he said. 'If you're ringing for an update then I—'

'That's not why I'm calling, guv,' Stevens interrupted. 'It's something else. Not long after you set off from here there was a serious incident at Neil Hutchinson's farm. The man himself rang the three nines claiming his house was under attack from a mob of hooded fox hunt supporters. They were throwing objects at the farmhouse and yelling for Mr Hutchinson to come outside. Several windows were smashed and vehicles in the yard were damaged.'

'Was anyone hurt?' James asked.

'Luckily, no. The attackers obviously knew we'd be called so they didn't hang around. By the time the first responders got there they were long gone.'

'Have you sent someone from our team?'

'DC Isaac and a couple of uniforms are on their way. In fact, they're probably there by now.'

'Jess and I will go there from here.'

'I thought you'd want to. But before you hang up, what's the news from there?'

'Confirmation that the body is that of Ted Rycroft and we now have two murders to investigate.'

CHAPTER FORTY-EIGHT

James briefed Abbott as soon as they were in the Land Rover. It was partly to remind himself what he knew about Neil Hutchinson.

'He's got a wife named Sheila and two daughters, Naomi and Faye,' he said. 'It's Faye who's dating Warren Spicer. Hutchinson is the nearest neighbour to the Rycroft farm, and the two men have been involved in a bitter feud for years over fox hunting.'

'And he accused Rycroft of vandalising his car, correct?' Abbott said.

'He did. And for all those reasons he's one of our suspects despite the fact that his family are providing him with an alibi.'

'Well, that could be why his home was targeted. It's probably common knowledge among hunt supporters by now that he's among the people in the frame.'

James nodded. 'That's the trouble. There are extremists on both sides of the great hunting divide and they're as bad as each other.'

Two patrol cars were parked in the yard when they arrived at the farm, their blue lights flashing. There were also three other vehicles – a Mini, a Skoda SUV and a Ford Ranger.

As James climbed out of the Land Rover, he saw that the windscreens on the SUV and the Ranger had been smashed. It made him feel like he was stepping back in time to when he'd arrived at Ted Rycroft's farm on Christmas Eve. And the feeling intensified as he approached the farmhouse and saw that three of the ground-floor windows had also been smashed and white paint had been sprayed on the front door.

Two uniforms were taking photos and making notes of the damage. They recognised James and Abbott so there was no need for them to flash their IDs.

'DC Isaac is inside,' one of them said. 'The family are very distressed.'

'Can you tell us who's here?' James asked him.

'Mr and Mrs Hutchinson, who own the farm, and one of their daughters,' the officer answered. 'Plus, a family friend who arrived not long before the attack. An Emily Monroe. You've probably heard of her, sir, since she's one of the county's most infamous hunt saboteurs. I know because I had occasion to arrest her once for abusive behaviour at a meet.'

James nodded. 'I thought that name rang a bell. I suppose we shouldn't be surprised that she's a friend of Neil Hutchinson.'

DC Isaac had been told that her boss was coming to the farm and she was ready to meet them when they stepped inside.

'I got here about fifteen minutes ago,' she said. 'I've had a brief chat with the family, but unfortunately there's not much to go on. The group who came here were wearing black balaclavas. There were about seven or eight of them and they arrived in a van with the number plate covered up. They started by shouting that they were hunt supporters and wanted Mr Hutchinson to come outside and tell them why he and his mates had kidnapped and killed Nigel Marr. They probably didn't know about Mr Rycroft's body being found.'

'I take it he didn't do what they wanted,' James said.

'He didn't dare. Instead, he called the emergency service, made sure all the doors were locked, and then moved upstairs with his wife, daughter and their guest, a Miss Monroe. The other daughter, Faye, is staying at her boyfriend Warren Spicer's home tonight.'

'Where is the family now?'

'In the living room. Phil sent me a text to let me know you were coming so I told them.'

The terrifying experience had obviously had a serious impact on all of them, but Hutchinson's daughter Naomi looked to be in the worst state. She was sitting on the sofa with her mother's arm around her, weeping into her hands.

Her father was standing to one side, shuffling from foot to foot, cigarette smoke jetting from his nostrils.

The woman who James assumed must be Emily Monroe was sitting on the floor with her back against an armchair and her knees pulled tight to her chest. She looked to be in her thirties and had short, jet-black hair, owl-like eyes and a silver ring through her nose. She may well have gained some notoriety as a hunt saboteur, but James had never come across her.

'I didn't expect you to turn up as well, Inspector,' Hutchinson said. 'But it's reassuring to know that the police are taking what happened seriously. Those bastards need to be found and locked up.'

'I'm sure my colleague has already told you that we will do everything we can to bring them to justice,' James said. 'I'm just glad that none of you are hurt.'

'They were clearly intent on causing us harm and I can't help but blame you for that, Inspector.'

'Really? I don't understand.'

His body stiffened and his voice became more strident. 'Because you virtually accused me of trashing Rycroft's farm and being involved in his disappearance. News of that would have spread and made me a target. And I expect it will carry on and get worse now that he's also turned up dead. All eyes will be on me and my circle of close friends.'

'I haven't accused you of anything,' James said.

'But you believe I've got something to do with it. Why else would you send people here to search the farm?'

'We're asking for permission to search all the farms in the area. I didn't realise a team had already been here.'

'They came about an hour before this happened and I let them look around. They found nothing incriminating, of course. So it was a waste of police time.'

'That's good to know.'

Rage burned in his eyes, but before he could respond, his wife spoke up.

'You really should make it known that my husband is not a suspect,' she said, her voice shaking with emotion. 'He's had nothing to do with any of it. And despite what you're probably thinking, we're all shocked and upset by what happened to Nigel Marr. And we just heard on the news that a photo of Rycroft's body is now being circulated. We didn't get on with them but we would never have wished them harm. And we're praying the others are still alive.'

Her daughter lowered her hands then and looked up at James. Her face was ashen and drained of blood.

'Please do something so that this doesn't happen again,' she pleaded. 'It was so scary. I thought we were all going to be killed.'

'I did as well,' Emily Monroe said as she chose that moment to stand up. 'I've been threatened more times than I care to remember over the years, but I have never been as frightened as I was earlier. It was horrible.'

James met her gaze and held it. 'And you are?'

'I'm surprised you don't know,' she replied. 'I've spent time in police custody often enough. My name is Emily Monroe. Miss. I'm a proud hunt saboteur. That's why I'm going to make sure the world and his wife are made aware of what exactly happened here. It's usually people like me who attract publicity and are labelled violent extremists. But this just shows that those people who condone fox hunting are not averse to stepping over the line.'

'When did you arrive here today, Miss Monroe?' James asked.

'Why do you want to know that?'

'I'm wondering if it's possible those people followed you.'

She shook her head. 'I don't think so. I came straight from my home in Bowness. I arrived here at least three hours before that lot turned up. And I watched your officers search the place.'

'Emily came straight over as soon as she heard that my nephew Shane was in hospital,' Hutchinson said. 'She's his friend and like the rest of us wasn't able to get in touch with him.'

'You're talking about Mr Logan?' James said.

'Obviously. And I know that you've got it into your heads that he's also involved in whatever has happened to Rycroft's crew. His wife told me you've been to see her, which is outrageous. It's got me wondering if his car crash wasn't an accident and he was targeted like we've been.'

'I doubt that very much,' James said. 'As I understand it, his car slid on ice and he lost control.'

'Yeah, well, maybe there was more to it than that.'

James felt it was best to leave it there and told them he had to return to the station.

'My colleague DC Isaac will stay with you and collate as much information as she can,' he said. 'Our forensics team will also want to have a look around and I'll see to it that someone comes to repair the windows. Is there anything else I can do for you?'

'There is one thing,' Hutchinson said. 'You can leave my nephew and his wife in peace. It's bad enough that he's seriously injured and in a coma. They can do without you lot making things even more difficult for them.'

CHAPTER FORTY-NINE

James and Abbott walked back into the office to find the team glued to the TV monitors. The latest press conference had just begun at Constabulary HQ in Penrith and Superintendent Tanner was doing his best to answer questions from an audience of fired-up reporters.

The discovery of the second body, along with another abhorrent photo, had propelled the story into the stratosphere. It was making headlines around the world and James was glad he wasn't having to face the cameras.

He'd been lucky in that respect since moving to Cumbria as Tanner had always elected to front the pressers. He claimed it was because his detectives found it uncomfortable. But everyone knew that it was really because he enjoyed being in the spotlight.

James wasn't sure he was enjoying it now though, as the questions came thick and fast, fired like darts at a board.

'Were those men murdered simply because they hunt foxes?' asked a reporter with the Press Association. 'And do you believe there's more than one killer?'

'What's your reaction to the furore that's erupted across social media?' This from a BBC journalist. 'Is it true that it's led to an increase in violent incidents between hunt supporters and protesters?'

James watched it through to the end and was impressed with his boss's performance. He said as much when he phoned him with an update.

'It's going to get much harder if this drags on,' Tanner said. 'I learned today that newspaper hacks and TV crews are pouring into the Lake District. Some of the smaller hotels are being block booked, would you believe?'

It was approaching six o'clock when James came off the phone and shortly after that he called the troops together for what he intended to be the last briefing of the day.

By then he had already been told that another blast of snow had forced the search and rescue teams to call things off again. And there'd been more discouraging news from DC Patterson, who rang from Penrith Hospital to say that Shane Logan was still in a coma. In addition, the digital forensics team hadn't yet gained access to the man's mobile phone because of the damage done to it in the crash.

'Let me start by asking if anyone has some positive news,' he said to the team.

But no one had. Warrants to search the homes of Karl Kramer and the Spicer brothers were still pending. And Francesca Marr's ex-husband Aaron Drax had gone on a trip to London without informing his supervising officer. It meant they'd been unable to interview him.

Abbott had updated the evidence board with photos of Ted Rycroft's body, so James began his spiel by pointing to the images and running through what Dr Flint had told him.

'It's the same MO for sure. He was dumped there after he was shot somewhere else. And Dr Flint believes he was dragged unceremoniously to the spot.'

He went on to describe the scene and to talk about the attack on Neil Hutchinson's farmhouse.

'This is yet another troubling development,' he said. 'It means we have to keep a tighter rein on the flow of information. It won't look good for us if another of our suspects is targeted in a similar way.'

He mentioned Emily Monroe and explained that she'd gone to the farm after learning that her friend Shane Logan, Hutchinson's nephew, had been involved in an accident.

'She describes herself as a proud hunt saboteur and we know she has form,' he said. 'We also now know that she's closely linked with four others on our list of suspects – Hutchinson himself, Shane Logan and the Spicer brothers. So, let's put her under the microscope. Find out what she's been up to and where she was on Christmas Eve. And check her social media activity.'

Another hour passed before he told those who had been on duty since early that morning to knock off.

'It'll be a six a.m. start again tomorrow, so try to get a good night's sleep because I fear that we're in for another demanding day,' he told them.

James messaged Annie to let her know that he'd soon be leaving and then set about writing his report. It only took fifteen minutes and after he sent it into the system, he got up to leave.

But as he did so, he received a call from the family liaison officer who was spending time with Dylan Payne's wife Maria at her home in Kendal.

'She wants to talk to you as a matter of urgency, sir,' the FLO said. 'She says it has to be face to face and that it's something you need to know about her husband and his friends. She refuses to tell me what it is, but it's clear she's desperate to get it off her chest.'

CHAPTER FIFTY

James decided to visit Maria Payne by himself while on his way home. She lived on the eastern edge of town just off the A684, which was the route he took to Kirkby Abbey.

He was curious to know what she wanted to tell him and why she was not prepared to confide in the family liaison officer.

He recalled meeting her when she came to the station with Owain Hughes. She'd revealed then how she had begged her husband not to go on the Christmas Eve hunt because the weather forecast was so bad, but he'd refused to listen to her.

She also made it known that as well as being threatened and attacked over the years, Dylan and the others had received an unremitting stream of targeted abuse on social media from anti-hunt activists.

'*We all live in fear of them,*' she'd told him.

A lot had happened since then. Two of her husband's friends had been murdered and seeing photographs of their bodies would have made it hard, if not impossible, for her to retain any semblance of hope.

Their home was a small but smart detached house within walking distance of the outdoor clothing shop that the couple owned.

It was the family liaison officer who opened the door to James. He knew Samantha Cooper well and rated her highly.

'Mrs Payne insists on speaking to you alone, sir,' she said. 'She's in the front room. I'll wait in the kitchen. Do you want me to make you a hot drink?'

'No, thanks, Sam. I'm already pretty high on caffeine.'

Maria was sitting on an armchair in her dressing gown when he entered the room. She looked up at him, her eyes plaintive and forlorn.

'Thank you for coming, Inspector,' she said. 'I appreciate it. Please sit down.'

Her face was gaunt and colourless, and it looked to James as though she had aged ten years since he last saw her.

'I gather you have something important to tell me,' he said when he was seated on the sofa facing her. 'Please take your time. I'm in no hurry.'

She dropped her gaze to the floor and the room filled with the sound of her heavy breathing. After some ten seconds she lifted her eyes and said, 'First, can you tell me if there's any news on Dylan? I know about Ted and that's why I wanted to speak to you. There's something you should be made aware of.'

'We're still doing what we can to find your husband, Mrs Payne, but I'm sorry to say that we don't yet know where he is,' James said.

Her lips tightened and she inhaled a long breath through her nose before continuing.

'I was hoping I wouldn't have to tell you what I'm about to,

Inspector, but I've come to realise that I might be withholding information that could be vital to your investigation.'

'And what is it?'

She fixed him with a hard stare and he saw tears pooling in her eyes.

'I'm afraid I lied to you when we last spoke,' she said. 'Owain raised the subject of that day five years ago when Ted's Jeep collided with that young woman. I insisted it was an accident and that she stepped in front of the Jeep deliberately to try to stop it.'

'I do remember that and it's what Mr Hughes and Mrs Marr also led me to believe. Are you saying it's not true?'

'I am. You see, it's what they told us. And Dylan maintained it was the truth right up until about a year ago, when he got drunk one night and let it slip to me that Ted did drive into her on purpose while she was walking along the side of the road.'

James was taken aback and said, 'He actually told you that?'

She nodded. 'We were talking about our biggest regrets in life and he said it without thinking. He immediately tried to backtrack, but I refused to let him because I'd long suspected that it wasn't an accident. It was the way that he and the others always tried to avoid talking about it. But the subject kept coming up because of all the accusations and abuse that was aimed at them on social media and when they went on hunts.'

'So, what did he tell you actually happened?'

She paused to clear her throat before continuing.

'He said they were all fuming when they drove away from the hunt in the Jeep because the protesters had given them so much grief. When Ted spotted the woman on the lane, he immediately saw red and lost his cool. Without warning, he stamped hard on the accelerator and instead of driving past her, he drove right into her. She didn't stand a chance apparently. Dylan said Ted slammed on the brakes straight away as though he'd suddenly realised what he'd done. He then begged them to lie for him and they did. And if that man Kramer hadn't witnessed it, I'm sure no one would have questioned what happened.'

'Do you know if Nigel told his wife or Rhys told his son?'

'I'm sure they didn't. And Dylan made me promise never to tell anyone. So, I haven't until now. And I'm doing so because I know there's speculation that what's happening now is in retaliation for what happened all those years go. And if so, then I feel it's important that you know the truth. It might help you to find out who's behind it.'

She lost it then and a howl of anguish escaped from her throat.

James stood up with the intention of trying to console her, but she pushed him away and dropped her head into her hands, her body shaking with huge, racking sobs.

It took him a while to calm her down with the help of the FLO, and once she'd stopped crying, James thanked her for being honest with him.

'I know it wasn't easy for you to betray your husband's confidence,' he said. 'But I can assure you that it was the right thing to do, Mrs Payne.'

CHAPTER FIFTY-ONE

When James returned to his car, he took out his phone and fired off a group email to the team. He felt it was important to let them know as soon as possible what Maria Payne had told him.

The revelation gave substance to the theory that the murders of Nigel Marr and Ted Rycroft could have been linked to that incident five years ago. And it backed up Karl Kramer's account of what he'd witnessed.

Cases of angry drivers mowing down pedestrians were pretty common, and those who didn't drive away were usually brought to justice. Ted Rycroft had been saved by his pals who had agreed to lie for him. James suspected it wasn't just because they didn't want him to face the consequences. They probably went into panic mode and feared that they'd be accused of being accessories.

Rycroft himself would have faced a range of charges, from causing actual bodily harm to attempted murder. So, James wasn't surprised that they had stuck by the story all these years.

But that didn't stop him wondering how each of them had managed to live with the guilt, especially after they discovered that Joanna Grey had suffered life-changing injuries.

The drive to Kirkby Abbey required all his concentration so he was forced to push the case to the back of his mind. It was snowing again, visibility was poor, and the roads were slippery. According to the dashboard temperature gauge, it was minus ten outside. Still, he got home safely and without incident.

Annie was clearly relieved to see him and she wrapped him in her arms even before he'd taken off his coat.

'You must be shattered both physically and mentally,' she said. 'After I put Bella to bed, I caught up with the news and I honestly couldn't believe what I was hearing. Of all the cases you've worked on since we've been together, this has to be the most shocking.'

Before he settled down to have dinner, he responded to those who'd replied to his group email. DI Stevens was one of several who wrote that they too had begun to suspect that what had happened five years ago might not have been an accident. And DC Booth told him that she would redouble her efforts to find out where Joanna Grey was now living.

Annie served up fish and chips and joined him at the table, and while they were eating she told him that her uncle Bill had once again refused to speak to her over the phone, but this time it hadn't upset her as much.

'I've come to accept that it's something I'm going to have to get used to,' she said. 'I just feel so sorry for him.'

And he felt sorry for her, so once again he decided not to tell her about the NCA job offer until she was in a better frame of mind. He also needed to give it more thought himself before taking it further.

After dinner they settled on the sofa and watched a recorded soap. But James found it impossible to relax with so many unanswered questions tumbling though his mind.

They both went to bed just after eleven, but he was still awake at midnight as Annie slept soundly beside him.

He was trying to work out why they hadn't made more progress and if they'd put the right people in the frame. It was a strange and fast-moving case, made all the more difficult because of the atrocious weather and the growing pressure from a febrile media.

CHAPTER FIFTY-TWO

Day Five

Thursday got off to a great start for James because his daughter woke up before he left the house. It gave him a chance to hold her and kiss her and to tell her how much he loved her.

And it gave Bella the opportunity to poke a finger in his eye and blow him a raspberry.

It cheered him up no end though and he was smiling as he climbed in behind the wheel of his car. But his mood inevitably took a dive as soon as he set off.

Snow was no longer falling, but there was still plenty of it on the ground, and the wind was whipping it up. He heard on the radio that the search for Rhys Hughes and Dylan Payne had yet to resume because the arctic blast had continued throughout the night. But at least the forecast conveyed a more upbeat message, with lighter winds, fewer snow showers, and a rise in the temperature.

It wasn't enough to encourage James to feel any less anxious about the day ahead, though. The dread was already ballooning inside him and his thoughts were spinning in all directions.

No one knew if another body was going to turn up, but it was highly probable. And there was no way of knowing where or when it would be.

He arrived at HQ at ten minutes to six and by twenty minutes past the team were gathered in front of the evidence board waiting for him to kick off the morning briefing.

He began with Maria Payne's revelation about what Ted Rycroft did to Joanna Grey five years ago.

'We now know that it wasn't an accident and that Karl Kramer, who witnessed it, told the truth. So perhaps what happened to the men is related to that awful event.'

'But that's not the direction the evidence has been taking us in,' DS Abbott said. 'The emails, the text messages, the word *murderers* scrawled on the hunting picture at Ted Rycroft's farm . . . They all suggest that the men have been targeted by extreme anti-hunt fanatics simply because they go after foxes.'

'There's no doubt in my mind that the perps are anti-hunt activists,' James said. 'I believe they're performing this horror show in order to draw as much attention to the issue as they can. But at the same time, it could be their way of camouflaging the real, underlying reason behind it, which is to exact revenge against those men for what happened to the girl. And they chose to do so on the fifth anniversary of the event.'

'There's something else to consider if we're going to treat this as a credible scenario,' Stevens said. 'It's the fact that Johnny Elvin wasn't hunting with the others back then. He didn't join the group until about a year ago. Maybe someone poisoned the cake to target him, so he would pull out of the Christmas Eve hunt?'

Maria Payne's revelation had certainly focused minds and the team discussed possibilities for another half an hour.

'I've made enquiries with the local police and council and I'm hoping they'll get back to me soon,' DC Booth said, updating the team on her efforts to trace Joanna. 'A couple of uniforms are also about to visit the street where they used to live in Milnthorpe to see if any of their old neighbours can tell us where they are now.'

James was then asked if Johnny Elvin and Karl Kramer should be informed of what Maria Payne had told them.

'Not at this stage,' he said. 'But I would like someone to tell Owain Hughes. I want to know if his dad confessed to him at some point during the past five years.'

The discussion then moved on to what was on the agenda for the rest of the day. Dr Flint would soon be carrying out a post-mortem on Ted Rycroft and they were due to receive a forensic report on the crime scene from Tony Coppell.

In addition, they were expecting an update on CCTV and traffic camera footage, plus more information on hunt saboteur Emily Monroe.

DC Patterson had reported in to say that he was on his way to Penrith Hospital, but he'd already been told that Shane Logan remained in a coma. Meanwhile, the digital forensics team were still trying to extract data from the man's broken mobile phone.

The briefing ended with news that warrants to search the homes of Logan, Aaron Drax, Karl Kramer and the Spicer brothers had been signed off. James instructed DCs Hall, Isaac and Sharma to go with the teams.

'We're particularly looking for any shotguns,' he said. 'And I want all their digital devices delivered to forensics as soon as possible. Let's find out if they've been sending anonymous emails and text messages and taking photos of dead bodies.'

He took time out to grab a coffee and a sandwich, but before he'd taken a sip or a bite he received a call from Superintendent Tanner, who told him the search for the two missing huntsmen was about to resume.

'I want you to join me in fronting a press conference this afternoon,' he said, and James felt his heart drop. 'I've decided to hold it in Kendal because the press office says the media are keen for you to make an appearance as the senior investigating officer on the case. I'll get back to you with the time. Meanwhile, what's the latest?'

After James had briefed Tanner, he took his coffee and sandwich over to the evidence board where he stood studying what had been gathered in the hope that he would spot something he'd so far missed. But he was distracted by the thought that before the day was over there were likely to be more photos and messages pinned to it.

He was still standing there and discussing various ideas with Stevens when a call came through from DC Hall, who had gone to Aaron Drax's home armed with the search warrant. Apparently, the former drug dealer and ex-husband of Francesca Marr had refused to let them in and when they tried to get past him, he punched one of the officers in the face.

'He's been arrested and we're bringing him in, sir,' Hall said. 'I'm assuming you'll want to grill him.'

CHAPTER FIFTY-THREE

Of all their suspects, James considered Aaron Drax to be the least credible. It was for the simple reason that, according to his ex-wife, he was a supporter of fox hunting, which didn't fit the profile of an anti-hunt extremist set on revenge.

But he had been a violent criminal who'd served eight years in prison for dealing drugs and possessing a firearm. And he'd only recently been released on licence. Then, three weeks ago, he had a brief and hostile encounter in a pub with Nigel Marr, Ted Rycroft and Dylan Payne.

There was also the not insignificant fact that he'd resorted to violence in order to stop police with a search warrant from entering his home. Did it mean he feared they would find something incriminating? A shotgun that didn't belong to him, perhaps?

James arranged for a duty solicitor to be on standby, and sure enough it was the first thing the man demanded when he was escorted into the building.

They gave the solicitor time to get acquainted with the

brief before he and Drax were brought to the interview room where James and Stevens were waiting.

Aaron Drax was a burly figure with broad shoulders and a pot belly. Despite his size, his features were chiselled with prominent cheekbones, a strong jaw, and a slightly crooked nose.

With him was duty solicitor Clive Edgar, a man both detectives knew well and had a lot of respect for.

When they were seated, James did the introductions and then asked Drax if he understood why he had been arrested.

'I'm not fucking stupid,' he said, his voice husky with emotion. 'I tried to stop a bunch of coppers from invading my father's house. The poor old sod was still in bed and it almost gave him a heart attack.'

'But you overreacted by assaulting a police officer, Mr Drax,' James said. 'And that is a serious offence, especially for someone who was released from prison on licence not so long ago.'

Drax shook his head. 'But they had no right to insist I let them in while waving a piece of paper under my nose and telling me they were going to ransack the house.'

'That was a legal document issued by a magistrate, as you well know,' Stevens told him. 'And given your criminal record, I'm pretty sure that it's not the first time police have turned up at your home with one in hand.'

Drax switched his small, fierce eyes between the two detectives.

'It wouldn't have been so bad if I knew I'd done something wrong,' he said. 'But I haven't. And I don't get why you think I might have been involved in what's happened to those huntsmen. I'm not some psycho and when it comes to culling foxes, I'm on their side.'

'My client has a point there, Detective Chief Inspector,' Edgar said. 'Would you please explain to both of us why he's regarded as a suspect in your investigation?'

'I'm happy to,' James said, before fixing his eyes on Drax. 'You see, three weeks ago, just two weeks after you were released from prison, you entered a pub in this very town where three of the men who went missing were having a drink. I'm guessing you knew they were there, which is why you turned up. You then had an exchange of words with one of them, Mr Nigel Marr. He's since been shot dead, along with another of the men, Mr Rycroft. And since one of the charges that got you jailed was possession of a firearm, it would have been remiss of us not to deem you a person of interest.'

'This is beyond belief,' Drax responded. 'I had nothing to do with it. Those guys went missing on Christmas Eve and I spent that day at home with my dad, just like I've spent most days since I got out. I've got nothing else to do. My movements are restricted, my daughter doesn't want to know me, and I no longer have any friends in this part of the world.'

'Then would you care to explain why you went to London yesterday without clearing it with your supervising officer?' James asked him.

'I was bored, so I went there to look up some old mates,' he replied. 'I didn't let on because I assumed I'd be told I couldn't go. There's nothing more to it than that. I went by train and was back home by eleven last night.'

'And have you had any more encounters with the huntsmen since you saw them in the pub?'

'No.'

'So, you didn't follow up on your threat against Mr Marr?' James said.

A nervous sweat now sparkled above Drax's top lip and his jaw pulsed.

'I didn't threaten the guy,' he said. 'Who told you that I did?'

'Mr Marr told his wife – your ex-wife. He claimed you warned him that he would regret it if he tried to stop you making contact with your daughter.'

'Well, it's not true. Look, I did want to see her but I've decided my best bet is to give Bridget time to get used to the idea that I'm now a free man. Her birthday is coming up soon and I plan to try and persuade Francesca to speak to her on my behalf. There's not much more I can do. I'm desperate to see her.'

They spent another half hour asking him questions and collecting information. They learned that he'd been driving around in his father's car even though he hadn't yet renewed his licence, he'd so far been unsuccessful in his attempts to secure employment, and he'd moved back to Cumbria because he had nowhere else to go. He also denied ever going to Ted Rycroft's farm and said he wouldn't know how to send emails or text messages that could not be traced back to him.

They'd started to press him for details about his movements over the past five weeks when DC Foley opened the door and said she needed to speak to James.

He stepped outside, listened intently to what she had to say, and then went back in.

James could tell from the look on the man's face that he knew instinctively that he was about to receive some bad news.

'We now know the real reason why you didn't want the officers to enter your home, Mr Drax,' James said. 'They've just found a bag of class A drugs, which tells us that you're back to your old ways already. Is that why you went to London? To pick them up?'

Drax slumped back in his chair, blew out a breath and said, 'No comment.'

James closed his notepad and put his pen back in his pocket.

'You'll need to stay here while I arrange for another officer to come in and interview you in respect of the drugs,' he said. 'You should expect to be charged and held in custody. I suggest Mr Edgar here lets your father know that you won't be returning home any time soon. But before we depart, is there anything else we're likely to find in the house that you don't want us to? A shotgun, for instance.'

Drax gave James a cold, implacable stare and said again, 'No comment.'

CHAPTER FIFTY-FOUR

James and Stevens were both of the opinion that Aaron Drax probably wasn't involved in the murders of Nigel Marr and Ted Rycroft or in the trashing of the farm. He'd more or less convinced them with what he'd said. However, they were not going to rule him out entirely until they'd finished searching his home and gone through his digital devices. They would also check CCTV and traffic cameras to see if his father's car was on the road on Christmas Eve in the area of Rycroft's farm or the locations of the bodies.

His father would also be required to provide a statement confirming what his son had said.

While they had been in the interview room, Superintendent Tanner's office had called through to say that the latest press conference would take place at 1 p.m. in Kendal. James was tasked with pulling together responses to the questions that were likely to be asked.

It didn't take him long since there hadn't been any signifi-cant developments during the morning. When Tanner arrived they talked it over in his office and the boss expressed his disappointment at the progress that was being made.

'The pressure is building by the minute and we need a result,' he said. 'We're all dreading the next instalment of this horrorfest, which is bound to include another photo and a third body.'

While they talked it through, news came in that search warrants had been executed on the homes of Shane Logan, Karl Kramer and the Spicer brothers, but nothing had been found to implicate any of them in the murders or the vandalism at the farm.

Despite the lack of progress, Tanner started the press conference on a positive note by saying that the search for the two missing men was once again under way and more people were taking part.

He then introduced James as the senior investigating officer and said his team were working around the clock to find out who was behind it all.

James, for his part, told the dozen or so reporters who were present that his team was following several lines of inquiry and that a number of individuals had been interviewed.

'Does that mean you have a suspect?' one of the reporters said, while another asked him if he believed that Rhys Hughes and Dylan Payne were dead.

James was reminded why he hated fronting pressers and once again it proved to be an unpleasant experience. He wasn't able to tell the hacks what they wanted to know and it made him feel like he and the team were failing in their task.

Afterwards, Tanner took him to one side and said, 'That actually went better than I expected it to. You did well, James, considering you didn't have any good news to offer up.'

Tanner then hung around for the afternoon briefing, at which Dr Flint confirmed that the shell found in Ted Rycroft's head was a match for the one taken out of Nigel Marr's chest.

'It's most likely they were fired from the same weapon,' she said.

The news was what they had expected and so too was the update from Tony Coppell. His SOCOs hadn't found any useful forensic evidence on and around Mr Rycroft's body.

'The same goes for the quad bikes at his farm,' Coppell said. 'They're riddled with prints because they've been rented out to any number of tourists. And we found no traces of blood.'

James made it clear to the team that they needed to spread the net wider.

'I know that our monitoring of social media has thrown up the names of a number of other people who've said, and are saying, bad things about those four men,' he told them. 'It's time we honed in on the ones who stand out as being particularly hostile – the extreme anti-hunt activists who are relishing what's going on.'

Tanner pointed out that officers from across the county were ready and waiting to be drafted in to help out.

'We're prepared to throw everything at this,' he said. 'I know it's a hard, strange case, but I have every confidence that you lot can solve it.'

James knew that words alone were not going to be enough to lift spirits among the team. In fact, just minutes after Tanner set off back to Penrith, their morale took another knock when DC Booth announced that she had made a breakthrough in her efforts to find out what happened to Joanna Grey after she moved from Penrith to Whitby.

'The local police just got back to me,' she said. 'But I'm afraid the news is not good. Joanna and her mother Alice are no longer alive. They apparently died within weeks of each other about nine months ago.'

CHAPTER FIFTY-FIVE

DC Booth's words seemed to suck the air out of the room as she revealed more of what she knew about the tragic life of Joanna Grey. She explained that the officer she liaised with in Whitby had spoken to the hospital that had treated her, and with a friend and neighbour of the family.

'The sequence of events was as follows,' Booth said, and then read from her notes. 'As we know, on Christmas Eve five years ago Joanna Grey, then twenty-one and working as a nursery school teacher, was run down by Ted Rycroft's Jeep. She suffered severe TBI, which is short for Traumatic Brain Injury. It was an awful time for her parents because while their daughter was in hospital, they were subjected to abuse from some extreme hunt supporters who claimed she got what she deserved for stepping in front of the Jeep.

'Joanna was eventually released from hospital, but her parents were told that she would never fully recover. Her cognitive abilities were severely impaired and she could barely speak or remember things. She also suffered persistent headaches, which got progressively worse as time passed. The family discussed moving away from the area and decided to relocate to Whitby, where the parents had previously lived. They put their house on the market and quickly found a buyer. But, before the deal went through, Mr Grey died suddenly from a stroke.

'It was another devastating blow. However, after his funeral Mrs Grey went ahead with the move. She rented a flat for her and her daughter and put the money from the sale of the house away for Joanna's future care. She also got help from her other daughter, Kerry, who returned from America after breaking up with, and then divorcing, her husband. Kerry moved in with them but unfortunately things didn't get any easier for Joanna. Her condition deteriorated to such an extent that she was admitted to hospital for end-of-life care. And during this period her mother, who was then sixty-eight, got into such a state one night that she overdosed on prescribed anti-depressant pills and painkillers. It was generally accepted that it was an accident and not intentional suicide. Sadly, Joanna passed away from her brain injury just a matter of weeks later.'

It took the team a few seconds to digest what they'd heard. And it was DS Abbott who broke the silence.

'We now have to wonder who was aware that Joanna died nine months ago,' she said. 'Perhaps one or more of the people who knew and were also convinced that she was deliberately run down, took the view that she was murdered because she eventually died from her injuries.'

'She moved away from the area three years ago, guv,' Booth pointed out. 'Since then, her name has cropped up online from time to time, but only when that Christmas Eve incident was mentioned or discussed. I couldn't find any reference to where the family had moved to and what had happened to them. And Joanna's death wasn't even mentioned in the local papers.'

'That doesn't mean that one or more of Ted Rycroft's enemies didn't learn about it and decided that it was time to make him and the others pay,' James replied. 'And then turned it into a ghastly horror show to bring the fox hunting controversy back into the media spotlight.'

Booth went on to explain that she was still trying to trace Joanna's sister, Kerry.

'My contacts in Whitby have so far drawn a blank,' she said. 'We know she moved out of the flat after her mother and sister died, but no one seems to know where she is now.'

'Keep at it then,' James said. 'The more we can find out about the family the better. For now, let's end here so everyone can grab a late lunch. I went without breakfast myself and my stomach is growling like crazy.'

He felt better after washing down a cheese sandwich with two cups of black coffee in his office. But sustenance wasn't enough to stop his mind from leaping all over the place. The case had more twists and turns than a big dipper and frustration was gnawing at his senses.

Over the next hour a few more updates came in. James was told that Owain Hughes was claiming that his father had never confessed to him that the incident with Joanna Grey was not an accident.

'He could be lying, guv, but I don't suppose we'll ever know,' DC Sharma said.

James also learned that Emily Monroe had been active on social media since Christmas Day. The infamous anti-hunt sab and friend to Neil Hutchinson and Shane Logan had posted a number of unpleasant comments about Ted Rycroft and co, including:

Sounds like it's payback time for the animal killers.

And:

I consider those men to be my enemies, so why should I feel sorry for them?

Following the discovery of the second body, the fox hunting issue had become even more frenzied. New videos were appearing online showing violence at meets that had taken place since Christmas Eve.

In one of them, masked sabs were seen pulling a huntsman off his horse and kicking him as he lay on the ground. In another, three hunt supporters were filmed attacking a woman who was holding a banner that read: *SCUM KILL FOR FUN*.

Furious debates were taking place across the internet and on the TV news and current affairs programmes. It was becoming so intense that the prime minister himself was asked to comment on the situation during a visit to a factory in Kent.

'My thoughts are with the families of those men who were murdered and those who are still missing,' he said. 'I fear that these terrible crimes are being exploited by people who want to add fuel to a dispute that is already overheated.

'I urge those on both sides of the hunting debate to show restraint. You are playing into the hands of the criminals responsible and by doing so you're causing more distress and harm.'

The man was clearly deeply concerned, but James doubted that his words would cool things down. And he became even more convinced of that an hour later when Gordon Carver alerted him to another anonymous email the *Cumbria Gazette* had received. Only this time it wasn't a photo that was attached to it.

It was a short video.

CHAPTER FIFTY-SIX

This time Gordon Carver didn't bother rushing over to head-quarters. Instead, he forwarded the video to James's phone.

It came through just as DI Stevens burst into his office to announce that the latest episode of the Lake District horror show was about to be aired.

'Have you seen it yet?' James asked him.

Stevens shook his head. 'The press office just alerted us. The papers have been on to them.'

James held up his phone. 'Courtesy of Gordon Carver. Let's watch it together.'

The first thing to shock them was the message in the email.

Let this be a warning to those who kill for fun. All creatures great and small deserve to live.

The video, which had obviously been recorded on a phone, began with an interior shot of an old brick wall before panning down to rough, stained floorboards.

'That looks like an old barn to me,' Stevens observed, and James agreed.

The camera then moved away from the wall and James caught his breath as the first body came into view.

'That's Rhys Hughes,' he said. 'I can tell from the grey hair.'

The camera dwelt on the body for just over five seconds from a distance that must have been only a few yards.

Hughes was lying on his back, his eyes closed and his arms outstretched. He was wearing a thick green coat that had been unzipped and pulled open to reveal a large, blood-stained hole in his beige sweater just above his stomach. He'd clearly been shot and James suspected he'd been lying there since Christmas Eve.

'Jesus fucking Christ,' Stevens muttered, and James reacted by squeezing his lips together.

The camera then moved to the right and they saw a back-pack on the floor before it alighted on the second body.

Dylan Payne, the youngest of the four huntsmen at just forty-nine, was on his side. He too was wearing a heavy outdoor jacket, but this time the camera moved in close towards a large shotgun wound just below his neck.

James swallowed down the rock lodged in his throat and continued to stare at the small screen as the person holding the camera stepped away from the bodies so that both men were together in the frame.

They were lying about ten feet apart and framed in such a way that their surroundings were not visible.

The shot was held for a further five seconds before the clip ended. But it was another ten seconds before James felt ready to release the air from his lungs.

The two detectives watched the video again and afterwards

James felt a cold numbness envelop him. He'd grown used to attending ugly crime scenes with blood-spattered bodies, but this was grotesquely different and it took several minutes for him to get his thoughts back on track.

A dull beat was thudding in his chest when he went out to address the troops after the video had been circulated.

Some of them were watching it on their phones and computers, while others stood around discussing it, their loud voices laced with expletives.

He waited for the hum of conversation to die down, and before he spoke, he had to exhale long and hard to dislodge the knot of tension inside him.

'I don't need to tell you all how despicable this video is,' he said, as his eyes flicked rapidly around the room. 'Or how much of an impact it will have when it's released. The psychos will lap it up.'

James rattled off a list of instructions that he wanted carried out immediately.

'Inform the FLOs who are with Owain Hughes and Maria Payne,' he said. 'Let them break the news, but I want two of you to go straight to their homes to offer both information and support.'

He pointed to DCs Foley and Hall, then turned to DC Sharma.

'Ahmed, I want you to forward the video to the search team leaders. They need to switch their attention away from the fields and woods,' he said. 'Those bodies are in an old barn or shed, for sure, but it's not necessarily a disused or abandoned building. It could be part of a working farm, one that they haven't been to yet, or even some kind of storage unit that's part of a commercial property.'

That was as far as he got before multiple phones started ringing, including his own.

'This was to be expected,' he said. 'We'll reconvene in fifteen minutes.'

James was already clutching his mobile so he answered it as he stepped back into his office.

'Hello, boss,' he said. 'I can guess why you're calling.'

'I take it you've seen it then,' Superintendent Tanner said.

'Gordon Carver forwarded it to me and I've just circulated it to the team. It's sick.'

'Damn right it is. I'm told it's been sent to the same news outlets as the photos were. They've all been on to the press office and the Chief Constable is trying to decide how to respond. Meanwhile, the email is with the digital crime team, but I've already been informed that it's almost certainly going to be untraceable.'

'I'm sending word on to the search teams to focus on old buildings,' James said. 'And we're taking steps to ensure that the families of the two men are alerted. I just hope it hasn't been sent to them as well.'

'Do you think that building is where all four of the men were murdered?' Tanner asked.

'Quite possibly. It could be they were either abducted and taken there or they went of their own accord without knowing what was going to happen.'

'Then why were these two not moved to outside locations and photographed like the others?'

'Could be because the killer or killers ran out of time, or maybe bad weather stopped them from doing so. Or perhaps they wanted a grand finale that would pack an even bigger punch and incite more violence across the country.'

281

CHAPTER FIFTY-SEVEN

Seconds after James ended the call with Tanner, his phone rang again. This time it was Gordon Carver who had some bad news to impart.

'Are you aware that the video has already been uploaded to the internet?' the reporter asked.

'Really? That was quick,' James replied.

'We've got a small team monitoring things and they've come across it on at least two social media feeds. And it's being talked about on Facebook, Twitter and Instagram.'

'Are the sites that are running with it censoring it in any way?'

'Nope. You can see the clip in all its gory glory. And on one of the sites, it's been viewed more than three hundred times in the hour since it was posted.'

James got Carver to give him the details of the two sites and then asked him how the *Gazette* intended to play it.

'The editor is on a conference call right now with the chief executive of the group that owns us,' Carver said. 'We haven't run anything yet, but a short headline piece is being pulled together as we speak. I suspect we'll publish heavily edited stills from the video, but even those are bound to make a lot of people uncomfortable.'

'Off the record, I'm still struggling to make sense of things, but I'm confident the search teams will soon stumble upon the location of the third crime scene.'

'And when they do, I reckon it will turn the current storm into a full-blown hurricane,' Carver said. 'I think it's fair to say that our readers are split down the middle on the issue of fox hunting and trail hunting. Exchanges between them have been lively and pretty disrespectful over the years. But what I'm seeing now is ugly and quite alarming. And the longer it goes on, the more damage it's going to cause within communities.'

James assured Carver that he would keep him updated and ended the call.

Adrenaline was pumping through his veins, so he sat back behind his desk and loosened his tie.

He was deeply concerned about the impact the case was having, but he couldn't allow it to distract him. The violence, the overt threats, the bitter exchanges and mud-slinging on social media . . . they were someone else's problem.

His job was to find out who had murdered those four men and to stop them using the crimes to spread misery and mayhem across the country.

He tried not to acknowledge the sense of dread that was growing inside him. But it wasn't easy. The video of the two dead men had left him feeling wired and jumpy.

It was a horrible thought that those bodies were out there waiting to be discovered. And he was sure they would have been found by now if the exceptionally bad weather hadn't impeded the search operation.

But it was not really a surprise since this was without doubt the worst winter he'd experienced since moving to Cumbria. And according to the long-range forecast, heavy snow, high winds and sub-zero temperatures were set to cause more widespread disruption throughout January and maybe even into February.

However, he was mentally crossing his fingers that the search would soon come to an end. The images from the video would hopefully make it much easier for search and rescue to find the location where the bodies had been sheltered.

Many properties, both old and new, had already been visited, so the teams could head for those that hadn't. And it wasn't as though there were thousands of them spread across the landscape.

He stressed this point to the team when he reconvened the briefing.

'We have to be ready for the call to come through at any time,' he said, willing the anxiety out of his voice. 'There's only about an hour of daylight left, but as long as conditions don't get much worse, the search will continue into the evening and perhaps overnight. Dr Flint and the SOCOs need to be on standby to go straight to the location. It's reasonable to assume that it's where all the murders have taken place, so there will hopefully be some uncontaminated forensic evidence for us to find. And that's something we desperately need right now.'

Desk and mobile phones continued to ring and proved to be a distraction as James relayed the gist of his conversations with Superintendent Tanner and Gordon Carver.

The callers included contacts, family members, newspaper reporters and detectives based elsewhere in the county who wanted to alert them to things they had seen and heard.

The team learned that social media platforms were fighting a losing battle trying to remove the video and photos of the dead huntsmen from their platforms, while at the same time the images had been uploaded to dozens of blogs and innumerable sites across the dark web.

The mainstream media, meanwhile, were struggling with their collective conscience over how much to show and whether what they dared to show would get them into trouble with the regulators.

For the dedicated news channels the story was manna from heaven. It had all the elements necessary to attract a big audience – murder, mystery, shocking images, and at its heart one of the country's most divisive issues.

Despite the interruptions, James managed to run through where they had got to with the investigation, while referring to the lack of evidence on the evidence board.

'It's hard to believe that after so many days we still have so little to go on,' he said. 'I fear that our suspects will soon start to fall by the wayside unless we can pull apart their spurious alibis.

'For instance, Liam and Warren Spicer claim they stayed at home with each other during most of the day on Christmas Eve, but Sonia Logan says her husband told her that they went out protesting with him. We won't know what he's got to say for himself until he wakes up. Meanwhile, we've had no luck with spotting their cars on traffic cams. So, if they did go out causing trouble, then who took them?

'And then there's Neil Hutchinson, whose alibi is provided

by his family. For all we know they're all involved, along with the Spicer brothers. Next, we have Aaron Drax, who also insists he stayed at home, but the person corroborating that is his own father. So, we need to make more headway.'

Greg Pike's name came up then and everyone was reminded that he remained a person of interest because he benefitted from the will Ted Rycroft drew up soon after he was diagnosed with terminal cancer.

'He's well known to most of Mr Rycroft's friends and associates,' Stevens said. 'They all describe him as a loyal employee and he's never fallen foul of the law. But we have found something interesting in his boss's files. Mr Rycroft apparently paid for Pike to have private treatment for an addiction to online gambling. This was two years or so ago and it ran to several thousand pounds. We also managed to track down a former girlfriend who now lives in Lancaster and she confirmed that one of the reasons they broke up was that he was always in serious debt.'

It struck James then that perhaps they should be giving more consideration to Greg Pike as a suspect.

'Maybe the treatment didn't work and he's still got a gambling problem,' he said. 'If so, then finding out that his boss had cancer and was leaving the farm to him in his will might have prompted him to come up with some diabolical plan.'

'That's not inconceivable, guv,' Stevens said. 'For all we know, he could have gone out with the guys that morning even though he told us he was at home. He also knew about his boss's shotguns and had access to the quad bikes.'

James considered this for a moment, then nodded. 'This is what I think we should do. Rather than bringing him in for questioning, send someone to his home in Windermere. Tell him we want to find out more about his boss and then bring it around to him and see what comes of it.'

'That makes sense,' Stevens said.

The names of several new potential suspects were put forward, but only because they had criticised or condemned the four victims through social media. They would still have to be checked out, of course, and that was going to take time as there was nothing else on the face of it to link them to what was happening.

Sunset was fast approaching when the Chief Constable got around to appearing before the cameras again, and just like the prime minister, he began by saying that his thoughts were with the families of Rhys Hughes, Dylan Payne, Nigel Marr and Ted Rycroft.

'I'm fully aware that a video claiming to show two of the men is being circulated and I would urge media companies to please refrain from showing it,' he said. 'Giving it exposure will serve only to make a bad situation much worse. These crimes, which have been committed by one or perhaps several deranged individuals, should not be allowed to cause such widespread hostility and unrest. It makes no sense.'

James tuned out at that point and told the team to get on with the tasks they'd been assigned while he got himself a coffee.

He was already mentally preparing himself for another all-nighter. He didn't want to be at home and in bed if the bodies were discovered in the coming hours. He needed to be ready to respond immediately.

To that end, he retreated to his office and called Annie to warn her.

'I do understand,' she said. 'It can't be helped.'

'Have you heard about the video?' he asked her.

'Indeed, I have. But I don't intend to go searching for it online. I know a lot of people will, though.'

'My advice is not to watch it even if it pops up on the telly or on your phone. It's extremely unpleasant and upsetting.'

'I guessed that much.'

'Is Bella okay?'

'She's great. I'm going to bathe her soon and hopefully give her an early night.'

'Well, kiss her for me and I'll try to let you know later when to expect me home.'

'Don't worry if you're not able to. I'll more than understand. Just stay safe and good luck.'

The evening drew in and the team remained on tenter-hooks as they waited for news on the search. Some officers were sent home when the night shift crew reported for duty. Those who were happy to go into overtime included DI Stevens and DS Abbott, while DCs Foley and Hall volunteered to stay at the homes of Owain Hughes and Maria Payne as they waited for news.

Meanwhile, DC Patterson was going to spend most of the night at Penrith Hospital where Shane Logan was apparently showing signs of improvement and doctors were suggesting he might soon emerge from his coma. And the techies had announced that they believed they were on the verge of gaining access to the man's mobile phone after carrying out some delicate repairs to it.

Time moved slowly and the team became increasingly disheartened as the weather outside turned nasty again. Snow started to fall in places and gale force winds whipped across the fells.

James had started to think that the bodies would lie undis-covered for yet another night when, at 10.30 p.m., the call they had been waiting for finally came through.

CHAPTER FIFTY-EIGHT

The call from Control was to inform them that the two bodies had been found some seven hours after the email with the video attachment had been sent.

The discovery was made by a police search team that entered a dilapidated barn about three miles north-east of Ted Rycroft's farm.

The location was in one of the many areas that had not previously been explored, and it was between the sites where the bodies of Nigel Marr and Ted Rycroft were found.

James did have the option of staying put and going over in the morning after the SOCOs had done their job, but he chose not to take it as he wanted to be among the first to see the victims in situ and to take a mental snapshot of the scene before it got disturbed.

He asked DS Abbott to go with him and DI Stevens to oversee the operation at base. Dr Flint and Tony Coppell had already been given the heads up and were preparing to set off.

More details of the location came through as James was getting ready to leave. The barn was part of a farm that had been abandoned several years ago and most of it had fallen into disrepair. It lay between two small areas of woodland, was not a visible feature of the landscape from any direction, and was accessible via a lane that was apparently still passable despite being under several inches of snow.

James instructed PC Malek to go and prepare the Land Rover and to put the address in the satnav.

'Make sure you're dressed for the occasion,' he said to Abbott. 'It'll be like the polar ice cap out there.'

'I'm always prepared, guv,' she replied as she held up a thick woollen hat with one hand and pointed to the boots she'd already put on with the other.

He grinned. 'Don't let me leave until I've retrieved my wellies from the car.'

His pulse was galloping as he threw on his coat and grabbed his gloves and scarf. Before heading for the door he instructed Stevens to let Superintendent Tanner and the Chief Constable know that he was on his way to the scene.

As soon as the town was behind them, it became obvious that it was going to be an unpleasant journey. The weather was merciless, with windblown snow forcing PC Malek to drive slowly.

The fifth day of Christmas was almost upon them and as the journey progressed, James reflected on a festive season that had been marked by savagery on a scale he had never experienced.

He'd been so looking forward to it, too, with Bella at that age where her joyous reaction to everything would have created lifelong memories for him. Next year she'd be sharing Christmas with a brother or sister and would not have his full attention.

'Do you ever regret moving to Cumbria, guv?' Abbott asked him as they got stuck behind stationary traffic on the approach road to Staveley.

The question made him think about the NCA job offer, which he'd put to the back of his mind.

'Why do you ask that?' he replied.

'Well, you've not had much luck during Christmas and New Year breaks since you moved here.'

He shrugged. 'It was usually the same when I worked in London. In fact I can't remember a Christmas when I wasn't called out to some ghastly crime scene. So, the answer to your question is no, I don't regret moving here. At least for most of the year, murders are not a daily occurrence like they are in the capital.'

'I suppose we are lucky in that respect,' Abbott said. 'I just don't want Christmas to become known as the killer season in Cumbria.'

It was a wretched thought and one that James was thankful he didn't have to dwell on once the traffic was moving again.

Superintendent Tanner called to let him know that the media had already been tipped off about the discovery of the bodies.

'As you would expect they're in full manic mode,' Tanner said. 'We'll have no choice but to stage another presser tomorrow, but me and the Chief will handle it from Carleton Hall. You just concentrate on finding the psychos who are behind this murderous fucking rampage.'

As soon as that call ended, he answered another, this time

from Tony Coppell who wanted to tell him that he and his team were minutes away from the location.

'I thought I should tell you that your favourite forensic pathologist collared a lift from us so we'll be arriving together,' Coppell said. 'We've all seen the video so at least we aren't going in blind. Let's hope that this scene will provide us with something useful.'

Once again, they drove past Ted Rycroft's farm and James's mind flipped back to when he arrived there the night before Christmas. Back then he was assuming it was going to be a straightforward case of four men who had lost their way during a hike. He expected them to turn up safe and well and that would be the end of the matter.

But that was before he saw the damage done to the cars and the farmhouse. And then the picture of the fox hunters with the word *murderers* scrawled across it.

He found it hard to believe that they still didn't know for sure if whoever was responsible then went on to murder the four huntsmen. There was good reason to draw that conclusion, but they needed more than that in order to establish a firm timeline and move things forward.

Beyond the Rycroft farm the lanes became harder to negotiate and conditions weren't far short of a full-blown blizzard.

However, they managed to reach their destination on the stroke of midnight, and as PC Malek steered the Land Rover through an opening where a gate used to be, James felt a chill seize his entire body.

CHAPTER FIFTY-NINE

Day Six

It was probably the first time the farm had seen such activity in years. There were four vehicles in the yard – two patrol cars and two forensic vans, and all sets of headlights were on.

They illuminated two brick-built buildings that had obviously been left to rot, like hundreds of other agricultural properties across the north of England.

The two-storey farmhouse was missing its roof and the doors and windows were just holes in the brickwork. Close to it was a single-storey barn that did have a roof, but its door was missing.

As soon as James and Abbott stepped out of the Land Rover, Tony Coppell was there to meet them.

He was already wearing his forensic suit and he had to raise his voice to make himself heard above the wind that was blowing snow into his face.

'I've been inside and it's not a pleasant sight, guys,' he said. 'You'll need to suit up. And the question as to what happened to the other hounds that went out with those men has been answered.' He pointed to a spot between the two buildings. 'They're lying dead over there and the bodies all have shotgun wounds.'

James suppressed a shudder as he and Abbott went over to one of the forensic vans to get their Tyvek suits and shoe covers. They then struggled to put them on over the heavy coats they were wearing.

James breathed in deeply through his nostrils as he took a moment to gather his thoughts and take in the scene. Despite the crazy weather, the SOCOs and uniformed officers were already going at it full-throttle. Figures in fluorescent jackets were searching the yard while others in white suits were gathered inside both buildings.

Abbott offered to check out the house while James headed for the barn, and the closer he got to it the more his heart rate increased and his breaths deepened.

He walked past the bodies of the dogs and watched as an officer brushed snow from the top of one of them.

Seconds later he and Coppell entered the barn just as two forensic halogen lamps on stands burst into life.

James felt his stomach clench into a hard ball as he stared at the scene before him. It was a large barn, about eighty feet in length by forty feet wide. Snow had been blown inside but it hadn't reached the corpses of Rhys Hughes and Dylan Payne, which were lying on the floor at the far end.

They were positioned just as they had been in the video and Dr Flint was standing between them taking photos.

Tony Coppell walked towards her and James followed, stepping around SOCOs who were picking up and bagging various items, including a single backpack and four damaged mobile phones.

'This is clearly where all four men and the dogs were shot

dead,' Coppell said. 'What's yet to be established is whether they came here willingly or were brought here by force.'

'What does your gut tell you, Tony?' James asked.

'Well, having already given this a great deal of thought, I reckon the most likely scenario is that they arrived of their own volition. It wasn't snowing on Christmas Eve morning, but there were some heavy rain and sleet showers. It could be they got caught in one of them and knew about this place so came here to get shelter.'

'And then what happened?'

Coppell shrugged. 'Perhaps they were being followed by whomever wanted them dead. The killer or killers then entered behind them and let loose with a gun or guns. Or maybe there was a fifth person with them who'd been waiting for the right moment to strike. And that came when they entered this relatively small space. The victims were all close together – easy targets for someone using a semi-automatic shotgun that fires multiple rounds.'

While they'd been talking, Dr Flint had hunkered down to examine both bodies. Now she stood up and turned towards them.

'It's the same MO as the others,' she said, pointing to Dylan Payne.

'So, is it your considered opinion that the murders were carried out at roughly the same time on Christmas Eve morning?' James asked.

She nodded. 'It's possible that this bloodbath lasted less than a minute. If the men were taken by surprise, then they were sitting ducks and could easily have been picked off one after the other before attention was turned to the dogs. And they either ran outside or actually hadn't come into the barn in the first place. I suspect the dog that survived was sprayed with their blood before she managed to flee the scene. As for the sound of the shots, well . . . this place is pretty remote and I doubt that anyone would have heard them.'

James took a few photos inside the barn, then went outside and took some more of the dogs that were lying close to each other.

Abbott then emerged from the shell that was once the farmhouse and informed him that there didn't appear to be anything of interest inside.

'Come and check out the scene in the barn,' he said. 'Then I'd like you to call Phil and tell him about the dogs and the discovery of four damaged mobile phones. It might be an idea if you go back to the Land Rover and phone from there. PC Malek has been keeping it warm for us.'

James and Abbott remained at the scene for another hour in order to gather more information.

Uniformed officers who had searched the surrounding area established that the old farm was easily accessible from most directions and not just via the lane. There were bridleways through the woods on two sides and beyond them fields stretching for miles.

This was significant because it showed that, as they'd suspected, the bodies of Nigel Marr and Ted Hughes could have been moved relatively easily on a vehicle such as a quad bike.

The weather was calmer when they finally set off back to Kendal. It had stopped snowing and the wind had become more of a stiff breeze.

During the drive James tried to concentrate on the positives in an effort to push the image of the two bodies out of his mind.

They now knew where the murders had taken place, what had happened to the dogs, and why the families hadn't been able to reach the men on their mobile phones.

Plus, James felt that the weight of guilt had been lifted from his shoulders because he knew now that he could not have saved any of them. It was clear they were all dead by the time he'd arrived at Ted Rycroft's farm on Christmas Eve.

'So, where do we take the investigation from here, guv?' Abbott asked.

'That's a good question, Jessica, and one we need to give a lot of thought to,' he said. 'Since we're no longer searching for the four men, we can devote all our time and resources to trying to find out who killed them. We need to reassess everything, starting with the suspects.'

'Do you still believe we have the right people in the frame?'

'Let's just say I think it's too early to rule any of them out. They all have questionable alibis. Plus, Karl Kramer, Shane Logan, Neil Hutchinson and the Spicer brothers never made a secret of the fact that they hated our victims. And we know that at least one of them – Kramer – is experienced with weapons and would have had no trouble pumping them all full of shells in less than a minute.'

Abbott pushed out a sigh. 'I just wish we could make a breakthrough for everyone's sake. The longer this case goes on the harder it seems to get. And it's infuriating to think that the perpetrators must be lapping up all the misery and controversy they're stirring up.'

James wanted to offer her some words of reassurance, but none came to mind. So, instead, he took out his notebook and said, 'Let's just focus on the day ahead and draw up a list of what needs to be done.'

CHAPTER SIXTY

PC Malek dropped them at headquarters just after 3 a.m. He was told to go home and get some sleep, which put a smile on his face.

James desperately needed a blast of caffeine, so he and Abbott got coffees from the vending machine on the way to the office.

Despite the hour, the room was still busy with detectives, civilian support staff, a couple of cyber technicians and a rep from the press office.

Some of them were glued to the TV monitors that were showing rolling news. And it came as no surprise to James that the discovery of the two bodies had ensured the story remained at the top of the bulletins.

'I've just been told that another press conference will take place at eleven,' Stevens said as he approached the DCI. 'You should thank your lucky stars that you won't have to front it, guv. I guarantee it will be a raucous feeding frenzy.'

He was looking up at one of the monitors and James

followed his gaze. Photos of Dylan Payne and Rhys Hughes were on the screen and James caught his breath as he listened to their names being read out.

Then the shot changed to show a stony-faced presenter behind her desk. As she spoke, her voice was low and solemn.

'In the last few minutes police have issued a statement confirming that two bodies, believed to be those of Mr Payne and Mr Hughes, have been found on a derelict farm near Kentmere, in Cumbria.

'The location is close to where the bodies of the other two trail hunters who went missing on Christmas Eve were found. It's understood that all four died from gunshot wounds.

'This latest discovery follows the distribution of a video purporting to show the two men inside what appears to be a barn. It was sent anonymously as an email attachment to various news organisations and websites. The BBC has taken the decision not to show it.'

The presenter then voiced over photos of Nigel Marr and Ted Rycroft before throwing to a reporter who talked about the murder investigation and how the case had increased tensions between pro- and anti-hunt activists. He even mentioned the attack on Neil Hutchinson's home and said it was carried out by masked men claiming to be hunt supporters.

James turned away from the screen and told Stevens to gather everyone together for a briefing. He then got himself another coffee and sent a text to Annie apologising for not contacting her earlier.

He did his best after that to instil confidence in the team even though his mind was fogged by fatigue and adrenaline. But it wasn't easy and it didn't help that they were all now feeling the pressure of a case that was attracting so much attention.

A perceptible sense of shock and despondency hung heavily in the air throughout the rest of the morning. Every member of the team was tired, frustrated and desperate to hit upon something that would lead to a breakthrough in the case.

As expected, the vultures started to descend on headquarters. By 7 a.m. there were two news satellite trucks parked on the road and reporters were doing live pieces to camera.

Everyone from the Chief Constable down was being chased for interviews by persistent journalists who were eager to put the police on the spot and get on-the-record answers to their questions.

Other hacks were outside the homes of Maria Payne and Owain Hughes, hoping to get them to face the cameras and share their grief with viewers. But unbeknown to them, Owain had allowed himself to be taken to the murder scene to formally identify his father and Mr Payne.

James spent some time on the phone updating Tanner ahead of the morning presser. As soon as their conversation ended, he took a call from DC Foley who had gone to Greg Pike's home in Ambleside. Her brief was to determine whether his status as a suspect needed to be upgraded following the revelations that he was the beneficiary of his boss's will and had accrued heavy debts due to a gambling addiction.

She began with, 'Correct me if I'm wrong, guv, but didn't Mr Pike tell us that he lived here by himself?'

'I distinctly recall that he did,' James replied. 'Why do you ask?'

'Well, it appears that he lied. A young woman answered the door to us. Pike has apparently popped out to the shops, but she's expecting him back at any minute. She's allowed us to come in and wait for him. And get this – she just let it be known that she's lived here for the past six months.'

'Well, that is interesting and more than a little suspect,' James said. 'Forget about talking to him there. When he returns, tell him that I need to speak to him urgently and then bring him to the station. But first, find out as much as you can about his house mate.'

CHAPTER SIXTY-ONE

Foley arrived back at headquarters in just under an hour with Greg Pike in tow. While he was taken to an interview room, she went straight to James's office to update him.

'Prepare yourself for yet another shock, guv,' she said and proceeded to provide details about the woman she'd spoken to at Pike's house.

'Her name is Polly Lomax, she's aged twenty-four, and she began by describing herself as his lodger. But after I fired a few questions at her she felt obliged to explain that the arrangement is not as straightforward as that.'

What Foley went on to reveal most certainly made James view Greg Pike in a new and unfavourable light.

'The guy had no choice other than to confirm to me that it's true,' Foley added. 'It was a closely guarded secret and he's clearly deeply embarrassed that it's now out there.'

*　*　*

The man's face was downcast when James and Foley entered the interview room and his demeanour reeked of contrition. He remained silent as they sat opposite him and his breathing was heavy and audible.

'I know that my colleague here has explained why she visited your home today, Mr Pike,' James said. 'We wanted to ask you some more questions about Mr Rycroft and find out if you still have a serious gambling problem. And we also felt it necessary to ensure that you had told us the truth about where you were on Christmas Eve.'

Greg contrived a weak smile and shook his head. 'I can't believe you think I had something to do with what's happened. Ted meant the world to me. I'm a farmhand, not a killer.'

'But you're also a liar. You told us, and you presumably told Mr Rycroft, that you lived alone.'

'I did . . . up until six months ago.'

'And that was when Miss Lomax moved in.'

He nodded. 'That's right.'

'And you wanted that to remain a secret because she's a prostitute and you've been letting her use the house to entertain her clients.'

Greg pulled his lips tight. 'I needed more money because the debts built up and the wage that I got from Ted wasn't enough to pay them off. I first met Polly a year ago when I used her services after I broke up with my girlfriend. I enjoyed her company and I became her friend as well as a regular customer. Then she had to move out of her rented flat and it was her who came up with the idea of moving in with me. At first, I told her no way, but when she told me how much she'd pay in rent and that I'd get regular freebies, it was a no-brainer. So she moved in and the arrangement has worked well.'

'Does anyone else know about it?'

'Of course not. It's not the sort of thing you boast about.'

James sat back and tapped his teeth with his pen as he considered what he'd heard. After a few moments, he said, 'Miss Lomax told us that you spent the whole of Christmas Eve at home with her. Is that true?'

'Yes, it is. She had no clients that day and I had nowhere to go. So, we played board games, watched telly and made out a couple of times. Then, in the evening, I got the call about Ted and the others and my world all but fell apart.'

CHAPTER SIXTY-TWO

James was prepared to believe what Greg Pike had said. Nevertheless, he instructed Foley to run a few checks before they ruled him out completely as a suspect.

'Get a formal statement from Miss Lomax and find out more about her,' he said. 'And we should talk to Pike's neighbours and view CCTV footage in the area from Christmas Eve. It shouldn't be difficult to establish whether or not he went out.'

James then returned to the office where he briefed the rest of the team on the Greg Pike interview before he sat down to watch the latest press conference.

The Chief Constable began by reading out a statement letting it be known that the two bodies found on the derelict farm were those of Rhys Hughes and Dylan Payne. Formal identification had been carried out at the scene by Mr Hughes's son, Owain.

The two officers then faced a barrage of questions from a room full of pumped-up journalists who wanted to know, among other things, why it had taken so long to find the bodies and if it had yet been established how many people had carried out the killings and the vandalism at the farm.

One reporter wanted to know if it was believed the men had been targeted simply because they were hunters or if the motive could have been personal.

'Some people on social media are suggesting the killings might be linked to an incident five years ago when a young woman was struck by a Jeep carrying the four victims,' asked a Sky News reporter. 'Is that a line of inquiry you're considering?'

The Chief dodged that question by saying that the investigation team were pursuing many lines of inquiry.

James's attention switched away from the TV when DC Patterson made a surprise entrance into the office. He was supposed to be at Penrith Hospital waiting for Shane Logan to emerge from his coma.

'The techies called to tell me they'd managed to gain access to Logan's damaged mobile phone,' Patterson said. 'After they briefed me on what they'd found I thought it best if I came straight here.'

'That sounds promising,' James said.

'It is. The last text message he received was on Christmas Day and it's highly suspicious. It refers to something he did on Christmas Eve and was from someone you met the other day.'

'And who was that?'

'Emily Monroe. The woman who likes to be known as one of Cumbria's most infamous hunt saboteurs.'

* * *

The text message that was flagged up on Shane Logan's phone was yet another development that raised more questions than it answered.

Emily Monroe had sent it to him at eleven thirty on Christmas morning, presumably when he was at home with his wife, Sonia.

James got Patterson to write it in large letters on the whiteboard and then read it aloud to the team.

"'Merry Christmas, Shane. I'm still buzzing from what we did yesterday. I hope you don't regret it or feel guilty this morning. Let me know where we take it from here.'"

James reminded them all who Emily Monroe was and that she was at Neil Hutchinson's farm when it came under attack from the group claiming to be hunt supporters.

'The first question that needs answering is what the hell they got up to on Christmas Eve,' he continued. 'Does it mean the pair of them trashed the Rycroft farm? Or even that they carried out the killings? Logan obviously didn't want his wife to know who he was spending time with so he lied to her about going out with Warren and Liam Spicer.'

DC Sharma had been tasked with finding out more about the woman and James asked him what he'd come up with.

'She's single and lives with her parents close to Bowness,' Sharma said. 'Her dad runs a factory near there that turns out confectionery products. She's been arrested and fined twice for abusive behaviour at trail hunt meets. And she does a podcast that slags off fox hunters and has almost a thousand followers.'

'So what we have here are two anti-hunt activists who met up on Christmas Eve,' James said. 'Just ten months ago Shane Logan was fined for smashing the windows of a fox hunter's home in Carlisle. He also used social media to attack our four victims for what happened to Joanna Grey. And then there's Emily Monroe, who said in a recent social media post that she considered Ted Rycroft and his pals to be her enemies.

'Given all that, and what she wrote in the text, it's not unreasonable to assume that they got up to no good. It could be that they vandalised the farm, and someone else abducted and murdered the men.'

'It's not clear from the message if it was just the pair of them,' Stevens said. 'So maybe they were part of a group.'

James nodded. 'That's a good point, Phil. Perhaps Logan didn't lie to his wife about meeting up with the Spicer brothers, after all. It could be they went out four-handed to wreak havoc. That would make more sense, I suppose.'

He picked DS Abbott to go with him to question Emily Monroe and asked her to get the woman's address and sort a pool car.

'I need to freshen up and make a couple of calls,' he said. 'We'll leave in fifteen minutes.'

The first call was to Annie, who was relieved to hear from him.

'So sorry for not ringing sooner,' he said. 'We had another rotten night.'

'I've seen,' she replied. 'It's just so dreadful.'

'Is everything okay with you and Bella?'

'All fine. There's nothing to worry about.'

'Good. I'll be home later and will call when I leave here. Love you.'

'Love you too.'

He then had a brief conversation with Superintendent

Tanner and put him in the picture in respect of the latest development.

'Let's hope it proves to be a game changer,' Tanner said. 'Ring me as soon as you've spoken to this Monroe woman.'

James went to the bathroom to rinse his face in cool water and comb his ruffled hair. His eyes were heavy and his joints were stiff, and the prospect of not being able to go home until the end of another long day filled him with dread.

Before he took to the road, DC Booth approached him with an update. As she spoke, he noticed how tired she looked. Her face was pale and drawn, and thick, dark circles hung beneath her eyes.

'I've heard back from the police in Whitby, guv,' she said. 'They managed to make contact with a former work colleague of Joanna Grey's sister, Kerry, who said that no one has heard from her since she moved out of the flat her mother had been renting. However, I did get the name of her ex-husband. It's Derek Chandler, and from that I managed to track him down. He's a financial adviser and lives and works in Los Angeles. I've got the name and number of his company, but the office is closed now. I'll try again later and see if he knows how we can make contact with Kerry.'

'No you won't, Elizabeth,' James said. 'I will. Send me the number. I want you to go home and get some sleep. You've done a terrific job.'

'Are you sure?'

'Absolutely. You'll be no good to me if you're dead on your feet for the rest of the day.'

'I appreciate that, guv. Working through the night really takes it out of me.'

'I'll see you in the morning, bright and early.'

CHAPTER SIXTY-THREE

It was becoming something of a media circus outside the station. There were now three TV news satellite trucks in the road, plus a small crowd of reporters and photographers on the pavement.

For the first time in what seemed like forever, the clouds had parted above the town and there were glimpses of blue sky. It meant the hacks were no longer having to shelter from the snow and belting winds.

Photos were taken of James and Abbott as they set off in the pool car and they heard someone shout, 'What's going on, Detective Walker? Is an arrest imminent?'

As James put his foot down and headed for Bowness, the adrenaline was making his heart pump. He wanted to believe that they were on to something, a game changer hopefully, and that an arrest was indeed imminent. But he knew better than to jump the gun.

'We never discussed Emily Monroe after we met her at Neil Hutchinson's farm,' Abbott said, breaking into his thoughts. 'What was your take on her, guv?'

James shrugged. 'There's no doubt she's strong-willed and more than prepared to speak her mind. She's also devoted to a cause that takes up a large part of her life. And she doesn't seem to care if the methods she employs to promote it cause upset. That's what makes her a credible suspect.'

'I know what you mean and I can believe that she dropped in on Ted Rycroft's farm when she knew he wasn't there and took a hammer to it. But I really can't imagine her murdering him and his pals. She didn't strike me as a homicidal maniac.'

James grinned. 'I'd like a pound for every time I've heard that said about someone who turned out to be just that.'

Abbott chuckled. 'You're right, of course. I've learned that myself from experience.'

They continued to discuss the case throughout the rest of the ten-mile journey to the house Emily Monroe shared with her parents near Bowness-on-Windermere. They also had the address of her father's factory and planned to go there if she wasn't at home.

The roads were still pretty challenging in places, with ice patches and some uncleared snow. But it was far less difficult than it would have been if the weather hadn't calmed down.

They were also able to take in the stunning landscape that attracted millions of visitors to the Lake District every year. Not that they were able to appreciate it, however, since their minds were dominated by bloodshed rather than beauty.

Their destination was just south of Bowness-on-Windermere off the A5074. The satnav told them they were approaching the house just as they rounded a sharp bend and were confronted by the alarming sight of two men brawling in the middle of the road, while another man and a woman were yelling at them to stop.

James had to slam on the brakes and bring the car to a sudden halt to avoid crashing into them.

He immediately switched on the siren in the hope that it would stop the fight and it did the trick. The pair jumped back from each other and turned towards the pool car.

'I don't bloody believe it,' James said. 'That's Warren Spicer and Owain Hughes.'

'And I'm guessing the other two are Liam Spicer and Emily Monroe,' Abbott said.

'Correct,' James told her as he pushed the door open and jumped out.

'What the hell is going on here?' he yelled at the two men, who were now standing feet apart and panting heavily.

As he rushed towards them, he saw that Warren's nose was smeared with blood.

'Get onto the pavement before you cause serious harm to yourselves or someone else,' James demanded of them.

He then instructed Abbott to get back into the car.

'Pull it onto the kerb and switch off the siren,' he said.

It was then that he noticed they were outside a large, detached house with two cars parked on the driveway and another across the entrance to it.

'You arrived just in time, Inspector,' Emily said as she handed Warren a hanky to wipe the blood from his face. 'It only just kicked off and I reckon you've done them both a favour.'

All four were staring at him now and James was sure that Warren's elder brother Liam was trying hard not to smile.

'Are you okay?' James asked Warren.

He took the hanky away from his face and nodded. 'Yeah, it's not broken.'

'That's a fucking shame,' Owain snapped at him. 'You're a piece of shit and you deserve to suffer big time.'

The pair stared daggers at each other, but they stayed well apart and James didn't think they were about to pick up where they had left off.

By now a few neighbours had ventured onto the street to see what was happening.

'I need to find out what this is all about so I suggest we take it inside where I can ask some questions and decide whether to arrest anyone,' James said.

'Oh, leave it out, Inspector,' Liam responded. 'It was an argument that got out of hand. That's all. No big deal.'

'I agree,' Emily said. 'Mr Hughes came here looking to give me grief and as soon as I opened the door to him he started swearing and calling me names. But he didn't know I had visitors and when Warren came out and told him to bugger off, it got physical.'

'And he was the one who threw the first punch,' Warren said. 'But it's over now and I'm not going to make a formal complaint.'

Owain started to speak then, but only two unrecognisable words came out of his mouth before his face crumpled and emotion overwhelmed him. He began shaking his head and sobbing, consumed no doubt by a bolt of adrenaline and the grief of losing his father to a callous killer.

'Is that your car?' James asked him and pointed to the Renault Clio parked across the front of the driveway.

Owain managed a nod.

'Then let's get you back in it, Mr Hughes,' James went on. 'You can give me your version of what happened here before you go home.'

James told Emily and the Spicers that he wanted to speak to them as well and asked Abbott to go into the house with them.

Seconds later he was sitting next to Owain who was behind the wheel of his car, rubbing his knuckles into his wet eyes.

James waited for the man to compose himself before asking him what had happened.

'I was in a terrible state after I went out to identify Dad's b-body,' he stuttered. 'When I got home I had to pass the news on to friends and family. It tore me apart even more. But one of them, an uncle, told me about the vile stuff that that bitch Monroe was posting online about Dad and the others. She made it clear that she was glad they were all dead. I was seized by the need to confront her so I drove straight here.'

'Did the family liaison officer try to persuade you not to leave the house?'

'She did, but I told her I needed to go for a drive to help pull myself together. I didn't tell her I was coming here.'

'And what happened when you got here?'

'As soon as Emily answered the door I let rip and told her what I thought of her. Then Warren appeared and I told him what I thought of him, too. He shoved me away from the door and kept pushing me towards my car. I lost it then and punched him and we started brawling. That was when you turned up.'

James saw no reason for action to be taken against either man, and told him so. He also offered Owain his sincere condolences for his loss.

'I promise to do everything I can to find out who did it,' he said.

'But that's the thing,' Owain responded. 'I believe it could be them. And I'm not the only one who thinks that. I'm sure that you do as well, which is why you're here.'

James wouldn't be drawn on why he and his DS had come to Emily Monroe's house and he made it clear that they still did not have enough evidence to bring charges against anyone.

'I can truly understand how you must feel about Miss Monroe and those two brothers,' he said. 'But now really is not the time to confront them. For your own sake, you need to stay well away from those people who are using what's happened to stir up trouble in the wider community.'

CHAPTER SIXTY-FOUR

James experienced a profound mixture of emotions as he watched Owain Hughes drive away.

He wanted to do more for the poor man than just offer up empty platitudes. What had happened to his father was going to blight the rest of his life. And he could well understand why Owain had felt compelled to lash out.

But now was not the time to make his own feelings known to the three people he was about to question. Three anti-hunt activists who were also suspects.

It was no longer just a case of finding out what Emily had got up to on Christmas Eve with Shane Logan. He now wanted to know why the Spicer brothers were here today. Was it perhaps to discuss some monstrous crimes they'd committed as a group – such as wrecking a farmhouse and murdering four men?

The question sent a shiver of anticipation through him as he walked up to Emily's front door and rang the bell. It was Abbott who answered.

'They're in the living room,' she said quietly. 'Is Mr Hughes all right?'

James shook his head. 'Not really. But he's on his way home now. I'll check on him later. Are Emily's parents in?'

'No. They went away for Christmas and won't be back until Tuesday. That's when their factory is due to re-open after the break.'

'Have you got much out of them yet?'

'I haven't broached the subject of Emily's text message to Shane Logan, but they're saying that they got together this morning to record something for her podcast.'

James followed his DS along a narrow, white-walled hallway into the living room, which was large and airy with a fireplace, polished wood flooring and a tall window overlooking the back garden.

Emily and the Spicer brothers were sitting together on one of two long leather sofas. They all seemed fairly relaxed and James noticed that Warren's nose was no longer bleeding.

'Are you going to keep us here long?' Liam said, as James sat on the sofa facing them while Abbott remained standing.

'Are you in a hurry to get away then?' he replied.

Liam nodded. 'Me and Warren have appointments to go to. We've already explained to your colleague that we came here for just a couple of hours and were planning to leave about now.'

'In that case I'll try to be quick.' James turned to Emily. 'What about you, Miss Monroe? Have you got things to do?'

'I intend to edit the conversation between the three of us that we recorded for the podcast,' she said, her voice clipped and devoid of emotion.

'May I ask what it's about?'

'I'd have thought it was bloody obvious,' Warren piped up. 'We want to make it clear that we had nothing to do with those murders. It's got out that we've been questioned and that's enough to convince a lot of people that we're guilty.'

'It was my idea,' Emily said. 'What happened at Hutch's place the other night really freaked me out. I'm worried that those nutters in their masks will turn up here next.'

'And this podcast is supposed to stop that happening?'

'We're hoping it will help convince people that we're not responsible. We make it clear that we all have alibis for when the Rycroft farm was vandalised. And that just because we speak our minds about fox hunting on social media, it doesn't mean we're murderers.'

'And to be honest, we're all now regretting some of the remarks and accusations we've posted online,' Liam admitted. 'None of us expected things to spiral out of control like they have.'

James wasn't convinced that he was being sincere, and it didn't help that he had a fixed, impenetrable expression on his face.

'I've already taken down several of the posts I put up over the past few days,' Emily said. 'I'm now praying that you find those responsible quickly so that this whole thing can die down and we won't feel threatened anymore.'

James raised a sceptical eyebrow. 'So, you accept that you've been helping to fan the flames?'

She met his gaze and held it. 'Yes, I do. We all do.'

James wanted to ask her about her text message to Shane Logan, but he didn't want to do it in front of the brothers.

Turning to them, he said, 'You can go now because we need to talk to Miss Monroe about an unrelated matter. We may want to speak to you again, so if you intend to leave the area for any reason then please make us aware of it.'

As the pair stood up, Liam placed a hand on Emily's shoulder and said, 'Give us a call later to let us know when the podcast is due to go online.'

She offered him a tired smile. 'Of course.'

The two men then left the room and Abbott followed them to the front door, closing it behind them.

'What's this unrelated matter you want to talk to me about?' Emily asked James.

He took out his phone and switched it on. As he started to speak, Abbott stepped back into the room.

'As you may know, your friend Shane Logan is still in a coma following his accident,' he said. 'As this is the case, we haven't yet been able to ask him what he was doing on Christmas Eve. However, what we have managed to do is gain access to his mobile phone.'

'And what has that got to do with me?'

'Well, we noticed that he received a message from you on Christmas Day.' As he started to read the message from his phone, her eyes bulged and the tendons in her neck stood out.

'"Merry Christmas, Shane. I'm still buzzing from what we did yesterday. I hope you don't regret it or feel guilty this morning. Let me know where we take it from here."'

He was surprised that she hadn't stopped him reading out the entire message, but he guessed it was because she was too shocked to speak.

Now her eyes were fixed on the ceiling, as though concentrating on a problem she couldn't solve.

'We've naturally jumped to the conclusion that you and Mr Logan, and perhaps several other people, are the ones who trashed Ted Rycroft's farm on Christmas Eve and then perhaps went on to slaughter the four huntsmen.'

A muscle flexed in her jaw as she lowered her eyes and shook her head.

'You've got it wrong,' she said. 'I swear. It's not what you think.'

'Really? Then what was it that Mr Logan might have regretted and felt guilty about?'

She twisted her mouth, searching for words, and then said, 'We slept together. Right here in this house.'

James felt his heart dip.

'What did you mean when you wrote that it had been a long time coming?' This from Abbott.

Emily threw out a long sigh. 'For months we've been meeting up at protests and we've had the occasional drink together. We struck up a relationship behind his wife's back. Then, when I knew that my parents were going to be away on Christmas Eve, I asked him if he would like to come over. He said he would, but that he'd already told his wife he wouldn't be working that day so I suggested he tell her he was going out with Warren and Liam. I knew she didn't have anything to do with them so I thought it would be unlikely she would ever find out.'

'Did Mr Logan respond to your message?' James asked.

She nodded. 'He called me and we talked about meeting up again. He said he was going to Cockermouth on Boxing Day to do a job and we hit on the idea of him coming here before going home. I was expecting him early afternoon, but he didn't show and wasn't answering his phone. I assumed he'd chickened out and it wasn't until the following day that I learned about the accident. That was why I went to see

Hutch. I wanted to know how Shane was. I didn't think anyone would find out what we'd done because he was always so careful about deleting messages from me. But for whatever reason he forgot to delete that last one I sent to him on Christmas Day.'

She stopped speaking and drew in a deep, shuddering breath.

James flicked a gaze at Abbott who gave a barely perceptible shrug.

'It really is the truth,' Emily went on. 'Shane and me spent most of Christmas Eve together. He arrived about nine in the morning and left about five. We didn't go out for fear of being spotted. When he comes out of his coma, he'll tell you that himself. And if he doesn't recover then you're going to have to take my word for it.'

CHAPTER SIXTY-FIVE

'That wasn't how I expected things to go,' James said when they were back in the pool car.

'Me neither,' Abbott replied. 'For what it's worth, I think she told us the truth.'

'Same here. But we still need to check it out. It'll help if Logan wakes up, of course. Meanwhile, let's view traffic footage in the area from Christmas Eve.'

Before leaving the house, they had noted down her car's registration and told her to let Abbott know when the podcast she'd just recorded would be aired.

'If she isn't lying then it would explain why Logan's wife believed he was with the Spicer brothers,' Abbott said.

James nodded. 'It sure would. But that won't take us any closer to solving the case. It'll just mean we lose a couple more suspects.'

James had asked Abbott to drive so that he could make some calls. When he opened his phone, he saw something he hadn't noticed earlier, the promised message from DC Booth with a workplace number for Kerry Grey's ex-husband.

He mentioned it to Abbott and said there was no point ringing now because the eight-hour time difference meant that it was only about three in the morning in Los Angeles where he now lived.

'So, you still believe it's worth our while trying to track her down?' Abbott asked. 'What do you think she'll be able to tell us?'

'I don't know, but as the only member of the family still alive she might have some useful information. Plus, I'm starting to wonder why she appears to have dropped off the radar.'

Abbott took her eyes off the road to look at him. 'I don't follow, guv. Do you think it could mean something?'

'Well, one possible explanation could be that it's intentional because she's somehow involved. I imagine that what happened to Joanna broke her heart. And after both her mother and her sister died, she presumably inherited some money. Maybe she paid someone to get revenge on the four men she held responsible.'

Abbott rolled out her bottom lip and raised her brow. 'That's not inconceivable, I suppose, especially when you consider that revenge is one of the strongest motives for murder.'

Before he could respond his phone rang with a call from DC Patterson.

'I was just about to ring you, Colin,' James said.

'I thought I should let you know that I'm on my way back to Penrith Hospital, guv,' Patterson replied. 'Shane Logan is apparently showing signs of coming out of his coma. What have you got from Emily Monroe?'

'Not what we were hoping to get,' James said, and went on to tell him what she claimed had happened on Christmas Eve.

'Do you believe her?'

'I've just been discussing that with Jessica and it's fair to say the woman convinced us both. So, if and when Logan does wake up, you need to see what he's got to say. And be careful not to let on to his wife. That's something for him to tell her.'

James then made two calls, the first to Superintendent Tanner to brief him on the interview with Emily Monroe. The second was to DI Stevens.

'We're just leaving Bowness, Phil,' he said. 'Bit of a disappointment, I'm afraid. I'll tell you about it when we get back. Any updates for me?'

'There is, as a matter of fact,' Stevens said. 'We had a call-out a short time ago to the home of Karl Kramer.'

'What's happened?'

'Well, someone has vandalised the front of his house with red spray paint. The word "liar" was scrawled on the front door, among other things. It was done during the night and spotted this morning by his next-door neighbour. She rang his bell, but when there was no answer, she got into a bit of a panic and called us. I've heard back from uniform who've now spoken to him. He was asleep when the neighbour tried to get a response and he reckons he heard nothing during the night.'

'So, it could be the handiwork of the same masked mob who turned up at Neil Hutchinson's farm.'

'That was my first thought. We'll check CCTV and a door-to-door is under way to see if any of the neighbours saw anything.'

'We'll drop by the place,' James said. 'I was planning to visit him again soon anyway. I want to tell him we've found out that Joanna died and that Dylan Payne's wife confirmed his account of what happened five years ago.'

CHAPTER SIXTY-SIX

'I completely understand now why Emily Monroe feels threatened,' Abbott said. 'I fear it's only a matter of time before her home is also targeted.'

'Let's hope you're wrong,' James replied. 'But she may well have left it too late to take down those provocative posts.'

On the way to Kramer's house in Kendal he recounted the conversation that he and DC Booth had previously with Karl Kramer.

'He was open about the grudge he held against Ted Rycroft and his pals,' he said. 'They made him out to be a liar and the flak he took on social media from hunt supporters, and the threats he received over the phone, drove him into an alcohol-fuelled depression that cost him his career in the army. But he strenuously denied killing them and trashing the farm.'

'You told us he actually knew Joanna and campaigned with her parents to try to get justice.'

'That's right. And it made things worse for him.'

They soon arrived at Kramer's end-of-terrace house near Sandlands Park and James was shocked to see the damage done to it.

The word 'liar' stood out in bold letters on the front door. The beige walls either side of it were smothered in red paint and so too was the window.

'What a mess,' Abbott said.

An empty police patrol car was parked outside and a couple of neighbours were standing on the pavement across the road, staring at the house.

Kramer must have seen them pull up because the front door opened as they approached it and he stood waiting for them in a baggy jumper and a pair of shapeless denim trousers.

'Your colleagues are knocking on doors,' he said. 'But I guarantee that nobody saw who did it.'

'May we come in, Mr Kramer?' James asked.

'What for? I've told them what I know, which is sod all. It must have happened after midnight when I was out cold.'

'There's some news we want to share with you. We won't keep you long. This is Detective Sergeant Abbott.'

Kramer frowned. 'Then you're not here about this?'

'No, we're not. It's something else. We happened to be close by when we were told about the graffiti.'

Kramer looked puzzled, but then gestured for them to follow him inside.

'Are you able to arrange for someone to repair the damage?' James asked him.

'I've told the landlord and he's sending someone out later to see what needs to be done,' he answered, as he led them into a small, cramped living room where he invited them to sit on the sofa.

When they were seated, he said to James, 'I hoped I'd seen the last of you. First you turned up here and more or less accused me of murder, and then a bunch of coppers arrived with a search warrant, but failed to find whatever it was they were looking for. And now . . .'

James raised a hand. 'Please stop there, Mr Kramer. You must appreciate that we had no choice but to treat you as a person of interest in the case. We could not ignore what happened five years ago and the things you said about Mr Rycroft and the others on social media.'

'Then I'll repeat what I've already told you,' he responded. 'I had nothing to do with what's happened to those guys. But as far as I'm concerned whoever did it deserves a medal. They were scum.'

'You've made it quite clear how you feel,' James said. 'But please put your feelings to one side for now while I tell you what we've discovered.'

Kramer drew a breath. 'Go on then. Let's hear it.'

'Well, firstly, one of the four men confessed to a relative that what happened to Joanna Grey was not an accident. He confirmed what you told the police and made it clear that Ted Rycroft drove into her deliberately. I won't reveal that person's identity at this stage, but I will apologise for the fact that my colleagues on the force didn't believe you back then.'

Kramer's body stiffened. 'Thanks, but it's a bit late for apologies. The damage has been done.'

James nodded. 'I know and I'm sorry.'

'They should have been held to account. What they did was sick.'

James allowed a pause before continuing. 'I've also got

some sad news to impart,' he said. 'You told me that you lost contact with Joanna's family. Well, we've learned that both Joanna and her mother are no longer alive. They died within weeks of each other about nine months ago. Joanna from the injury she sustained when she was struck by the Jeep, and her mother from what appears to have been an accidental overdose of anti-depressant pills. That's why you never heard from them again.'

He reacted to this by clamping his lips together and shaking his head. 'I did wonder if something like that had happened. I knew that Joanna would never recover, which is why I didn't want those men to get away with what they did to her. And I could tell that the impact it had on her mother would cause lasting damage. I'm just sorry that I didn't get a chance to say goodbye.'

He perched himself on the armchair facing them and James could see the glistening shine of emotion in his eyes.

'We're currently trying to get in touch with Joanna's sister, Kerry, who separated from her husband some time ago and returned from the States. We understand she was living with her sister and mum when they both died. But no one seems to know where she is now.'

'I wish I could help, but I don't know either. Look, it's been all over the news about the two bodies that were found last night, but nothing about how close you are to finding out who did it. Does that mean you still don't have a clue?'

'I'm afraid I can't provide you with details of an ongoing investigation, Mr Kramer.'

He was going to add that he was confident the perpetrators would face justice, but got distracted by the sound of a toilet flushing in the room above them.

'Oh, I'm sorry,' he said. 'I didn't realise there was someone else in the house.'

Kramer shrugged. 'It's a friend. She arrived yesterday. It was bad timing, though, and she was understandably upset when she saw what the bastards had done to the place.'

'Is she staying long?'

'A few days. We decided to keep each other company into the New Year. She said she'd wait upstairs out of the way until the police had gone so I'd better go and check on her. Is there anything else you want to tell me or ask me?'

James got to his feet and Abbott followed suit. 'No, there isn't, but we may well have to speak to you again at some point.'

As soon as they stepped outside, Kramer closed the front door without so much as a goodbye. As they walked up to the pool car they were met by the two uniformed officers who had been calling on neighbours.

'Nothing to report, sir,' one of them said. 'None of those we've spoken to saw or heard anything last night. The culprits probably pulled up in a car or van, did the damage without making a sound, and then shot away.'

'Well, file a report and let me know if anything turns up,' he told them.

As he was about to climb back into the passenger seat of the pool car, he glanced back at the graffiti across the front of the house.

'That won't be an easy job to get rid of,' he said to Abbott.

Before turning away, he noticed someone looking out of one of the upstairs windows. It was a woman with a sweep of dark hair and an inquisitive look on her face. But that was about as much he was able to take in before she stepped hurriedly out of sight.

CHAPTER SIXTY-SEVEN

On the way back to headquarters they stopped at a café to grab some lunch.

James had a large sausage roll and Abbott got her teeth into a hot pasty. And they drained two glasses of water each.

Their visits to the homes of Emily Monroe and Karl Kramer had given them plenty to talk about, but if everything they had been told was the truth, then it hadn't been a very productive morning.

'I forgot to ask if you also smelt the booze on Kramer's breath, guv,' Abbott said as they left the café.

James nodded. 'It was the same when I first went there. The guy has obviously still got a drink problem. That's probably why he slept through what happened last night. He was pissed.'

'Or too busy enjoying the company of his lady friend.'

Abbott explained that she had also seen the woman at the window and, unlike James, had noticed that she'd been wearing a dressing gown.

'I reckon the guy deserves to have some fun after what he's been through,' he said. 'But I very much doubt that his troubles will be over if he doesn't stop savaging those men on social media.'

The press and TV crews were still gathered outside the station and luckily for them the bad weather hadn't yet returned.

Inside, the tired team members were still hard at it, chasing up leads, monitoring social media and CCTV footage, reviewing all the case notes and seeking out new suspects.

Tony Coppell had filed a forensic report in which he pointed out that no breakthrough evidence had been found at the abandoned farm or on the bodies of Rhys Hughes and Dylan Payne.

Gathering everyone, James told them about the conversations they'd had with Emily Monroe, the Spicer brothers and Karl Kramer. And he pointed out that the investigation appeared to have hit the buffers as there were no fresh lines of inquiry to follow up.

The mood in the office was one of gloom, mixed with a weird sense of not knowing what to expect next. The bodies of the four missing huntsmen had been found, so did that mean that the horror show was over?

Would the killer or killers consider it job done? Had their gruesome objective been achieved? And for how long would the repercussions continue to be a source of concern?

There seemed to be no let-up in the exchange of insults, accusations and threats on social media between pro- and anti-hunt activists. Plus, the murders continued to be headline news and the break in the weather was enabling camera crews to get close to the crime scenes.

In addition, everyone was fearing an outbreak of violence at trail hunt meets over the forthcoming New Year break.

The team listened to the podcast aired by Emily Monroe and it came across as somewhat cringe, she and the Spicer brothers all denying any involvement in the killings and saying that they themselves were the victims as they'd been targeted by pro-hunt extremists.

'I for one intend to set an example by opting out of this whole toxic debate, at least until things have calmed down,' Emily said as the podcast wrapped up. 'Too many bad things are being said and too many bad things are happening as a consequence.'

At 4 p.m. the Constabulary released another media statement saying that the investigation was making steady progress under the leadership of Detective Chief Inspector James Walker.

At 5 p.m. James called the number DC Booth had given him in Los Angeles for Derek Chandler, Kerry Grey's ex-husband.

He was told the man wasn't yet in the office but that a message would be passed on to him when he arrived. Whoever had answered the phone declined to give out Chandler's mobile number.

At 5.15 p.m. James called Owain Hughes to see how he was and he said he had calmed down and was now at home with his aunt and uncle.

It wasn't until 6 p.m., just as James was preparing to go home, that he received news that Shane Logan had at last emerged from his coma and might soon be able to answer questions.

CHAPTER SIXTY-EIGHT

James didn't intend to hang around. He was dog-tired and in desperate need of some sleep.

He told DC Patterson to call him on his mobile if he was able to question Shane Logan. Or to send a text if it was at an ungodly hour.

Then he and the others who'd been working without a break for over thirty-six hours took their leave.

It had started snowing again, but not hard enough to hamper his drive to Kirkby Abbey. Along the way his mind refused to let go of the case.

The team needed to turn things around, but the longer they went without a significant breakthrough the harder it was going to be.

He was just glad that cases like this – cases involving multiple crimes, lots of viable suspects and a serious lack of solid forensic evidence – were few and far between.

It bugged him that there remained so many unanswered questions, including whether the murders had been carried out in revenge for what had happened to Joanna Grey.

It was this last question that was dominating his thoughts as the lights of Kirkby Abbey appeared in the distance.

They now knew that Ted Rycroft did drive into the young woman deliberately and that his friends covered up for him. They also knew that on the fifth anniversary of that event the four men were slaughtered.

An image of the damage done to the Rycroft farm rose unbidden in James's mind and he saw again the picture of the huntsmen with the word *murderers* scrawled across it. James had assumed that it was referring to the fact that Rycroft and the other men hunted down and killed foxes. But he now wondered if there was more to it.

What if the perpetrators knew that Joanna had eventually died from her injuries? Did that mean that, in their eyes, she was effectively murdered? And was that why they defaced the picture with the one-word accusation?

James was still pondering all of these questions as he arrived home and pulled onto the driveway. As he climbed out of the car, he told himself that it was time to stop thinking about the case and pay some attention to his wife and daughter.

And that was when he saw them at the kitchen window. Annie was holding Bella in her arms and they were both waving at him.

It lifted his spirits and he waved back. But at the same time the image brought to mind the woman he saw earlier looking out of the window at Karl Kramer's house.

And it suddenly occurred to him that he'd perhaps missed something crucial by not enquiring as to who she was.

*　*　*

He got to spend at least half an hour with Bella before they put her to bed. He and Annie then had dinner together and once again he resisted the urge to tell her that he had been offered a job that would entail them moving back to London. That was just going to have to wait.

As soon as they had finished eating, DC Patterson called him on his mobile with news about Shane Logan.

'The guy is awake, but the doctors say there's no way they'll let me talk to him just yet,' Patterson said. 'He's confused and suffering some memory loss, and can barely string two words together. They're confident he'll improve overnight, but we won't get any sense out of him right now.'

After the call, James's mind was back on the case and when Annie said that she was going to bed he told her he wasn't quite ready.

'If I go up now I'll be awake for ages,' he said. 'I need to make a couple of calls and note down some thoughts. It won't take long though and then I'll join you.'

He kissed her goodnight and when she went upstairs, he retreated to the study. It was usually where he ended up when he couldn't clear from his mind a particular train of thought or an image that posed a question.

In this case it was the woman he'd seen at the window in Kramer's house. Gut instinct told him that since she was staying with one of their main suspects, he should have found out something about her. What was her name? Where did she live? How long had she known him?

But it wasn't just that. She had suddenly appeared on the scene just as he'd started to turn his attention to another unre-solved issue – the whereabouts of Joanna Grey's sister, Kerry.

Was it possible, he wondered, that after her mother and

sister died, Kerry moved back to Cumbria? Did she then team up with Kramer – the man who bore witness to what had happened to Joanna – and together they hatched a plan to get their revenge?

Sure, Kramer had said he'd lost touch with the family and he hadn't been aware that Joanna and her mother had died. But maybe he'd lied.

The wheels began to turn sharply in James's head and he tried again to reach Kerry's former partner, Derek Chandler, in Los Angeles. This time he was told that his earlier message had been passed on to Mr Chandler, but he'd been in meetings all morning and was now out to lunch. And once again James was told that company policy was not to give out personal phone numbers of members of staff.

'Please can you tell Mr Chandler that I need to speak to him as a matter of urgency?' James said. 'It's a police matter and has to do with his former partner, Ms Kerry Grey.'

Next, he called DC Booth even though he suspected she'd be asleep. But much to his surprise she answered the phone within seconds.

'I'm so very sorry to disturb you, Elizabeth,' he said. 'But there's something I need to ask you.'

'It's no problem, guv,' she replied. 'I slept all afternoon and woke up about an hour ago. I'll give it another hour and then go back to bed. So, what's the question?'

'I'm still trying to track down Joanna Grey's sister, Kerry. And I've yet to speak to her ex in the States. But I want to know if you came across any photos of her when you were dredging up information on the family.'

'No, I didn't. I think I mentioned to you before that there were very few pictures of any of them online. I only came

337

across a couple of Joanna and her parents. I can only think that Kerry chose to stay out of the spotlight. And since I couldn't find any photos, I assumed she'd never had a presence on social media or at some point she'd removed all trace of herself.'

It was another half an hour before James hauled himself up to bed and by then his head felt like it was going to explode.

Despite that, he did eventually drift into a shallow sleep, only to be woken at five in the morning by a call from across the Atlantic.

CHAPTER SIXTY-NINE

Day Seven

James rushed downstairs with his mobile phone to take the call, leaving Annie lying awake in bed.

'Thank you for getting back to me, Mr Chandler,' he said. 'What time is it there in Los Angeles?'

'It's nine in the evening and my apologies for not ringing you sooner,' he answered. 'There was a bit of a misunderstanding at my end. The assistant who took down your first message only passed on your name and number and omitted to tell me that you were a police officer, so it didn't convey a sense of urgency. I only just returned to the office to collect some papers before going home and your second message was handed to me. So, what is it all about? Has something happened to Kerry?'

'I don't believe so, Mr Chandler. I know that you and she got divorced and she moved back to the UK, but can you tell me when you last heard from her?'

'That would be when she rang to tell me that her mother and sister had died,' he replied. 'She thought I should know. She was naturally very upset.'

'Well, I'm trying to trace her, but nobody seems to know where she is.'

'She was living in Whitby at the time of their deaths. She told me she was planning to move away from there, but she didn't say where she was going. I did try to ring her again a month later, but I got no response and thought she must have changed her number. I'm really sorry I can't help you.'

'Actually, you still might be able to, Mr Chandler. You see, Kerry's name has come up during the course of an investigation and I need to know more about her.'

'What kind of investigation?'

'Have you heard about the murders of four men that have taken place here in Cumbria since Christmas Eve?' James asked. 'It's been all over the news.'

'Murders? No. I've not paid much attention to the news during the past week. Why? What on earth would they have to do with Kerry?'

'I take it you know about the incident in which her sister Joanna was hit by the Jeep five years ago?'

'Of course. It was a real blow to the family and Kerry never stopped talking about it. She was convinced it wasn't an accident, for one thing. There was a witness who claimed the Jeep was driven into Joanna deliberately by a group of fox hunters because she'd been protesting at one of their meets. Joanna was in a terrible state. She couldn't speak or communicate. But what happened to her impacted badly on Kerry as well.'

'In what way?'

'As Joanna's condition worsened, Kerry's character seemed to change. She became more volatile and unpredictable, and was often depressed. It led to arguments between us and after her father died and her mother moved to Whitby she felt guilty because she was living so far away and wanted us to move back. It really put a strain on the marriage because I didn't want to. I'm happy here. I have a great job and I felt it would be a huge mistake. In the end she decided to go by herself and asked for a divorce. I'm guessing that after Joanna and her mum died she fell into a pit of despair.'

James thought about this for a moment and said, 'Well, for your information, Mr Chandler, the four murder victims were the men who were in that Jeep that crashed into Joanna. And for that reason, we've been trying to find out if the killings could possibly be linked to that incident. We hoped that as the only family member still alive Kerry might be able to help us.'

Chandler remained silent, clearly lost for words, but James could hear him breathing rapidly into the phone. He waited several seconds before asking another question.

'What else can you tell me about Kerry, Mr Chandler?'

'Well, only that I did truly love her up until the relationship was making us both unhappy,' he replied.

'Can you tell me what colour hair she has?'

'Dark brown and shoulder length.'

Just like the woman in the window.

'And does she have a career?'

'She did, but I don't know if she does now. She was an IT technician and used to work for a digital device repair company.'

James felt a flash of hope. Whoever had sent out those emails and text messages, and created false internet accounts, would have had to be proficient in the use of modern technology, including mobile phones and computers.

'Did she ever give you the impression that she might one day seek revenge against the men who effectively ruined her life?' James asked.

'Are you serious?' He gasped. 'Do you really suspect that Kerry might have killed those men?'

'Not at all, Mr Chandler,' James said. 'But we have to consider the possibility that she might have been involved somehow.'

'But that's plainly absurd. How were those men killed anyway?'

'They were shot with a semi-automatic shotgun while they were sheltering from the rain inside a barn. The details are in all the news stories online.'

There was another long silence before Chandler responded, and James detected a marked change in the tone of his voice.

'There actually is something you ought to know then, Detective Chief Inspector,' he said. 'Kerry has always been fascinated by guns. Her father owned a shotgun and she got me to take a photo of her with it. Then, when we moved over here, she bought a rifle and a pistol and we would often go to the ranges together. I remember on one occasion she actually told me that given the chance she would happily shoot dead those men who destroyed her sister's life.'

CHAPTER SEVENTY

Before hanging up on Derek Chandler, James asked him if he still had any photos of Kerry.

'They're on my old mobile phone, but it's at home,' he said.

'I'd like you to send a couple to me, Mr Chandler, including the one of her with her dad's shotgun. As soon as you can.'

'It'll be in about an hour, if that's okay.'

'That's fine.'

He gave the man his email address and asked him not to speak to anyone about what they'd discussed.

'I'll make sure to let you know what comes of this line of inquiry,' he said.

James called the office and got them to send a surveillance team to Karl Kramer's house in Kendal.

'I want them to report back immediately on any comings and goings,' he said. 'But they are not to approach anyone because it's possible that one or both of the occupants are armed.'

After that he had a quick shave, jumped in the shower, and got dressed in record time.

'It seems we may have had a breakthrough in the case,' he said to Annie when he was ready to leave. 'I haven't got time to tell you about it now, but I'll call later.'

'I'll be rooting for you, my love,' she said before pulling the duvet over her face.

As James clambered into his car, the blood pulsed and hammered inside his head. What Derek Chandler had said about Kerry Grey was enough to convince him that she was now their prime suspect. She had motive, she'd dropped off the radar, and she had even told her ex that she wanted them to pay with their lives for what they did.

And it made sense that she would get together with Karl Kramer to exact revenge. What happened to Joanna had wrecked his life too. Maybe Kerry had been living with him for weeks or months. Perhaps they had even struck up a relationship as they planned their revenge.

James called the office on the hands-free and said he wanted a message to go out to every member of the team.

'Tell them we have a new lead and we will have to act on it quickly,' he said. 'I want them all in as early as possible for a briefing. And alert armed support. I think we're going to need them.'

The snow had stopped falling during the night and the new day was pretty calm so there were no hold-ups and he made good time. As he drove into the town his whole body felt like it was humming with electricity.

Most of the team had arrived before him and as he entered the office, he sensed an air of nervous energy.

DI Stevens was the first to ask him what was going on.

'Let's get everyone together so that I won't have to repeat myself,' James told him.

All the main players were there and hoping he was going to make their day – DS Abbott and DCs Foley, Booth, Sharma and Hall. DC Patterson was watching via his phone from Penrith Hospital where he was waiting to interview Shane Logan.

James began with a recap of the Joanna Grey incident five years ago. He then told them about the woman he and Abbott had seen looking out of the window at Karl Kramer's house, a detail he hadn't thought to mention during the last briefing.

And then he dropped the bombshell, the revelations from Derek Chandler about his ex-wife. This sparked loud gasps and raised eyebrows across the room.

'We can't be sure that the woman staying with Kramer is Joanna's sister as we only glimpsed her briefly, but I reckon she's about the same age, in her late twenties or early thirties. And she has dark hair, as did Kerry when she was living with Chandler. He's due to send me photos of her about now.'

It was another ten minutes before the email from Chandler came through with two photos of Kerry attached.

When James opened them up and looked at them, a shiver skittered down his spine and bile rushed into his throat.

'Oh shit,' he said aloud when he saw that the woman in the photo was not the woman who had peered out of Kramer's window.

However, he realised immediately that Kerry Grey was familiar to him. In fact, he'd met her several times over the past few days.

The name she was now using was Rebecca Carter, and for months she'd been employed as Ted Rycroft's part-time clerical assistant.

345

CHAPTER SEVENTY-ONE

It came as a shock to everyone in the room, especially those who had met her.

Kerry Grey had given an award-winning performance as Rebecca Carter, the distraught employee of Ted Rycroft.

'So, it would seem that she had everyone fooled,' James said. 'First Ted Rycroft and then us.'

'But what about the two texts she received?' Foley said. 'The second one suggested that her boss was about to turn up dead.'

James shrugged. 'She must have sent them to herself or got an accomplice to do it for her to throw us off the scent.'

There was no time to have a lengthy discussion about this unforeseen development. They needed to bring the woman in for questioning as soon as possible.

James had her address in Windermere and as far as he knew she lived alone.

'It will take us about fifteen minutes to get there,' he said, and picked Stevens and Abbott to go with him. Then he told the others to arrange for uniformed backup and armed support to follow on.

It was still dark as they set off for Windermere, sunrise still at least an hour away.

James and his two colleagues shared a pool car, with Stevens driving. Two patrol cars and an armed response vehicle were close behind. Blue lights were flashing but the sirens were mute.

James was still trying to come to terms with the dramatic turn the investigation had taken. All he could think about was how Kerry Grey, aka Rebecca Carter, had succeeded in pulling the wool over their eyes by being clever and manipulative.

James thought back to some of the things she said to him during their three brief encounters.

'I've really enjoyed working here . . . Ted has been like an uncle to me. I just hope that he and the others are all right.'

Her reaction upon seeing the vandalism inside the farm-house: *'I don't believe it. Who would have done such a thing?'*

Her reaction to the picture of Nigel Marr's body: *'I couldn't stop crying after I saw the photo of Nigel on the news.'*

It was all a devious act that she had pulled off brilliantly. But now he wanted to know how she'd pulled off everything else. Luring her four victims to the abandoned farm. Killing them there. And then moving two of the bodies to other locations. Had she acted entirely alone or was there an accomplice?

The address she'd given James was just off the A591 on the approach to Windermere. They were a mile away from it when the blue flashing lights were switched off.

James had been communicating by radio with the armed response officers and it had been agreed that it would be too risky to simply knock on the woman's door and then arrest her when she opened it.

They had no choice but to treat her as a suspect who was potentially armed and dangerous. The plan, therefore, was for armed officers to force their way in and surprise her.

The street had rows of terraced houses along both sides and the fleet of vehicles pulled up just short of Kerry Grey's. As soon as James and his fellow detectives stepped out of the car, they slipped on bulletproof vests.

They then followed behind the armed support officers who rushed along the pavement to number five, a two-storey property with a small front garden and no driveway.

And then came an explosion of noise as they started to force open the front door with a ram. Within seconds they were inside and yelling at the tops of their voices.

James and the others stood outside listening as the officers hurried from room to room and lights were switched on.

But after just a few minutes it was determined that the house was empty. And when the senior support officer emerged, he said, 'It doesn't look to me as though the place has been occupied in the recent past, guv.'

James felt his heart drop and confusion pulled at his face. He was about to respond when his phone rang, so he tugged it from his pocket. He didn't recognise the name, but as soon as he heard her voice he know who was calling him.

'Would I be right in assuming that you know I've been pretending to be someone else, Inspector?'

James waved his arm as a signal for those around him to stop speaking and put his phone on speaker.

'Yes, you would, Kerry,' he said. 'What's going on?'

'I would have thought that was obvious,' she replied, her voice cracking with emotion. 'I gave you the wrong address. You just raided the second home of a family who live in London. I'm next door at number six and now that you know my real identity, I see no point in carrying on. My life is as good as over, but at least I can now rest in peace.'

'Please don't do anything stupid, Kerry,' James said. 'Let me come in and talk to you.'

'Why? You know what I've done. That's the reason you and all those armed coppers I saw from the window have come to get me.'

'But I want you to tell me what made you do it, Kerry. Surely it will help to get it off your chest after so long.'

'Nothing will help me now,' she said. 'I half expected it would come to this. That's why I kept one of Rycroft's shotguns. The one I used to kill them all.'

'Please, Kerry. I beg you to let me come in.'

She didn't respond immediately, just breathed heavily into the phone for several seconds. Then: 'Very well. The front door is open. You're welcome to bring one of your armed bodyguards with you. But I promise I don't intend to shoot anyone but myself.'

And with that she hung up.

CHAPTER SEVENTY-TWO

'There's no doubt she's planning to kill herself, so I need to go in,' James said. 'Maybe I can talk her out of it.'

It was really the only option open to them other than to storm in and risk multiple casualties or stay outside and wait for a shot to go off.

'I'll go first,' the senior armed support officer said. 'I've been in this situation before.'

The tension built as the officer walked over to number six and pushed open the front door, then stepped inside armed with a semi-automatic carbine.

James followed close behind, his nerves jangling, heart pounding.

'I'm in the living room,' Kerry called out.

It was a short hallway and when the officer reached the first doorway, he peered inside.

'Just come in and let's get this over with,' James heard her say to him.

The officer did just that and a moment later James entered

the room himself to find Kerry Grey sitting in an armchair in her dressing gown. She seemed fairly relaxed even though she was holding a shotgun on her lap. Her finger was on the trigger and the barrel was pressed against her chin.

James realised immediately that there was no need for him to fear for his own life. If she redirected the gun at him she would be cut down in an instant with the carbine that was aimed at her.

He stepped forward and sat on the sofa facing her. The armed officer stayed where he was just inside the door.

He saw then that Kerry's eyes shone with unshed tears and the hand gripping the gun was shaking.

'First, can I ask how you found out who Rebecca Carter really is?' she said, her eyes fixed firmly on James.

'We linked the murders of the huntsmen to what happened to your sister five years ago,' he said. 'Then we discovered that Joanna and your mother had died and we tried to track you down. But we got nowhere until we spoke to your ex, Mr Chandler. He told us some stuff about you and how your own life had suffered as a result of what Ted Rycroft did. And then he sent us a photograph of you.'

She nodded. 'I always knew there was a possibility you'd uncover the truth. I just prayed it wouldn't happen before I finished what I set out to do. That's why I gave you the wrong address. I didn't want to be caught off guard if you turned up here.'

'So why do you now feel the need to end it?' James asked.

'I've had suicidal thoughts for a long time,' she answered. 'Those men destroyed my life. What Rycroft did to Joanna was unforgiveable. She meant everything to me. But he got away with it and his friends helped him.'

'But you didn't know that for sure.'

'Karl Kramer was a witness and we all knew that he was telling the truth when he said the Jeep drove into her on purpose. I'm in no doubt that the strain it put on our father brought on his stroke. Poor Joanna lived the last few years of her life as a vegetable. It was too much for my mother and it caused my own marriage to break down because I didn't want to live so far away. Those bastards took everything from me.'

'So, you decided to seek revenge.'

'It was after I found myself all alone and came very close to committing suicide. What stopped me then was the thought that those four would never be brought to justice. It wasn't fair and I realised I would never be able to rest until I did something about it.'

'So how did it all start?'

'The first thing I did was tell people who knew me that I was moving away from Whitby, but I didn't say where to. Then I changed my name by deed poll before moving back here about seven months ago. I started renting this place and found a job at a store in town. We'd lived in Milnthorpe before and I didn't know anyone in Windermere.'

'What then, Kerry?'

'I spent most of my free time monitoring the social media accounts of Rycroft and his friends. I needed to find out where they lived and what they were up to so that I could decide how to go about it.'

'And I take it that was when you saw the job being advertised at the Rycroft farm?'

'That's correct. A stroke of luck. I applied and got it because there were no other applicants. But working for him even for just three days a week was unpleasant and the longer it went on the more I hated them. On one occasion I heard Ted and Nigel Marr discussing what had happened to Joanna and that backed up Karl's account that he drove into her on purpose.'

'And where did it go from there?'

'I had to bide my time until I could get them all together and when they began planning the Christmas Eve hunt things started to work out. And the more I thought about it, the more ambitious I became. I decided it wouldn't be enough to just kill them. I wanted to drag it out, get an audience and as much publicity as possible. It got to the point where I suddenly had two objectives – to kill those men and to put the fear of God into all those who take part in any form of animal hunting.'

'Hence the photos of the bodies and the video,' James said.

'Exactly. I acquired a couple of burner phones and set up some fake email accounts. It was easy enough because, as you probably know, I've worked in IT for years.'

'This was all very elaborate, Kerry. Did you have an accomplice?'

She shook her head. 'It was all my own work, I'm proud to say.'

Her words sat cold inside James and he noticed a tear escape from her right eye and cascade down her cheek.

'I take it you sent those messages to yourself to ensure that we didn't regard you as a suspect?' he said.

She nodded. 'But also so that I could get close to you and find out where you were with the investigation.'

'One of them landed on your phone when you were in the car with your colleague, Greg.'

'I had two phones on me and the burner in my pocket was

already set up to send the message to my everyday phone. I just had to press the button and he knew nothing about it.'

She suddenly let out a weighty sigh and more tears streamed out of her eyes.

'Any other questions, Inspector? Or shall I end it here?'

Her finger tightened ever so slightly on the trigger, and James swallowed sharply, his mind whirring through his options. He needed to play for time, and it was running out.

'Tell me how it all came together on Christmas Eve,' he said.

She wiped the tears from her face with her free hand and said, 'When I decided to go ahead with it the first thing that I needed to do was to make sure that Johnny Elvin didn't go with them. He wasn't in the Jeep with them five years ago and didn't deserve to die. So, I made a fancy cake and left it outside the door to his kennels. I filled it with rotten eggs and other stuff that I knew would give him food poisoning. And I'm pleased to say it did the trick.'

'And what would you have done if you hadn't managed to make him ill?'

'He would have become collateral damage. You see, by then I felt compelled to go ahead with it on the fifth anniversary of what they did to Joanna.'

In a voice that shook with emotion, she went on. 'I intended to turn up at the farm on Christmas Eve morning just before the men were due to set off.

'A few days before, I took this shotgun and box of shells from the cupboard in the trophy room. I knew where he kept the key so it was easy. I also knew he was unlikely to open it and discover anything missing. I then hid them in the boot of my car.

'I'd planned to enter the farmhouse and shoot them all after explaining who I really am and why I wanted them dead. But they were already outside by the time I got there and two of them were rounding up the dogs.

'I could have shot them there and then outside, but that wasn't how I wanted it to be,' she said. 'They needed to be together so that I could tell them what I thought of them . . . so I told Ted I'd gone there to pick up some documents from the office. And I still thought it was too good an opportunity to pass up so I asked him if I could go with them out of curiosity. He said I could and I came up with the idea of following them on one of the quad bikes in the hope that I'd get lucky. And I did when a heavy rain shower forced them to seek shelter in the abandoned barn.'

'And that's when you decided to strike,' James said.

Another nod. 'It was so flipping easy. I had the element of surprise and they were big targets in a small space. They didn't stand a chance. Before I started firing I told them who I was and then shot Rhys Hughes and Dylan Payne in quick succession. Ted tried to run so I shot him just outside the barn. Nigel Marr fell over Ted's body and I blasted him as he begged me not to.

'The dogs ran outside then and I shot three of them, but one escaped.

'My intention was to move the bodies to different locations and take photos of them to ensure that it made headlines around the world. So, I attached Marr's body to the back of the quad bike using a length of old chain I found in the barn. Then I dragged him to the first location. I followed this by dragging Ted Rycroft to the second location.

'But it was much harder than I thought it would be. I decided to leave the other two in the barn and shoot a video of them instead.

'When I returned to the farmhouse, I decided to trash it in the hope that it would make the police believe that it had been carried out by anti-hunt extremists. I also took the other shotguns from the trophy room and later threw them into a lake. It felt so good. Once I started, I couldn't stop.'

'And what about the word *murderers* scrawled on the picture?' James said.

She shrugged. 'I couldn't resist it. That's what they were, after all. They killed my sister, didn't they?'

Kerry then heaved a breath and stiffened her spine.

'It's time to leave me alone now,' she said. 'I'm sure you don't want to see my brains splattered all over the room.'

'You don't have to do that,' James said. 'Just put the gun down and come with us.'

'What for? I'll spend the rest of my life behind bars and I don't want to.'

James felt his jaw go tight, making it hard to breathe. He didn't know what to do next and when he glanced briefly at the officer to his left he realised that he had no idea either.

But then a thought jumped into his head and he said, 'You must realise, Kerry, that to a great many people you're a hero for killing those men. And I'm sure their numbers will grow once your full story is out there. We've already had it confirmed that what Karl Kramer said was the truth. Dylan Payne confessed to his wife and when it's made public you'll attract more sympathy, I'm sure.'

Her demeanour abruptly changed and her wet eyes narrowed inquisitively.

'Look at it this way, Kerry,' James continued, while trying to keep the desperation out of his voice. 'The longer you're alive, the more attention you'll be able to draw to the crusade against cruel sports, which as you well know would make your sister happy.'

She sat there, as if lost deep within herself, while her finger hovered dangerously above the trigger.

James took a long breath, struggling to keep the panic in, and it struck him that he had one last card to play.

'There's another thing you should take into account, Kerry,' he said. 'There'll be plenty of opportunities down the line to take your own life if you still want to.'

Another long, agonising minute passed before she lowered the shotgun and dropped it onto the floor.

CHAPTER SEVENTY-THREE

Events moved rapidly after James told Kerry Grey that she was under arrest and placed cuffs on her wrists. As soon as she was led away the house was sealed off and a forensics team was summoned.

Neighbours started to appear on the street and within half an hour the first reporter arrived, having been tipped off by one of them. James wouldn't be drawn into answering any questions and told her that a statement would be issued soon.

He left Abbott at the house and Stevens drove him back to headquarters. On the way he was suddenly beset by a stream of conflicting emotions. He was delighted that the case had been solved, but he was also fearful that the shocking outcome was not going to ease tensions between the pro- and anti-hunt supporters.

The rest of the day was manic for James and the team and the level of interest in Kerry's arrest was nothing short of hysterical.

She was charged with four counts of murder and one count of causing criminal damage to property.

She broke down twice while being interviewed under caution, but at no point did she show any contrition for the men she'd killed and their families.

'I don't believe the wives, sons and daughters didn't know what those men did,' she said to James. 'So why should I feel sorry for them?'

Superintendent Tanner staged a press conference late in the afternoon and by then the forensics team had unearthed a wealth of evidence at Kerry's home.

They found the burner phones and laptop that had been used to send the vile messages, photos and video clip, plus the documents relating to her name change.

Two loose ends were tied up towards the end of the day.

The first was that DC Patterson at last managed to question Shane Logan at Penrith Hospital and he confirmed what Emily Monroe had said. The pair had indeed started a relationship behind his wife's back and they spent Christmas Eve together at Emily's home. He also admitted that it had been a mistake to tell his wife that he went out that day with the Spicer brothers.

The second was the identity of the woman James had seen looking out of the window at Karl Kramer's house. It turned out she was exactly what he had said – an old friend from his days in the military – and she had recently moved to Cumbria.

So, all in all, it was a constructive day, but neither James nor any of his team were in the mood to celebrate. The case had taken it out of them and the denouement had come as a brutal shock. It didn't help that the story sparked a fresh explosion of outrage across the internet.

Predictably, there were anti-hunt activists who were full of praise for what Kerry had done and said the four men had received just punishment. Hunt supporters, on the other hand, described her as a psychopath and there were those who said they hoped she'd be murdered before she got to stand trial.

James was relieved when he finally got to go home, but it was too late to spend any time with Bella. Instead, he sat up with Annie and they watched the story play out on the news until it was time to go to bed.

CHAPTER SEVENTY-FOUR

Day Eight
New Year's Eve

Sunday was something of an emotional roller coaster for James as he visited the homes of Owain Hughes, Francesca Marr and Maria Payne. He wanted to be the one to tell them about Kerry Grey before the details were drip-fed to them by the media.

Naturally, they were all in a state of shock, and for Francesca it was made worse when she learned that her late husband had lied to her about the Jeep incident.

'I never doubted him for a single second,' she sobbed. 'But I'm sure that if he had told me I would have kept it secret too.'

James's last visit of the day was to Greg Pike, who was having a hard time accepting what his boss had done five years ago. But it was learning the truth about his colleague that really got to him.

'She seemed so genuine,' he said. 'I can't believe she was living a lie. Her performance was surely worthy of an Oscar.'

James made an effort to push all thoughts of the case from his mind when he finally returned home. Annie had prepared a special New Year's Eve meal for him and after Bella was put to bed, they cracked open a bottle of prosecco.

James felt they deserved it and he even managed to relax for the first time since the night before Christmas Eve.

EPILOGUE

One week later

There had been no let-up in the weather as snow and strong winds had continued to batter the Lake District.

It had added to the workload of the Cumbria Constabulary because of the sheer number of road accidents and cases of hikers getting into difficulty on the fells.

But at least the biggest and most disturbing investigation they had ever had to deal with was behind them.

Kerry Grey had appeared in court and was now being held in custody, waiting for her trial date to be set.

Funerals were being arranged for her four victims and more information about the murders and what had led to them was gradually being released, ensuring that the story remained at the top of the news agenda.

Unfortunately, the war of words between the two factions in the hunting debate showed no signs of abating and there had been more violence at recent meets.

However, James was able to move his mind beyond the gloomy news when the sonographer who was carrying out the ultrasound scan on Annie pointed to the screen next to her hospital bed, and said, 'You're having a baby boy, Mrs Walker. And he looks fighting fit to me.'

James couldn't have been happier and tears welled in his eyes.

'That's terrific,' he said to Annie as he leaned over and kissed her. 'I can't wait to tell Bella.'

Annie laughed. 'Let's hope the lad brings some luck with him and that we get to spend next Christmas together as a family . . . Which reminds me. You need to book it off as annual leave. I want us to spend it somewhere warm, sunny and crime free for once.'

Yet again James chickened out of telling her he'd been offered the job in London. That was now going to have to wait for at least a few days more.

THE END

ACKNOWLEDGEMENTS

Once again, I'd like to thank Molly Walker-Sharp who has been my editor on all four of the James Walker books. It's been such a pleasure working with her and I've really appreciated the help and encouragement she has given me.

If you've enjoyed *The Night Before Christmas*, then why not head back to DI James Walker's first case?

Twelve days.
Twelve murders.

THE
CHRISTMAS
KILLER

ALEX PINE

A serial killer is on the loose in Kirkby Abbey. And as the snow falls, the body count climbs . . .

One farmhouse. Two murder cases.
Three bodies.

THE
KILLER
IN THE
SNOW

A FAMILY
SLEEPS.

A KILLER
AWAKES.

ALEX PINE

DI James Walker knows that to catch this killer, he needs
to solve a case long since gone cold . . .

Christmas has arrived in Cumbria,
and wedding bells are ringing.
But an ice-cold killer is waiting in the fells . . .

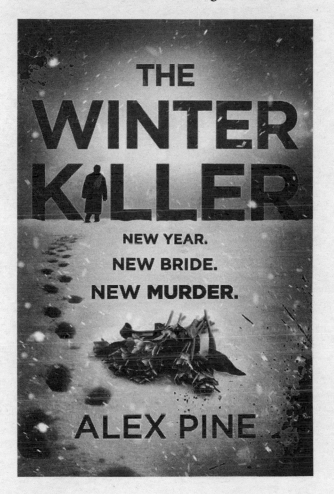

Something old, something new. One guest is a killer.
The question is: who?